The Salvation Mongers

Common Threads in the Life

Ronald L. Donaghe

Writers Club Press
San Jose New York Lincoln Shanghai

The Salvation Mongers
Common Threads in the Life

All Rights Reserved © 2000 by Ronald L. Donaghe

No part of this book may be reproduced or transmitted in any form or by any means, graphic, electronic, or mechanical, including photocopying, recording, taping, or by any information storage or retrieval system, without the permission in writing from the publisher.

Published by Writers Club Press
an imprint of iUniverse.com, Inc.

For information address:
iUniverse.com, Inc.
620 North 48th Street
Suite 201
Lincoln, NE 68504-3467
www.iuniverse.com

This novel is a work of fiction. All characters and incidents described are strictly the creation of the author, and any resemblance to real people, living or dead, or real incidents of similar nature is purely coincidental.

ISBN: 0-595-09835-5

Printed in the United States of America

Dedication

This book is lovingly, belligerently, dedicated to gays and lesbians the world over and for all time—especially to those who know the ache and emptiness of self-loathing.

Contents

Chapter I	The Belly of the Beast	1
Chapter II	New Friends and My False Confession	15
Chapter III	Who is Paul Romaine	37
Chapter IV	The Routine and Those Who Fail	45
Chapter V	Learning to Love Oneself and What is a Man	59
Chapter VI	Rewards for Right-Thinking	75
Chapter VII	Punishment for Wrong-Thinking	89
Chapter VIII	The Aftermath	113
Chapter IX	Watch for Dust Rising in the East	127
Chapter X	Cat Piss	147
Chapter XI	Storm Coming	155
Chapter XII	The Hot Seat	173
Chapter XIII	One Shall be Taken	187
Chapter XIV	Found	197
Chapter XV	Barbed Wire for a Crown	219
Chapter XVI	Look Who's Laughing Now	231
Afterword	The Salvation Mongers—the Real Thing	249
About the Author		259

Foreword

While this is a work of fiction, the kind of "ex-gay" ministry portrayed in this novel is all too real. The "Eighteen Steps to Salvation and Cure" is based on a real program from one of these ministries. I am indebted to all the people who have participated in such programs and have written about them.

Ronald L. Donaghe, 2000

I

The Belly of the Beast

Lion's Mouth Christian Ranch
Guadalupe Mountains, New Mexico

Saturday, June 6, 1998

Collect call from William... These are the words that ended it all or, perhaps explain how it all began, because when William came on the line, all I heard before the gunshot was his sobbing. That was October 1, 1997. By then, I had known William for a little over six years. What I did after that night and how I ended up here in the middle of nowhere in an army tent with ten other guys, scribbling these words on a sheaf of blank paper is the subject of this journal.

I listen to the silence of the night outside the tent. Inside are whispers or silence from the other guys. Under the shadowy light of a string of naked bulbs, eleven of us are spending our first night at Lion's Mouth.

I am a recruit (so they think) at LMCR—a retreat created solely to "cure" homosexuality through Christian belief and practices. Josh Rafferty of the Light of Christ Ex-gay Ministries of Albuquerque, New Mexico, and the Assembly of God Almighty of Carlsbad, New

Mexico, have established a fellowship here in southeastern New Mexico in the Guadalupe mountains.

While massive, forbidding, and covering thousands of square miles, the Guadalupes are encircled by even more forbidding and vast stretches of salt flats and desert. In all these thousands of square miles, the terrain is dotted with struggling farms and ranches. The famous Carlsbad Caverns lie south of here. The city of Carlsbad is east of us on the plains with the main mass of the mountains to the west.

Tonight, in the city of Carlsbad, no doubt, numerous families who attend the Assembly of God Almighty are talking about us in the privacy of their homes; no doubt they hope there will be more of us wayward homosexuals staying at their "ranch" in the future. We're supposed to come in small groups, every nine weeks and stay for eighteen. I guess it's supposed to take a week to make each step in the program and, by week eighteen, when I become a "people helper" (becoming a people helper is the last step in the program), I'll be cured of my homosexuality and will be a real Christian to boot, according to the teaching of the "Light of Christ." What happens to each recruit (or should I say patient?) after their eighteen weeks at the ranch is of little concern, however, to the wonderful brotherhood of "ex-homosexuals" that results. There is no real follow-up on those who graduate. I ought to know, since William was one of Rafferty's first victims.

We're cut off from the outside world—as part of the agreement we all had to sign to be admitted into this program. We're supposed to be able to write letters home, although they're to be screened by the Rev. Rafferty. But since I've got plans to keep this journal (unbeknownst to the retreat leaders), I'll need to write some letters to avoid arousing suspicion. I'm completely on my own for the next eighteen weeks, except for my contact with a guy by the name of Charlie Hays, who has agreed to keep these journal entries for me. Since he's a foreman here and no one suspects *him* of being gay, I'll pass these illegal pages to him whenever I get the chance. If I get caught with them, the worst thing to happen will probably be getting kicked out of the program and escorted off the ranch. If that happens, I'll never be able to find out how they did what they did to my sweet William. Again, this isolation is "voluntary," which they call "Step number 10: Avoid homosexual hangouts and friends."

I know it's outrageous for me to subject myself to this ex-gay program when I don't want to be turned heterosexual or, for that matter, *saved*. But after what Rafferty's program did to William, I knew someone had to investigate—not only for William's sake, but for all these others, here.

* * *

William was my lover for over five years before he decided to join Rafferty's program which, at that time, was in Albuquerque. It was also eighteen weeks but, back then, the recruits stayed in a house in the city and were not isolated as much from the outside. So, even during that time, I was able to see William off and on; and it was painful for me and him, both, I think. But I loved him enough to let him see it through, and I didn't pressure him to quit, even when I began to see the changes in him. It was even more painful when he "graduated," because by then he was committed to leaving behind everyone he had known when he was a "practicing" homosexual, which meant me, mainly, and a few guys we had been friends with over the years.

In August of '97, he was pronounced cured and sent on his way. He was supposed to mingle with his "new friends," which I'm sure he did for awhile. But I never lost hope that we might one day get back together, because he could never quite stop his contact with me—sending me little notes about how wonderful it felt to be normal, that he was dating women and, "yes, Kelly, I'm really really enjoying it." But then just two months later, I received that awful telephone call in the middle of the night from God-forsaken Oklahoma: *"Collect call from William. Will you accept?"* I remember fiddling with the telephone, trying to wake up and listen, expecting William's voice to come on the line, only to hear his sobbing and that impossibly loud explosion. He must have held the receiver with one hand and the pistol to his head with the other, because when it came, I knew precisely what it was.

Yeah, Rev. Rafferty, you did William a big favor, subjecting him to your eighteen steps. You didn't tell him the only thing that lasts is the guilt.

* * *

I listen to the whispers. I write down my thoughts. But I don't know how to begin. A whole new future lies ahead, most of its features indistinct.

I've come to get a record of this place, and I haven't come with an open mind, although I'll have to act like it's wide open so they can pour their poison into it. I have to make myself vulnerable enough, however, to feel what William must have felt, but not so vulnerable that I end up blowing my brains out as he did. When I walk away from this place, I will know what they do and how they do it, and I will be able to fight them before they destroy too many other lives.

I suspect—

Cut that thought. I can't suppose anything about what will go on here over the next few months. But it seems wrongheaded, anyway, to set up a camp like this, to try to cure people of their attractions to members of the same sex. Judging from my own experience, my homosexual *nature* sort of hit me over the head when I was a senior in high school. No way did I one day decide, "Hmmm, I think I like boys. I think I'll practice homosexuality." Nor was I invited to try it by anyone that I ever recall. Oh, I did fight it for awhile, but realized two things: first, I couldn't suddenly not like liking boys; and second, I *like* being gay. These other guys *are* here, I assume, because they hate being gay and believe they can be cured. I'm here to see what happens when they try.

I don't know how Josh Rafferty plans to accomplish this. But since the ex-gay movement has been so visible in the last couple of years, despite the criticism it gets even from former members and founders, Rafferty must believe that he's going to be successful. What that success actually consists of is beyond me. That the recruits get cured of being gay is the greatest lie about this whole movement. Yet it seems that every wild-eyed fundamentalist wants to cash in on it.

Beyond the fact that the ex-gay programs just plain don't work, this movement has a dark side. And here I lie on the edge of that darkness, peering ahead into the next few months, wondering what it will be like and hoping (with great dread) to find out what lurks in this darkness.

* * *

The eleven of us in this tent arrived at the ranch this afternoon on an old yellow school bus that had been converted to the work of Rafferty's Light of Christ ministry by having someone paint in lavender on its side: Lion's Mouth Christian Ranch. We left the pavement somewhere near the entrance to Sitting Bull Falls State Park around three o'clock this afternoon and continued on for an additional forty miles, churning a funnel of dust behind us all the way as we got deeper into the Guadalupes. We rocked and rolled over dirt ruts, patches of gravel, and rocks the size of footballs for at least three hours, sometimes getting up to twenty miles-an-hour, but more often grunting along at five or ten. We arrived by late afternoon, the bus shivering and farting puffs of black smoke behind it as we entered Lion's Mouth Canyon, itself. Although the sun was still visible above the western horizon, its light was already turning from white to golden as we came to a halt in front of a row of drab metal buildings. When the driver turned the ignition, the engine chugged and coughed, ending in a death rattle, and the bus threatened, for its final act of life, to tumble over and lay dead on its back like a giant cockroach. The dust we'd churned up caught up with us, drifting down like volcanic ash, caking the windows and filling the inside with a brown, choking cloud.

It was a perfect end to our trip which had been hot, grimy, and depressing. I was the first one out of the bus and the only one to climb on top of it to begin unloading our luggage, which reminded me of the same multi-colored suitcases I saw upon my arrival in boot camp a few years before this. Except now, the luggage was a uniform gray. The once gaily painted signs on the sides of the bus that said "Lion's Mouth Christian Ranch" were gray. The faces of the recruits were gray, too, as they stepped off the bus into the powdered dirt—some of that hopeless, cheerless color *was* dirt, but I think most of it was the fear they tried to keep hidden beneath the dust and the sweat. All of us knew that this particular ex-gay ministry, according to the brochures that Rev. Rafferty has each new recruit read and sign, is not like many of the other ex-gay programs. The good reverend will tell you himself that it's more like boot camp than a religious retreat. "We practice tough love, son," he told me. " 'Tough love'. But since you've been in the army, you know what I'm talking about. The foundation for a strong heterosexual identity in men is true masculinity, just like they practice in the army. We mold you to your role as men, and send you off into the world as soldiers. Difference is, our enemy is Satan. So, don't sign that pledge unless you're ready to destroy your effeminate identity."

William had said as much, and part of the change I saw in him, the part that hurt the most, I think, was that he'd hardened on the outside, too. Or at least had tried to keep up that appearance the last time I saw him. I was aching to hug him, but when he said good-bye, before getting on the bus and heading for his home in Oklahoma where he would later call me from, all he would do was shake my hand—one hard pump and then he released it. Turning slightly on the step as he boarded he flashed me a brave smile, but I caught a glimpse of a tear shining on his face. "You take care of yourself, Kelly. I will never forget you."

* * *

No sooner had I untied the ropes on the luggage when a man in a bright green suit stepped outside one of the buildings and came quickly across the yard where we waited. I should have known who it was, but the Rev. Rafferty looked different here, out of place from the cool of his pale green office in Albuquerque. Now, the beet red of his face, the watermelon rind of his jacket and (believe it) a peach-colored pullover knit shirt, made him appear gaudy, undignified, and plump, making me wonder just what kind of masculinity *he* considered himself in possession of. I hated the sight of him and his ridiculous outfit, and I wanted to cry out, "Murderer!" I fought back a jolt of anger, thinking of how William must have felt on his first day in that house in Albuquerque—what I can only think of as Rafferty's proving grounds, since following his success there, he'd apparently been able to get funding from other sources to take on this more ambitious program.

For a moment, I thought the preacher had lost his voice as he stood before us squinting at our expectant faces. Or maybe his jaunt across the yard had taken his breath away. The air was so hot, you couldn't really draw a clean, deep breath, and I'm sure the air is thinner in this high desert mountain range. In the next instant, he forced a hardy laugh and said, "Gawud be praised! Welcome, men!"

Then he turned away, motioning for us to follow. At the entrance to the same building he'd come out of, he told us to wait, then disappeared indoors.

Most of the guys trudged toward the shady ground on the east side of the building, where they assembled and began milling about or sank wordlessly and wearily to the ground, some raking fingers through sweaty hair, others stretching out on the stingy plot of grass that clung desperately to the edges of the building.

We waited. Each silent, or emitting sighs of relief. After what seemed about ten minutes, I climbed back on top of the bus, just couldn't stand being close to the others after the eternity it took to get here from Carlsbad.

I was going to keep a low profile, especially on this first day, try to blend among the rest, but I just had to see the place we had come to.

The ranch is located in what appears to be a small, round valley, encircled by rocky bluffs and rough hills. Toward the west lies the trail we followed through Lion's Mouth Canyon, but it was invisible within the late-afternoon shadows cast by the canyon walls. As I looked around, I could plainly see that the canyon trail is the only path a vehicle can follow to get inside the valley. If there were a rock slide within the narrow canyon (which looks likely given a hard rain) no bus, no vehicle of any sort, would be able to get in—or out.

Long tongue-like shadows from the throat of the canyon lapped across the trail, casting deceitfully cool-looking shade across the burning sand. It was hot as hell. Along the northern ridges, rocky cliffs hover against the glaring blue sky like the edge of a hand. Toward the east, the hand's fingers become sloping, creased fissures of hills. From where I stood atop the bus, I could see the hills and higher ridges tumble away endlessly in mesquite, cactus, yucca, and sickly clumps of juniper. Southward, the mountains rise brown and purple, their western faces turning pink by the fast-setting sun.

The valley, itself, like a giant crater or an open wound in this endless sun-baked nowhere, holds the only signs of human activity. On the south edge, where we stopped, three metal buildings stand like some twentieth-century military outpost, without the protective wall, however. They're small buildings—or appear to be, huddled against the upward slope of land behind them. On the first building, where the others milled about, is a cross, devoid of the Christ, stabbing the sky.

The brochure Josh Rafferty handed me several months ago in his Albuquerque office called this a "chapel." Next to it is the largest building, full of windows and painted a grim beige: "the activity center, complete with showers, gymnasium, and classrooms," the brochure said. Farther east is the "dining hall"—a pale blue structure with a low-slung porch on which a row of twenty or so metal chairs face the center of the valley. On the north side of the valley, appearing to be cupped by the rocky "hand" stand two drab-green army tents, which the same brochure said were temporary "barracks." These reminded me of those I stayed in one time in Oklahoma when our unit was on bivouac, training to become medics.

Between the metal buildings and the tents, the earth looks freshly clawed. I would say plowed, having seen freshly plowed earth back on the farm where I grew up, but whoever did this doesn't know shit about plowing—or worse, it was done by hand, by the back-breaking labor of the recruits who came before us. There are crops in these fields, what might be corn or grain, alfalfa, and pitifully scrawny looking beds of what might be squash, but in the heat, everything looks to be on the edge of death.

I could have invented the phrase on the spot, "Abandon all hope, ye who enter here," as I surveyed the land. And I recalled sitting in Rafferty's office back in Albuquerque a few months earlier, trying to appear enthralled as he talked about the thriving ranch he had started, when all I wanted to do was kill him as dead as William. *"You see, ah, Kelly, ah, the Lord will work miracles for the righteous."* Seeing it now, I felt vindicated. If the Lord does work miracles for the righteous, these squalid crops at least proved what He thought of this particular group.

The entire valley—an area of what appears to be no more than three hundred acres—is flat, dry land. Rafferty said it would soon grow corn and vegetables and alfalfa. But in this June heat, I have my doubts. I wouldn't give any crop much chance of thriving if it isn't up by June.

A fearful thought struck me as I continued to survey my new home, causing my empty stomach to churn with hunger. The brochure had also said, "The recruits will live off of what they produce, becoming a community of men thus committed to the Lord, living off the fruits of their labor—and none else." In a pig's eye. Unless we're to starve or eat manna from heaven, we're going to have to ship a lot of food in here.

For all I care, this valley will repel us, as it must have done since people first saw it. In the silent, hollow air, where even a slight breeze felt like the hot breath of a beast, I began to have serious doubts about Rafferty's sanity, if he thought this place was a thriving anything. To a jaundiced eye like mine, it looks like a death trap.

When Josh emerged again, he stood straight as he motioned us to assemble. I felt conspicuous on top of the bus, apart from the herd, so I climbed down hastily and took my place near the others. He didn't give me a second glance, for which I breathed a sigh of relief. My throat ached for water.

* * *

The light inside the chapel was murky. The planners had made no pretense with huge windows, but instead had created an interior as protected from the desert valley as a cave. Only in front of the chapel had they placed tiny windows on either side of the podium. In place of gleaming pews were backless benches of thick pine. The interior was large enough to hold fifty or so closely packed worshippers. The walls were finished with sheetrock, painted white, and still newly-done looking. Behind the podium in gay lavender were the words, "God is Love."

As I took a seat, I looked over the heads of guys I'd come in on the bus with, at the other guys already seated in front of us. There were about fifteen of them—recruits that must have been in this program, now, for about nine weeks. Rafferty had mentioned them when I'd asked about joining his program back in Albuquerque. As I looked at them, I was reminded yet again of being in boot camp. These were the toughened troops who had come before us. They were uniformly dressed in gleaming white T-shirts and Levi's, reminding me, not of military men, but of basic trainees.

It troubles me that they're all so damned young. First, it's disturbing to think that someone barely in his twenties could be so full of self-hatred and willing to subject himself to this "tough-love" conversion program. Second, it's distressing to think that programs such as this are more effective with young minds. They're much easier to mold.

Anyway, as we shuffled around noisily to get seated and settled down, I was struck by how eerie it was that none of the older recruits turned around to watch us file into the seats. This seemed to me to be a bad sign. So soon, that universal urge for gay men to check out new guys to see if any of them are cute seemed to have been snuffed out of these guys. Every head was cut uniformly short, each bowed as though in deep meditation. In contrast, we new arrivals seemed motley with sweat-drenched shirts of all colors, hair wildly raked and dirty from the long trip. Around me, I smelled the sweat of heat and fear and the sickening sweet odor of cologne—probably all coming from us new recruits.

I tingled with anticipation of what a couple of months had done to the first set of converts. Were they well on their way to becoming cured of their homosexuality? Had William been so easily cowed? Were these guys more like William or less, or did it really matter? Could even the most stubborn-minded hold out very long against the peer pressure and the holy brow beating? If they were successfully being cured as they apparently wished to be, had they become like other good, queer-hating Christians? When this movement began, I think all the way back to 1978 in Dade County Florida, where Anita Bryant ran her successful "Save Our Children" campaign, I was only fifteen, but I remember hearing about the bumper stickers that appeared on cars bearing messages like "Kill a Queer for Christ," and I thought how, in William's case, he had become a self-hating queer and had obligingly killed himself.

The Rev. Rafferty took the podium with relish, gripping the edge of the lectern with both hands, elbows out like wings. He leaned toward the lectern staring at us, smiling broadly.

"None of you is a homosexual!" he shouted, suddenly, causing even my reverie to shatter.

I listened, waited. But he said nothing else. He just looked at us, taking his time to let his smile and eyes rove over us. Silence ensued like that in a tomb, until I thought he'd forgotten his lines, or was waiting for us to disagree.

"NONE of you is a homosexual!" he shouted, again. "There is no such THING! There is no THIRD SEX! You are not now, or have you ever been, homosexuals!"

Got it, Rev, I thought. *The old Nature argument.* Clever of him to begin with that premise.

"Homosexuality is be*hav*ior, something you *choose* to engage in. No one is born homosexual!"

Tell it to William, Rev.

"In the next few weeks, my sons, we shall together learn that your homosexuality is a sham. Deep within your troubled hearts you know the truth. You are all heterosexual as surely as I am. And that is what you have come here for. Isn't it? And with the power of Jeezuss! And with your own reawakened will power you will learn this truth. And this truth shall set you free!"

William tried to believe you, Rev. Look where it got him.

"You are not born a homosexual. You are led into it. And if you do not withdraw from it..."

Yes? Reverend death, tell us.

"If you persist in such behavior, it becomes a habit, then an addiction, and all along this iniquitous path, you are slowly dying."

And then what happens you murderous dog?

"Your mind becomes dark, rebellious, angry, until you *think* you are homosexual. Your illness is the wages of your sin. But my children," the preacher said, slowing the assault on us, "Before it is too late, you must be told. You must KNOW. You must never forget. You must look for the one small truth in the grimmest, blackest part of your reprobate hearts...The ultimate wages of sin are death."

At that, he stopped again, giving us time to absorb his words, to turn them over in our minds, to feel their sharp edges. And I felt them all right, just as, at that moment, I felt William sitting beside me, his presence telling me to do something. I looked around without moving my head, wanting to jump up and shout to all the young men to get up, right now, and head for the door, before it was too late. But for my dead William's sake, I kept my mouth shut.

Then Josh went on with a kinder discussion of becoming new Christians, beginning to feel the heat of God's love burn out our sin. He ended in tears that made me shake my head in disgust. He was one of those crying preachers extolling us to better ourselves, to live whole lives. He claimed the Light of Christ ministry could deliver us from the jaws of hell.

***

After the short service, we were herded from the chapel to the activities building where they gave us haircuts. It was flashback time to boot camp. I could shut my eyes and conjure up the same fear that gripped me as I went through each of the rituals of boot camp. Just as I had then, I felt I was being changed, step-by-irrevocable-step, as our civilian clothes were taken away, then our appearance changed by the man behind the barber's chair. When we were done and were herded outdoors, again, I looked around at the recruits I had come in with, and I scarcely recognized any of them.

After our haircuts, when we were still itching from the hair that had fallen down our necks, we were marched to the chow hall and fed a supper that could have been wonderful, except that we were sweaty and itchy and tired. I couldn't even smile at the beaming church women behind the counters who dished the beans and roast beef and mashed potatoes onto my plate; and even though Rafferty announced second helpings, the only guys who hurried up to the counter were the first recruits and one fat guy from our group. I almost gagged when he sat down at the table across from me with another full plate. But I watched him eat, could even hear him grunting a little as he forked the food down his throat.

Tears brimmed on my eyelids as I watched the fat kid. Maybe he was trying to hang onto his identity by walling himself off from the world with a layer of fat.

But there seemed to be a conspiracy against those of us who would keep something of ourselves intact. As it was coming on full dark outside, we were marched to the showers, where we new recruits had to strip naked in front of the fully clothed group of older recruits who, rather than looking sick from their suppers, began to look…what? In control?

They stared at us as we pulled off our sweaty clothing, each of us having to hand it to one of them, then walk through the facility naked. It was embarrassing and made me feel vulnerable in the presence of those who seemed to act with one mind, to carry out their duties as if they were receiving input through subcutaneous implants. Our clothes were taken away, including the contents of our pockets. When we came out of the shower, we were given Levi's and white T-shirts—and in the space of a few hours at the ranch, our individuality had been reduced to mere body type, or quality of voice. Maybe even in the privacy of our thoughts, some of us wished only to belong to the group that emerged. So strongly was I reminded of boot camp in the army by the haircuts and getting our uniforms, that I began to feel extremely uneasy. If this place was as efficiently run as boot camp, within days, not weeks, none of us would be clear-minded. All of us would be disoriented. And so, the indoctrination began.

II

New Friends and My False Confession

Lion's Mouth Christian Ranch
Sunday, June 7

Step No. 14: Find one or more intimate new friends. And a companion to this step is number 15: give check-up privileges to one or more of these new friends.

I'm beginning to realize, quickly, that enforcement of the eighteen steps to salvation is not going to be our choice. These two rules are even more insidious than "avoiding homosexual hangouts and friends."

* * *

The older recruits from our first day came for us at sunup. A dedicated group, those guys from the other tent must have got up at five a.m. to be all clean and dressed and fucking chipper to get us out of bed. As soon as the tent flap was opened to a burst of sunlight like a nuclear blast, they came in screaming at us. The shock of being in boot camp momentarily seized me and, for an instant, I was about to jump out of bed and begin dressing, trying to do it under one minute as we had been expected to do in the army. Then I realized who it was and where I was, so I propped myself up on an elbow and watched the others in my tent flying out of their beds with a mixture of fear and confusion.

Our tent looked as it did the night before; clothes strewn over the bare ground floor, suitcases lazily shut with bits of clothing sticking out, shaving kits, dirty socks, even a few pair of underwear lay around, wadded up and damp from the previous day's sweat. From one end to the other of the forty-cot tent, Pandemonium reigned as the yelling continued, and members of our group fell over each other trying to get dressed, some of us half clad, dancing around with one foot in a pants leg; others colliding.

"Get UP, Brothers! The Lord can't waste a day on you!"

"Not that shirt, you stupid lamb of God! Wear your *issued* attire!"

And so the screaming went, and the scrambling around, and the confusion.

I found it easy, once I'd regained my reason from my momentary lapse, to get dressed efficiently. But I did shudder as I looked across the tent at a figure standing in the entrance; the sun at his back, he was a distorted shadow; yet I felt that he was staring directly at me. His stillness in the chaos disturbed me, the way his shape never wavered in the five or ten minutes it took for my group to get dressed. I felt his presence as a threat; so I hurried through the crowd to the exit, to see what he looked like in the daylight.

When they lined us up outside in the rosy dawn, I saw that the shadow man was the leader of the other group and, as it turned out, our leader as well. Although he was a scrawny little chipmunk-faced man, I guessed his age to be that of Rafferty's, around 50, and I thought it odd. He looked suspiciously like a practitioner of BDSM, straight off Folsom Street, rather than a minister of some sort, and that disturbed me. He had thinning (almost balding), pasted-down mouse-brown hair, a mustache, with a patch of gray-flecked hair beneath his lower lip, and a beady-eyed concentration that gave him a quiet, spooky look of authority. I was sure I had not seen him the day before, because his was the kind of face one doesn't forget. No one spoke after he raised a hand to silence us. My group took its cue from the others, who stood at attention, their eyes rigidly fixed ahead. I didn't have to wait long to find out his name was Paul Romaine, as he introduced himself before calling out our names from a clipboard.

For a moment, I couldn't concentrate on what it was we were supposed to be doing. *Paul Romaine.* The name had a such a familiar ring, I was sure I had heard it before. I would think of where later.

Each time one of us stepped forward, one of them took a name tag from Paul and pinned it on his assigned recruit; then the older recruit introduced himself as Brother so-and-so, and took his recruit across the valley to the chow hall, where we had eaten our first supper the night before. As each pair walked to breakfast, the recruit was informally "interviewed." This is how it went with me.

Brother Jerry instantly became my intimate "new friend," but pissed me off immediately on our walk across the valley. It wasn't because he dropped my name tag as he fumbled at my T-shirt, apparently nervous about slipping his fingers inside my shirt and touching my chest, nor because he handed it to me to pin on myself (I guess he was a little flustered at my willingness to sort of lean against him to have him "do" me). It wasn't so much because he pushed too hard in the first five minutes of our walk to be my intimate friend, either. Rather than beginning with something personal between us, like a real introduction and a real desire to get to know me, he was too quick to ask the questions printed on an index card. Then he didn't seem to be that interested in my answers. I would have felt sorry for him, but I thought of how fucking sincere William would have been with his interviewer, and so I hardened myself against this guy, refusing to let him get close to me. I understood that he had duties, but he couldn't seem to get my name right, and that pissed me off, too.

"How long have you been a practicing homosexual, ah, Kerry?"

"That's Kelly, Jerry."

"No. We don't call you by your last name."
"O'Kelley is my last name, Jerry. My first name is Kelly."
"That's a strange name, isn't it?"
"I'm full-blooded Irish on both sides of the family."
"Oh, I see, Kelly, how long?"

I must have looked at him blankly, because he repeated the question almost immediately. Actually, the question was stupid. I hadn't forgotten.

"You mean when did I come out?"
"You know, when did you get involved with practicing homosexuals? Someone must've recruited you into the lifestyle."
"Is that another question?"
"Er..." he glanced down at the card. "Yes. So it is."
"I wasn't recruited."
"Then how did you get started?"
"Let's see, Brother." I thought hard, stalling for time as we walked. I was determined to make a mess of his interview. We had already reached the clawed earth, which should have had knee-high corn by now. There was corn, but it was about a foot high and wilting. The sun was fully above the dun-colored hills to the east and, except for the shadow cast by Jerry on my left, I could feel its warm rays in my hair. I bowed my head a little, to compose a story. I thought quickly, knowing Jerry waited for an answer so he could ask his next question. Then I hit upon a good one that makes me laugh even now.

"I had a single uncle," I began. "We used to share my bed when he came to visit. He slept naked and, of course, being curious, I began to hurry to the bedroom before he came to bed. I would pretend to be asleep and peek out from the covers, hoping to see his...his, you know, cock...I mean, penis. I was hoping to see his penis."

I took a quick look at Jerry, who was all serious. "Is it okay to be so blunt...to mention his penis?" I asked, studying his face, hoping for a hint of red.

He rewarded me with glowing ears. "Sure. I don't see how else to get it out…in the open. Go ahead."

"Okay. Well, anyway, one night when my uncle undressed, I feigned sleep but watched him through my eyelashes as he played with his ding-dong, you know, sort of pulling on it, like he was milking a cow. He kept glancing my way, and I kept my face buried in my pillow, hoping to fool him. But I wasn't sure, you know, because he seemed to be doing it for my benefit. Pretty soon, he had a big hardon, like a general at attention. My little pecker was hard by that time, too, but wasn't much—maybe a second lieutenant." I paused, trying to keep from laughing.

Jerry's mouth was hanging open, lips parted. He licked them and shut his mouth. "G-go on."

"Well, he played with himself a little more, standing in front of the mirror, while he stuck his finger up his…his…"

"Anus?"

"Yeah, Jerry, his ass. And when he crawled in next to me, he sort of forced my head down to his crotch…like…since I was asleep, he could get me to suck him off without me knowing I was doing it, or like *he* was asleep and didn't know he was horny. Maybe he groaned and pretended my head was his cover, because he shoved pretty hard considering that he was supposed to be asleep. Anyway, I slid down there, and I think…yes…I was grinning to myself thinking what I was going to do. The first thing I remember, besides how big his cock was when my mouth went around it, was the smell."

Jerry swallowed. "The smell?"

"Yeah, Jerry, don't you remember your first—"

"Let me ask the questions!"

Woops. "Okay. It smelled like warm bread, fresh out of the oven."

My new friend gulped like he was getting hungry or about to throw up, but he pushed on bravely. "How old were you when you had your first homosexual encounter?"

"You mean when I gave my uncle a blow job?"

"Yes, your first homosexual act."

"Eight, maybe."

"Did you...what did you do after that? How did you feel? Guilty?"

"I loved it, Jerry. I mean, you know, an eight-year old boy falls in love with his first sex partner, doesn't he? I wanted to keep it up all night."

"No. You must've felt guilty."

"Really?" We looked at each other for a moment. Jerry's lips, which were full and luscious, tightened in disapproval. I decided to back off. "Well, yeah. I forget the details. I guess there was a lot of shame involved." I pretended to muse. "But I still *thought* I liked it. I became obsessed with sucking uncles."

"With other uncles?"

"Well, at that time, I lacked imagination. I thought you had to have an uncle, so I always hoped another one would visit. They did, but they didn't, you know, want anything. So all I did after that was just sort of wait for that particular uncle to come back. He never returned, though. He was killed in Vietnam, I think."

"Then, when did you first begin to feel that you were committing abominable acts?"

"You mean when I first wanted to stop?"

"Well, yes."

"Not for a long time, Jerry. Remember, I *thought* I liked it. Pretty soon, I was cruising the guys at college and hanging out in the men's bathrooms in the library. I never thought that two guys could fall in love with each other, but I guess they can, huh? Did you fall in love with a guy, Jerry?"

"No! No. It's not love, Kerry, it's lust."

"It's Kelly, Brother," I said, feeling angry at him for denying the best part of what two gay men could share. I'd felt nothing but love for William. And I like to think that, even after he'd gone through this kind of hell, and even during his tryst with women and his blush of salvation, that he still loved me; he'd continued to drop me little notes, even after he'd moved back home with his parents in Oklahoma, and he'd called *me* in his darkest and loneliest moment on earth, just before he pulled the trigger.

I shook my head. "Next question."

"Oh, yeah, thanks," Jerry said, and looked down at his card.

We walked on in silence for a minute and I took a good look at him. He was blond, a cute guy. Nice ass. Nice face. Long lashes fluttering a little with embarrassment. He had tanned skin and nicely developing muscles (probably from the work here). We walked on.

Ahead of us, other pairs of "new friends" followed the same trail through the field. Overhead, birds called to one another, cutting through the clear, hollow air. I wanted to stop right in the middle of the field and tell him I'd been lying—that there never had been any child-molesting uncle to introduce me to something I would discover for myself, before I even had a name for what I felt for certain boys in high school. I wanted so badly to tell Jerry and every other recruit on the ranch that I was glad to be gay—proud, in fact—and that they would all be a lot happier accepting themselves, that despair and suicide waited for some of them at the end of this program.

I was also becoming curious about Jerry. Why had he come here? Was he almost cured having been here nine weeks or so? Or just afraid to face the fact that it wasn't working? What was so awful about his life on the outside? What could have brought him here, to the middle of nowhere? Had he lost a lover, and the only way he could handle it was to deny his hurt, or to blame his being gay on an illness? I had a thousand questions.

The next question on his list was when had I realized that homosexual acts were abominable.

I squared my shoulders, prepared to tinker with his mind. "Oh, I guess I should say…I should tell you something like I eventually saw the gay world for what it is," I said.

"Being?"

"A place where a lot of good people get hurt. Did you get hurt, Jerry?"

"Yes." His face went putrid with memories, or disgust.

A cutting engine made us both look toward the ranch house. About a quarter of a mile away, a Jeep was churning dust along the driveway in front of the chapel. It stopped briefly at the chow hall, and I saw Josh Rafferty, unmistakable in his bright green jacket, hop into the Jeep. The Jeep turned around and flew past the buildings, heading west along the trail we'd come in on. It sped toward the mouth of the canyon that, even in the bright daylight, was a black gap in the ridge of cliffs.

"Where's he going?"

Jerry watched the Jeep get lost in a cloud of billowing dust; then he turned back to me. "It's Sunday. He's probably going to Carlsbad today to meet with the church people."

"Oh."

"Yeah, he probably needs to prepare them for your first visit."

"Me?"

"No. All of the new arrivals. Once a month, we go into Carlsbad. The church sponsors us, and they like to see how we're doing."

"You mean whether we're getting cured or not? Do we have to take a test?"

Jerry looked flustered. "You'll see. They know we'll be cured. It's just that they own the land and want to know how things are. Men from the church oversee our work."

"And the men from the church, do they know that *everybody* here is gay?"

He sighed. "Yes, Kelly. They know all about us."

I smiled to myself, at least having Jerry unintentionally tell me that he was also gay."

We walked on a little farther.

"So when did you want to stop being homosexual?"

I was tired of answering questions. Why couldn't we enjoy the beautiful sunshine? But I knew it was hopeless, so I tried a new approach—poisoning my lies with the truth. I said, "I decided I wanted to come here when a friend of mine said he'd been saved, claimed that he actually enjoyed dating women, once he went through this program. He was convinced that turning to Jesus was the first step on the road to salvation. It is, isn't it?"

Jerry beamed at me. His was a beautiful smile. Too bad it was wasted; he must've thought that he'd scored a victory in the battle for the Lord. "So, you've already taken the first step. Then what did you do, contact the Rev. Rafferty in Albuquerque?"

"Yes. But not right away. It was a very emotional thing for me to have my friend turned…into a Christian. I thought about this a long time, because everything else I had ever tried didn't work."

"Like what?"

"Oh, the usual things. Dating women, going to psychiatrists. Things that, when they fail, make you want to blow your brains out."

He nodded. "I'm going to tell you something important, Kerry…er, Kelly, now that we've got this far. I think you're ready now."

"I hope so," I said. Then I set my teeth for the sermon.

"Those other solutions never work. And do you know why?" (I started to answer but realized it was a rhetorical question.) "They don't work because they are not the work of God. They are worldly and subject to the whims of Satan."

"Wait, Jerry. You're going too fast. You mean Satan would be pleased that I dated women? I thought he'd want me to keep sucking guys off."

Jerry looked frustrated. "Nonono. It's…It won't work. Not until you accept Jesus as your personal savior, that's number one. Number two is be continually controlled by the Holy Spirit. Can you do that?"

"What? Number two? Now that you mention it."

"Huh?"

"Never mind," I said.

Jerry was frowning, now, and I knew I'd gotten under his skin, so I smiled as brightly as I could. "Go on, Jerry."

"Number three is walk in the spirit. Number four, admit homosexuality is a sin and confess it. Are you ready to do that?"

"Yeah, I guess so."

Jerry nodded. "Let me hear you say it. You've got to say it aloud."

"Is that rule number five?"

"No. It's kind of a basic approach. You say something; then you become committed to it."

"Oh. Okay. Homosexuality is a sin. How's that?"

Jerry chuckled like a little Reverend Rafferty, and I wanted to slug him. "That's fine, Kelly. Now, when you say it in front of the church, today, in Carlsbad, it'll come easier. You see? The Lord is already working changes within you. Dating women will be a beautiful and wonderful experience when you leave here."

"You mean I'll actually *want* to? Like my friend William did? And not want to blow my head off in the middle of the night?"

"After you have been cleansed by the spirit, through repentance, through participating every day. See?"

"I guess I do." I tried to look relieved, as though I were hearing something new. "It's a cleansing process then?"

Jerry was beaming now, like an older brother. He put a firm, brotherly hand on my shoulder that felt warm and other than brotherly. "So, after you contacted Josh's office, then what happened?"

Oh, puh-leese! I thought. "More questions?"

He nodded.

I wanted to tell him that I'd contacted my other gay friends and told them I'd gotten into the program, that I would be writing a report one of these days. "Well, I contacted the Rev. Rafferty, but he said I'd missed the first cycle, so I had to wait nine weeks for another group to be assembled. I often wondered why they don't let people come here whenever they want."

"Each group has to begin a cycle together, like a semester at school. You go through the program one step at a time."

"Oh. Like that sermon last night, where we had to repeat all that stuff?"

"Yes. Where you said, 'Lord, I have sinned,' then you repeated the Plan, the Eighteen Steps. That's exactly right."

"And the next step?"

"You'll see. But first, as I say, you have to have your meeting in Carlsbad. And it works, Kelly. It really does. You will become committed to your own salvation."

Jerry told me this in an offhand way, but my stomach jerked suddenly, and cold fear spread down my back.

I thought about a guy I'd known in Texas whose father was a preacher. The preacher's son admitted his homosexuality to a gay friend of mine by some dumb luck, not because he knew my friend was gay, but I think because he had got a mad crush on him, and must have thought my friend would be the understanding sort. After that, he tried to become part of the gay crowd in that small college town.

But he didn't like the bars we went to. He didn't like the drinking or the pot smoking. He didn't like the cussing, the campy humor, and he hated the endless talk of sex in the era of AIDS. For a sheltered romantic like him, I imagine it did seem crude. It was.

He tried to take it all in stride, I think, still hoping for a romantic, unrealistic meeting of his Prince Charming, but his little sheltered world had been torn apart. He came to the only conclusion his life as the son of a fundamentalist preacher had prepared him for. If you were gay, you had to do things decent people wouldn't; you had to become degenerate. I saw this warning sign when he began making excuses for invitations. I tried, but not hard enough, to get him to slow down, to convince him he could find some nice gay boy, like himself, eventually, if he would just give it time.

On impulse, I think, he went through a big confession in his father's church. He asked his own congregation to forgive him. Once he'd done that, as Jerry had just pointed out, he became committed to his confession. To love men, he now seemed to believe, he would have to reject his family, his religion, and his system of values. I was sick. He had nothing more to do with any of us. I saw him on campus occasionally. We would speak, but it was always guarded questions from me and pat assurances from him that he was fine, just fine. Before I graduated, I saw him for the last time escorting a pretty girl to an evening fellowship at his church on campus.

For the religious and the straights, that would have been a neat ending, but a few months later, after he married the girl, she caught him wearing one of her dresses. I got this from a reliable source, and I believe it. Suppress something long enough, and it seeks another outlet.

Oh, God—damn it! In writing this, I also remember thinking that if I ever had a lover, I would try to make sure he would be self-assured and proud of who he was. But in the case of William, it didn't work out that way. I was twenty eight when we met in a little hidey hole in Albuquerque, New Mexico. At the time, I was working as a mechanic at a Volkswagen dealership; he was fresh out of college and looking for work, still torn between staying in Albuquerque where he'd gone to school, or going back to some little town in Oklahoma, where his parents lived and trying to get a start from there with his new B.A. in English. He was scarcely twenty-two. But I was so attracted to him, his clear blue eyes, his jaunty-cut brown hair, and his perpetual sweatshirt and Levi's, that I overlooked the nearly seven years difference in our ages.

He seemed so self-assured and rebellious about his religious background (his parents belonged to the Assemblies of God, which he called "holier-than-thou rollers"), I never dreamed he carried so much guilt around with him about being gay. Although I wasn't his first lover, most of the others had lasted a semester or two in college and, he claimed, the *other* guy would break it off after awhile claiming to be straight or running off with their next conquest. The more we saw of each other, the more convinced I was that he was the person I had been looking for in the last decade of my life. After we moved in together and we both let down our defenses as we tried to open up to each other,

I began to see that he was troubled about being gay. We would be out for an evening at one of the gay clubs and he would be nursing a beer, frowning. When I'd ask him what was wrong, he would say, "nothing I can do anything about." If I pressed, we would end up leaving, stopping off in some straight club for a couple more beers, then go home.

When I wanted to celebrate our first anniversary, he seemed to droop a little. "Do you really think it's like we're *married*, Kelly?" Of course I did, but I realized he didn't. Even though he told me he loved me quite often, he wouldn't treat our relationship with the same kind of wonder and legitimacy I did. Then we celebrated (or I did) our second anniversary, then our third, and our fourth, and I began to realize with each passing year that William just wasn't convinced we had something that would last into old age.

I could have attributed his difficulty in believing in our relationship to the differences in our ages. But in a lot of ways, he was more mature than I was. If I wanted to splurge for a new television or spend the night in some expensive hotel, he would draw in the reigns. "We can't afford it," he'd say—or worse— "We can't just walk into a hotel and register, Kelly! They'll know what we're up to. We might get in trouble."

Then in the fifth year of our relationship, William was depressed a lot. I tried to get him to tell me what was troubling him, and he would give me his stock answer. "Nothing I can do anything about." But apparently, toward the end of that fifth year, which would have been in May, he did think he could do something about what was troubling him. I came home from work one afternoon, opening the front door and yelling, "Babe! I'm ho—" then stopping in my tracks with my work shirt pulled half way off.

He was on our sofa, seated between two clean-cut young men in their early twenties, with dress slacks, white shirts, and military haircuts, in the middle of reading from a Bible. After my entrance, the two guys got up, looking smug, and said good-bye to William, calling him Brother.

When they were gone, I asked for an explanation and, as it came pouring out of William's mouth, I could only stare at the stranger that had taken over my sweet William's body, shaking my head. "No. No. William, you don't know what you're saying." But he was adamant that he could go through a recovery program the two young men had been telling him about, run by a Reverend Josh Rafferty, who was getting recruits from the area. They would all live together in a house in Albuquerque, while keeping their present jobs.

William actually tried to talk me into the wisdom of it by kissing me on the lips, sobbing into my shoulder. "If it doesn't work, Kelly, I'll know. Then we can get on with our lives, okay? But I've got to try."

* * *

When Jerry and I reached the chow hall, I wondered if he had done his job as he was supposed to. He seemed at ease when he left me on the low-slung porch with all the chairs and the other recruits. He followed the chipmunk with the clipboard inside.

I waited on the porch with the rest of the guys and looked out over the field. In the early morning, the air was still cool, but the sunlight was warm and comfortable on my skin. The big, drab-green army tents across the valley had already begun to give off silvery waves of heat. Behind them, the "hand" of cliffs and bluffs looked as if it had splayed its fingers in the morning light. These long hills looked more than ever like fingers clawing into forever. That endlessness would be impossible to walk over, especially the sand and rocks. No human could get far in that purgatory without dying of exposure. I tried to envision the fields in front of me alive and cool green and inviting, growing strong in the sunlight. But it was as wilted and hopeless looking as the view of the hills.

From the chow hall, the smell of sausage and bacon filled the air and its smell reminded me that I was hungry. At the moment, I felt trapped and dependent on whatever it was Josh and his first converts were cooking up, besides the breakfast. The last few pairs of intimate new friends came across the field. I watched for a guy named Michael, whom I'd met on the bus trip from Carlsbad the day before.

The bus ride in the sweltering heat had been one of those times when I felt awkward having to talk, or worse, not talking. Michael had come through like a charm, however. He was one of those friendly sort of boys—and too pretty for his own good. A few miles into our trip into the unknown, he had us laughing at our predicament.

"I mean," he had said, grasping the front of his shirt with long bony fingers, "Honey! You girls better live it up now, because when they finish with us…"

His threat suggested an unspeakable horror, but I had laughed at his motherly warning and fought back the urge to spill my guts about William to anyone who would listen. Instead, I sought release from that ever-present sadness by letting someone like Michael capture my attention.

"Dear, I was Miss Houston for three years!" he'd said, somewhere along the hot, sweaty trip. "I do sooo hope I get a sex change." Then someone had asked to which sex, and that joke spread through the bus, until even the ones who were shocked at Michael's irreverent humor had smiled.

I felt sorry for him, too. What could he be expecting, really? He was the kind of gay boy people would always pick out as a fag, even if he wasn't—or, at least, even if he didn't want to be.

Last night in our tent, Michael had chosen a cot next to mine, and we had talked under the naked light bulbs until the bugs had become so thick he had shrieked in disgust. Again, I wondered just what he was hoping would happen to him here, what changes.

This morning, when he reached the porch, he smiled sweetly at his intimate new friend and, for one horrifying instant, I thought he was going to kiss him. They merely hugged and his companion rushed off, red-faced, to see the chipmunk.

Michael saw me and waved wildly, as though we were long lost friends. He fluttered into a chair next to me.

"Oh, Kelly, hon, I think I've made a very big mistake."

That threw me. "What?"

He leaned over to whisper. "I think I'm in love."

I wanted to laugh, but Michael had such a serious face I couldn't. "You're supposed to be getting cured, remember?"

"I know, hon, but give me a break." His face betrayed regret. "He's so cute!"

"Who?"

"My sister, hon. Alex."

"The guy who interviewed you?"

Michael just nodded and settled back in his chair studying his nails, holding them out in a fan in front of his face.

"But Michael, you'd better fall out of love, quick, before you get hurt." I laughed, but I meant it.

Michael looked contrite. "I know. But it's going to be hard with all these men around."

"Except," I said, "you can't forget why you're here."

He looked at me with such disgust, I wondered if I had angered him. "I haven't forgotten for one instant why I'm here, hon, if you know what I mean. It's just that I'm tired of being a *girl*, and this is my last chance. So if this is what it takes to get a decent job, and to be liked by people, I'll do it. I'm tired of being dirt underneath people's feet. The Rev. Rafferty says Jesus can cure me, then by God…" He stopped and grinned at the appropriateness of his oath. "Then I'll do it."

I felt William tugging on my heart, to tell Michael there was little chance he would find the cure he wanted, but I kept my mouth shut. I wasn't ready to tell anybody about William. *Good luck*, I thought, smiling at Michael, feeling sorry for him again, especially how violated he looked with his head shaved, where just the day before had been a head of luscious, curly auburn hair that any woman would have killed for. If I had to pick out Josh's first casualty in our group, I would choose Michael.

When the last pair reached the chow hall, and the older recruits had, I supposed, compared notes about us, they called us inside to eat. I tried to get into the line with the older recruits, who were being served at a counter where they were dishing up pancakes and sausage, but Jerry frowned at me and indicated another line farther down, where each of us new recruits was being dished up some gelatinous glob of beige paste. "We must earn our luxuries," Jerry said.

"And how are we sup—"

"Silence!" said the chipmunk behind me. I turned and locked eyes with him, and felt myself staring into some empty, plastic mannequin's eyes. "Neophytes do not argue."

* * *

After what passed as breakfast and a ten-minute number one and two break, we spent an hour of praying in the chapel. I was so angry with the way we had been treated at breakfast, I refused to bow my head even to pretend I was praying. But I was praying very hard that I could hang onto myself for just one day, without exploding and risk exposing my real purpose for being here. As the prayer session continued ad nauseam, my anger gave way to the threat of tears, but I blinked them back thinking, *poor William, poor Michael, and all you other poor damn bastards.*

Later, we were divided into details, with a foreman in charge of three of us and three of *them* (the older recruits). Note: I think I'll refer to them as the S&Ms, which seems more appropriate. Although there has been no truly overt roughness, or "tough love," there's an undercurrent of it in the air. After reading the pamphlet that Rafferty had given me, with his quite clear explanation of the program and mentioning boot camp several times, I had no illusions that this program was going to be like other ex-gay programs, where the overt emphasis is on love (although there is, to my mind an undercurrent of psychic cruelty). Here, however, physical violence seemed to be lurking just under the surface, just as it had in boot camp. Rafferty didn't have that tenderness when he was in his Albuquerque office, and he didn't display it here, either, except for his crying jag in the chapel yesterday. So as the heat rose in the valley, so did my sense of foreboding. I had quickly put up my guard at the breakfast, seeing that the S&Ms got the sausage and pancakes and such with some sort of tokens that looked like ordinary poker chips. So as we gathered in groups for our work details, my anger was already difficult to contain. I hate being told when I can take a shit, or when I can and can't talk, or for that matter, being fed pig slop.

Once our work details were established for the day, we toured the ranch, which I actually enjoyed.

It's surprising what this valley has hidden in it when you get a good look around. It is not quite so simple and barren as it might appear. Nor is it just one big flat bottom as I'd thought when I looked at it from on top of the bus. My S&M, Jerry, stuck close to me like stink on shit and yammered in my ear his endless questions, which I was beginning to tire of. I was no longer taken with his beauty so much as reminded that beauty only runs skin deep. Apparently, at the pre-breakfast meeting, the S&Ms were told to keep working on us. That annoyed me, especially when I was trying to listen to the work-detail foreman in charge of showing us the place.

The new barracks, which we'll be building, are south of the chow hall on the crest of a hill. It's a good site with pine trees and grass. They can't be seen from the low part of the valley where the present buildings stand. It's a soft spot. In the late afternoons, when the sun is sinking, and the air becomes cooler as it does in the desert, we'll be able to relax and maybe play volleyball before our sermons or discussions. Les Hunter, a man from the church in Carlsbad, and supposedly a crack carpenter, showed us the foundation for the barracks and the blue prints. I liked him immediately, maybe because he reminds me of

New Friends and My False Confession

my father who is also a sometime carpenter. I've helped my father build houses, so I figure I can do a good job on these.

Charlie Hays (my friend, confidant, and keeper of my journal) and his brother, David, own a farm somewhere near here. Charlie is the youngest brother. During the tour, he spoke softly, with a kind of down-home shyness I liked. At the same time, I pitied him, knowing what I knew about him. Anyway, he watched us openly and smiled at me when I caught his eye.

Later, our group was handed off to another foreman by the name of Alton Drigger, in charge of the livestock. The corrals and pens are also hidden from the floor of the valley behind a hill on the east end of the ranch. He drove us out to the site, then showed us the present livestock.

Although I was taller than Drigger by several inches, he was lithe and his forearms were roped with muscles. Like some of the drill sergeants in boot camp, he was small but compact, like a coiled spring might be, ready to spring, as drill sergeants often did, pushing themselves right into the face of the basic trainee, neck tendons taut, blood vessels popping out on their foreheads, as if they *hated* the recruit as they screamed at him. This was Drigger. Coiled and ready to spring or strike. His whole demeanor said, "WATCH OUT!" He mentioned our homosexuality frequently, which wouldn't have been so scary, except that he spat the word at us, pronouncing it "homa-sexshul," as if it churned up gall in his mouth. I've worked for some pretty foul bosses in the army, so I figured I could dig in and deal with him if he tried giving me a hard time.

* * *

The meeting at the church in Carlsbad took up the afternoon. It was just a typical church. The people were friendly and curious, but the questions they may have been dying to ask seemed to die on their lips. We performed our duties in front of the church, formally taking the first of the eighteen steps, saying, "I accept Jesus as my personal savior," then confessing to being sinners—pretty much as Brother Jerry said it would go. I swallowed my pride and spoke with the same mealy-mouthed sincerity of the others, although I was probably the only one who meant to be mealy-mouthed.

I kept having to remind myself that we had not been forced to join, but it reminded me of the often repeated argument in the army that no one had forced that choice on us, either.

Once we got back to the Lion's Mouth Christian Ranch, around nine o'clock that night, supper was served. The evening meal was at least palatable, but nothing to compare to the dinner we'd been offered the first night. Now I understood why, when Rafferty had announced seconds, the older recruits had, to a man, gone back. Our portions this night were inadequate, at best, to quite stop the hunger that had been gnawing at me all day.

The chow hall is a good indicator of what Rafferty's got planned. A hundred people could fit in the building, elbow to elbow, at the long tables. Presently, there are around forty of us, including the new recruits, a somewhat larger number of S&Ms, the foremen, and the LMCR staff.

After we had cleared the dishes from the tables and had taken them to the kitchen, where the work detail assigned KP duty began their chores, one of the S&Ms brought out a guitar.

We were given photocopied sheets of music from which we sang songs, not of protest or dreaming, but what I'll call "Caucasian gospel"—a simple one-step or two-step beat, slowed down and dragged out so that I yawned frequently, especially when stretching out one-syllable words to three or four, like "Lo-or-ord." Caucasian gospel is like the background music one hears in elevators and ignores. One thing, though: I love to hear the soft masculine movement through the scales. Apparently, they do a lot of singing here. The S&Ms sound pretty darned good, kind of like the Hitler Youth must've sounded to the people of Germany 60 years ago—yummy and wholesome (if you could ignore the stench of burning human flesh in the ovens). At first hearing, Caucasian gospel doesn't sound too intimidating, either. But to enjoy it, I had to think down, concentrating on the male voices and the way they blended together with a masculine resonance.

Michael and I shared a sheet of music. He sang the high notes, and I sang bass. Not that I have a bass voice, but Michael needed a bass for our side of the circle. There was a lot of smiling tonight, and maybe it was sincere for those of us who want to be cured.

For moments at a time, I found myself drifting into the spirit of the thing and, at those times, I imagined what this place would be like if it was a gay radical faerie gathering or a Burning Man festival. We'd have a nude barbecue, and then we would have danced till dawn, pairing off and, in some cases, grouping off. I couldn't smile about that. In comparison to the wholesome, if boring, fun we had tonight, the tendency for gay men to think SEX all the time in cloistered settings like this did seem a little degenerate. It seems to me that when Christians point the accusatory finger at us, they're referring to our unfettered sexuality, not to our homo-sexuality. When we gay people point back at the religious, we refer to their prudery—not their Christianity, per sé.

* * *

Gotta stop, since I'm getting a little preachy. It's lights out in half an hour, and there's something I've got to do before that. There's a guy (Larry, I think) a couple of cots down from me who is crying, trying to hide it and doing a bad job of it. He's been looking stricken all day—since breakfast. He is the fat kid who went for seconds last night. I forgot about him during supper and the sing along, but now I can't take my mind off him. I guess I'll go check on him. No one else seems interested. Step No. 18: Become a people helper.

I think I like that one just fine.

I kind of wish Charlie Hays were here, tonight, instead of home in his bed. If you're reading this, Charlie, this is just to let you know that I'm thinking about you!

Kelly

III

Who is Paul Romaine

Lion's Mouth Christian Ranch
Monday, June 8

    Sometime after I went to sleep last night, after seeing about the kid, Larry, and after relieving myself under the covers from the anxiety of the day (yeah, I do that from time to time, especially since William's suicide and being too gun-shy to commit to another man), I broke out into a cold sweat. Paul Romaine's face appeared to me in the darkness, almost as though he were standing over my bed and peering down on me with those cold, beady eyes. I *had* heard that name before, and it still bothered me that I couldn't think of where. And it nagged me all day. Each time I saw him around the ranch, but especially in the chow hall and tonight at our Bible study, I remembered how I learned about him—or at least someone like him with the same name.

    It was when I met a long-time gay couple in Common, New Mexico. It's funny how things work out. Now that I'm inside the same program that killed my sweet William, thinking about him is easier than it has been. Right after that awful night, when William killed himself, I called his parents in Oklahoma. I didn't tell them who I was but pretended to be an old friend from college and wanted to get in touch with William. His mother confirmed that William had died, but she said in an accident.

I had to choke back my tears, to pretend shock and sympathy for her, although I wanted to scream at her to stop lying. I just had to know about him during his last days, but she clamed up, except to say that no one would be allowed at the funeral except family.

So I said fuck it and headed to San Francisco. I think I intended to drown my sorrows in a sea of penises and, once I'd arrived in SF, that's exactly what I began to do. Of course, I insisted on safe sex (it's appalling that so many men in the big cities are into "bare-backing"). Only prowling the mostly twenty-something gay clubs and having one-night stands wasn't the balm I needed for what hurt me about William and the way he ended his life. After a month of trying to live in that crazy city, I began to realize I couldn't forget William by fucking my brains out and, since I've never been a drinker or a drug user, I didn't even try to get solace from that. I was about to pack up and leave the state, when I met Pete Thompson. Pete was up front about telling me he was HIV positive, which I appreciated. And with the sex-thing removed between us, we ended up talking—a great deal. I couldn't help talking about William, and he seemed willing to listen to me, so I told him what had happened and how I felt. I spilled my guts about how much I hated William's religion for raising him to feel ashamed of himself; then I told him about the program that had put the nail in William's coffin and about his fucking parents who, even with William's suicide, wanted to whitewash his life so *they* wouldn't look bad.

That's when Pete told me about the couple in Common, New Mexico, saying that even though he hadn't lived there for 33 years, he stayed in touch with them. He talked about a guy named Paul Romaine, too, explaining how it was him who was responsible for a lot that transpired in the small town of Common. Pete insisted that when I made my way back to New Mexico I should look up the gay couple, should tell them my story of William, too, since one of the men in the relationship had been a preacher's son, and he told me how this Romaine guy had eventually gotten the preacher to disown his son because of their homosexuality.

I've never had the stomach for the fundamentalists, especially with all their anti-gay rhetoric over the years, and how they've been using this mythical "gay agenda" to bash gays. But I did want to hear this couple's story, especially since one of them had been raised in a fundamentalist church as William had. I thought it would do me more good to get to know them than it would to continue trying to meet someone in San Francisco.

So I headed out for New Mexico in late November and stopped in Common. I was looking forward to meeting two guys who had actually been together for over 30 years and, according to Pete Thompson, had remained faithful to each other. Now in their 50s, I was a little nervous about meeting them. I'm 15 years younger than they are, and I was afraid they would consider me too immature to bother getting to know—or something like that, anyway, because when I arrived in Common at the truck stop, filled the pickup, and peed, I hovered around the pay phone for ten minutes before I could work up the courage to call. I don't know what I expected to happen, but as soon as I mentioned Pete Thompson, the guy on the other end, Tom Allen-Reece, began giving me directions to their farm, and called to his mate, Joel. They both got on the telephone, saying that Pete had already called and to expect me. They had my room prepared, wanted to know what I liked to eat and before I got off the phone, I felt like I'd known them forever.

It gives me a great deal of pleasure to take a break from writing about this program here at LMCR and, I know I digress, but I wish I could explain to all the young people living in places like San Francisco, LA, and New York, and other places I've never been what a wonderful life two men can share if they look to the future together and consider themselves married even if, in the 90s, we're barred from doing so in most states. It was the kind of relationship I had always wanted with William.

It was odd, therefore, and a little distressing when I was actually sitting in Tom and Joel's living room, sipping on some kind of imported beer from Australia that I began to feel more depressed and leaden than

I had after William left me, and as close to tears that first night in their home as I had the days following William's suicide. I stayed with them a week, and would have been content to become an employee of theirs (they repeatedly offered me a job); but I became more determined than ever to get on with my plans to investigate Rev. Rafferty's program.

Tom and Joel had a daughter, whom they had mutually conceived (at least that was about all I could understand from what they'd told me, and probably isn't appropriate for me to go into much detail about). Pete then was wrong about their never allowing a third person into their relationship. Because in a technical sense, they had both conceived their daughter by having relations with her mother. They also had loving parents in Eva and Douglas Reece; and Tom informed me that, after the birth of their daughter, his own estranged mother had come back to Common to become a grandmother to their daughter, Shara. Her husband, the preacher, had died of a stroke about two years after they had disowned Tom when they were living someplace in Arizona.

Tom and Joel's house was a magnificent adobe structure, which they had built during the eighties, laughing at how they just hadn't wanted to leave their first house, which meant so much to them, "since it was where we grew from boys into men," Joel had said. Apparently they had lived in a small house for 15 years, adding on as they made room for their daughter when it was their turn to have her, while her mother was attending university. What they settled for in the adobe structure would put the most affluent Santa Fe snobs to shame. Built in the classical pueblo style, it encompasses thousands of square feet of living space, from its 5 bedrooms and six bathrooms, to a great room with a ceiling that reaches 20 feet to a second level of rooms where they have their offices, library, and a tower that leads to the roof. We spent most nights on the roof looking out over the valley, upon a night sky that took my breath away, filled with a frothy Milky Way. And even at night, the Florida Mountains sit on the edge of the valley, a jagged silhouette to the night sky, stars crowning their peaks.

I was tempted several times to take them up on their offer of a job, but I finally left eight days after I had arrived. It was on the evening of the last night with them that I remembered to ask Tom about Paul Romaine.

Even after all those years, Tom's face, which seemed generally unmarked by his age, suddenly turned serious—so deadly serious, I was afraid I had offended him by bringing up the subject.

When I said so, he smiled wanly, as though looking back through time, nodding his head. We were on the roof, as we had been most nights, even though the weather that fall was cold. They have a kiva fireplace there, which we huddled around, warmed also that night by hot-buttered rum (and me warmed also by the two of them, who sat together legs intertwined like newly weds, looking for all the world like middle-aged farmers). I secretly found it amusing to consider telling them they should get a web page and do a few naked photos of themselves, and charge other men to view the "hot gay farmers." But I digress.

Considering my question, Tom untwined his legs from Joel's, placed his drink on the table in front of him, and sat forward, looking across at me. He took a deep breath. The light from the fireplace flickered on his skin, making his eyes twinkle and, at times, his tears to shine.

"Pete was right, Kelly," Tom said. "If it hadn't been for this Paul Romaine, Joel and I would have had time to sort through our feelings for each other, and probably would have been able to begin our life together a little more rationally. I might not have lost my parents—been disowned, that is—if it hadn't been for Paul."

Joel leaned forward as well, taking one of Tom's hands, and putting his arm around Tom's shoulders. I almost burst into tears as I watched the two of them. I couldn't help but imagine myself and William together, like them, a little gray, foreheads lined from years of life, yet not washed out; faces grown older, but still hinting at the beautiful youths they had been. Joel didn't say anything, but Tom settled back naturally into his arms; I felt myself sigh with sadness, scarcely able to recall a single time that my sweet William had been so at ease with me.

"After everything went down, and Joel and his family took me in," Tom said, sighing, "before we had ourselves a daughter or anything, I tried to keep up with some of the true Christians in my church. It turns out one of them was Paul's father, Leon. I had thought that, like my own parents, they might be grieving over their son, because he had pulled enough horrible stunts and got involved with…well, the guy that killed this family down the road, that they sent him away, to a place in Georgia, I think.

"So one day, I was visiting with Mr. Romaine and I mentioned his son.

"I already told you about all the trouble Paul caused me with my father's church. When he told everyone in the church about me and Joel being gay, his father, Leon, was just about the only man in that congregation who exhibited forgiveness toward me. I came to the conclusion years ago that Paul is a homosexual, although I don't think his father knows that. I've reflected on Paul's obsession with me when I knew him, how he was always trying to get us alone, how jealous he was of my friendship in high school with Joel.

"All I know is that Leon sent his son to that retreat, because he thought Paul was spiritually ill. But then, when I was visiting with him, he said Paul frightened him, that he would never forget that look of hatred in his son's eyes when things were going down at the church about me.

"So then I asked him if he thought the retreat had helped Paul.

"Kelly, the man broke down and cried. 'I lost him!' he said, and went on to say that Paul was into some things that frightened him and his wife. 'Like what?' I asked. The man actually shook as he took me by the shoulder and walked outside with me.

"'He used to come home for Christmas and such. Just short visits,' Leon said. There were tears in his eyes, and I thought the man was sorry that Paul rarely came home. But when I asked him about that, his eyes widened in horror. 'No, Tom. We're relieved. We'd never disown him, of course, the way your father did you. But we're glad he doesn't come around any more, talking that nonsense about the white race. It's just plain Nazi business. We didn't raise him to think that way.' Kelly,

Mr. Romaine couldn't even talk about his son in a normal voice. He kept it low, as if to speak too loudly, someone might hear. He finally asked me, 'Son, why are you interested in Paul? Didn't you get your fill of him years ago?'

"I told Mr. Romaine I was full to here with what Paul had done. I was honest with him, Kelly, but he didn't seem to mind my honesty. In fact, he nodded, agreeing with me.

"'I would've thought my son had his fill of that subject, too, since he hated it so much in you, and I thought once he'd gone through that program, he'd get on with his life, son. But now I know that if he couldn't get you to renounce your homosexuality, he would prefer to see you dead.'

"I asked if he didn't mean the death of my spirit. But Mr. Romaine shook his head, looked me straight in the eye.

"'No, son. Not a bit. I've got my theory that he's hooked on this homosexuality business—for the harm he can do people. I think my son is interested in death, itself, and precious little else.'"

For a moment, Tom was silent, and I thought he'd finished his tale about his meeting with Leon Romaine. But then, just as he said Mr. Romaine had lowered his voice, Tom leaned closer toward me, lowering his.

"What interested Paul even back then, Kelly, was the Nazis. Mr. Romaine told me Paul wasn't so much interested in their military machine, or even their desire to rid the world of the Jews. He was fascinated with their methods, their experiments." Tom shuddered visibly, and Joel wrapped his arms around him. In turn, I felt the hair rise on the back of my neck as a breeze came over the roof. It had an icy breath.

"I'm telling you, Kelly," Tom said, Paul was much sicker than Joel or I ever thought, if his own father is afraid of him. I just thought Paul was spiteful. I didn't dream he would be the kind to become interested in the dark side of things—especially in things having to do with torture, like the medical experiments of the Nazis.

"But as I said, he did get involved with a fellow here in Common at the same time he was trying to force me back into the church—a guy by the name of Kenneth Stroud. Kenneth killed his parents and a younger brother and then committed suicide. But we always figured it was a passion killing and not something he'd planned. The children Joel's parents adopted were the survivors of that family."

This time, Tom settled back, sighing once. "I guess that's the most I've recalled about Paul in a long time. The thing that makes me sad is that if Paul is a homosexual, he's one of the most tortured gay people I know. And it's doubly sad, since his shame makes him want to hurt others as he did me and Joel."

* * *

Whether this Paul Romaine at LMCR is the same person Tom knew, I cannot say, until I have had a chance to talk with the Paul Romaine, here. But, tonight, as I write this, I am afraid it's the same person.

And if he is the same person, that's bad news for the recruits. But even if he's not, the chipmunk-faced man, whose spirit apparently awakened me last night, causing me to break out into a cold sweat, will suffice. What might otherwise be the standard ex-gay program of love and light and dollops of reparative therapy as Exodus International practices could well be much worse because of him.

I will have to see. Can this possibly be only the third night I have spent in this tent?

Like the poor fat kid on his cot next to the open tent flap, I'm hungry, too, and fear there might not be enough to eat in the coming days to sustain my energy. Maybe not enough protein to keep the mental edge I need to investigate this place without giving in to it.

Maybe I should have taken that job Tom and Joel Allen-Reece offered.

IV

The Routine and Those Who Fail

Lion's Mouth
Thursday, June 11

After I left Common on my way to Albuquerque where Josh Rafferty has his main office, I thought about backing out of this thing altogether. By then it was fall in New Mexico and coming on winter. After I climbed out of the Chihuahuan desert of southern New Mexico, heading north on I-25, and the altitude continued to rise, the air got cooler and I could actually taste winter in the air. To be sure, the highway heads almost due north between mountain ranges where it is still desert, but the Rio Grande river meanders along a few miles to the east, and I could see the bare trees and copses of evergreens along the river in the Bosque del Apache wildlife refuge. I thought about backing out of this thing, since I was returning home and could easily re-establish a normal routine.

It wasn't that I was going to let my memories of William die with him. But I think it would have been all right with him if I had given up and tried to find someone like Tom Allen-Reece or Joel, his mate (they called each other "husband," which was quaint to me, but intrinsically lovely, too). And with the wind blowing through my pickup bringing the smell of burning wood on whiffs of cold-tainted air, reminding me of someplace cozy and warm, I felt it would be possible to find my own husband.

I was beginning to think I would just get on with my life as I entered Albuquerque, making a sharp eastward turn as I-25 crossed the river; but as I turned north again, and I came into the middle of the city to the dreary downtown huddled off to my left and the rest of the city all around me, my optimism began to sink, and William was sitting beside me in the pickup and we were on our way home after leaving a gay club. He was glum and when I asked him what was wrong, he said: "Nothing I can do anything about."

I began to cry and scream at him, now, on this fall afternoon. If anyone had looked closely at me as they whizzed past, they would have sped up to get around and away from the madman, gesticulating to no one there in the seat beside him. "That's how you left the world, isn't it William?! You couldn't do anything about being homosexual, and you couldn't do anything about not being able to go straight. Your precious brother in Christ left you in the lurch, and so you blew your beautiful head off!

"Why didn't you come home to me?

"Why couldn't you value what we had?"

My heartbreak gave way to anger, and I drove straight to Rafferty's "Light of Christ" ministries, which was in a 1950s ranch-style brick home in the heart of one of Albuquerque's old tree-lined neighborhoods, part residential, part offices and, these days, part gay ghetto, where gays had begun to move in and renovate the more salvageable older homes. Rafferty had parked himself right on the outskirts of this area, knowing that he would find takers there, as he had William, sending out his best-looking converts to knock on the doors and proselytize for the Lord.

***

No, I couldn't let someone else do what I'd planned. So, here I am filling page after page with penciled scrawl, squashing bugs into the sweat on my neck and arms. Maybe other people don't think this retreat of

Rafferty's is very important, but it meant William's life—literally—as I think it is going to mean the lives of many others. It certainly doesn't get the attention of the gay media in the big east- and west-coast cities, until there's a bashed gay somewhere, dead or castrated, or mutilated in some other way. And then it's only a sensation, as was that gay serial killer, recently. So what if a few unhappy fags want to try to get themselves converted?

People have been trying to cure gays for a long time and, worse, gay people have many times willingly submitted themselves to the most outrageous of cures including castration, electric shock, drugs, aversion therapy—you name it. There's nothing new, really, about this ex-gay movement—except that it is well funded and the anti-gay scare tactics is a good money maker for the fundamentalist movement.

And again, there is this Paul Romaine. Tom was right.

* * *

Step No. 7: Learn to control your mind.

In the few days I've been here, I have counted about fifteen of the S&Ms, though it's a little hard to keep track of so many new faces the way they break us up into small groups every morning. We all wear Levi's and white T-shirts. If it wasn't such a disgusting thought, I'd say that Josh is a Levi's queen and the reason we dress like this is because it gets his rocks off. There are eleven of us new recruits. That was easy to count because we all came in on the bus from Carlsbad together.

Of the church staff there's Josh Rafferty, Paul Romaine, a few women who work in the chapel and the kitchen; and then there are the members of the church in Carlsbad who are our foremen, including the Hays brothers (Charlie and David), in charge of the farming, Alton Drigger in charge of the livestock, Les Hunter in charge of the carpentry, Frank Mann in charge of the kitchen, and "Sharp" Jones, a black man, in charge of maintenance, janitorial, and sanitation.

Every day the new recruits and the S&Ms are grouped off with each of the foremen and, for that particular day, we perform those duties the foremen charge us with. Except for Sundays, which is a day of worship and rest.

On a typical day, we're up at sunrise, roused from the tent by our S&Ms. I don't know what goes on in their tent after lights out each night, but I know we new recruits are tired by the end of the day and that all we want to do is get eight hours of sleep, but it's more like five or six. Maybe the guys in the other tent can handle it, because they're not really human at all and, at night, they're turned off and stood in a corner. The new recruits are paired off with the S&Ms, appropriately drilled with questions as we make our way to the chow hall for breakfast.

Breakfast is a time for getting the work roster settled, questions asked and answered, followed by a brief prayer session, and about fifteen actual minutes to choke down the goo they serve us. It's interesting that, since that first breakfast, all of us have been fed the pig slop, even the S&Ms, unless they have those poker chips to buy meat or eggs or milk. I've begun to think the S&Ms must have had to work pretty hard for that one small reward on our first morning. Allowing them to have the real food, while we were fed the slop, might even have been a way to make us feel cheated and to aspire to being like the S&Ms. At any rate, food is used to reward and punish, and to keep us striving for it.

What work each recruit and his paired S&M does depends on what detail a person is assigned to; then it's lunch, prayer, and back to work. The work is hard. As I suspected, we do as much of the labor by hand as possible. I found out that the row beds in the fields were not done with a tractor at all, but built up with hoes and shovels, which accounts for their scraggly appearance. In passing, Charlie Hays (my buddy) has told me that he objects to it. As a real farmer, he's incensed that Rafferty requires such methods to be used. Charlie says, "They ought'a care whether we can raise good crops." I don't think Charlie quite gets *why* Rafferty insists on doing things the hard way. But that is the whole point.

Of course, we take showers in the heat of the afternoon, so that by the time we are allowed to go to bed, we won't rest quite as well as we might. [Note: I must continually try to find the cynical explanation for everything here; otherwise I might lose my mental edge.]

After a long, tiring day, we're again insulted by the shit they sling at us for supper. The excuse they make is that until we have brought in our own produce they must depend on the generosity of the church people in Carlsbad to supply our sustenance.

Devotionals take up most of the evening, and is the most intense time of indoctrination; it includes prayer, biblical discussion and, of course, confessionals. I have a feeling that one by one, each of us will be put in "the Hot Seat." Let me explain: one person is set off in the middle of the dining hall each evening. While he is eating, he's required to answer any and all questions put to him by any other person in the room. He is drilled by Josh on the eighteen steps and which step he feels he has accomplished. It's too early to tell, but I think this procedure will be repeated on each recruit during this eighteen-week, eighteen-step program.

It's hard to realize how long eighteen weeks of indoctrination is until you've been through just a few days out here. It's twice as long as military boot camp. It's already fuzzy in my mind about what the outside world is like. It seems that I've always been here and that everything that went before was a dream, including my time in the army.

I'm afraid the very repetitiousness of this routine will dull my senses; afraid, too, that my writing will become dulled, my purpose forgotten.

* * *

Today, I was assigned to Alton Drigger at the stock pens. As I said, they're hidden from the main part of the valley on the east end by a low rise of earth that breaks off into short cliffs. The pens' location is sensible considering the destructive force of blowing sand across this semi-desert valley; in the open, the air can be abrasive, with gypsum flecks that swirl in small tornadoes, electrified by the sun and wind.

Out in it from the open air of the Jeep, the valley is a lot bigger than it appears. It will require many hands and many months to transform this place into a real farm, and with hoes and shovels, it's daunting just to think about. This place is not a ranch, except in a city dude's mind like Rafferty's. The buildings and the tents are like a huddled camp. The valley is not so circular, either, as I thought the day I arrived. Small canyons break into the valley walls and lead to dead-ends, where rain and blowing sand have worked endlessly blasting through the turmoil of the seasons.

The stock pens are built close to the face of the cliffs. And in this area, the land is richer, full of healthy grass, amid piñon trees, yucca, and weeds.

Three of us recruits—me, the guy named Larry whom I hear crying every night, and an athletic Adonis named Donald—were assigned to three S&Ms, including my good friend Jerry. Today, we were supposed to clear the stock pens of weeds, mend the fences with new planks of wood, and reinforce the cow shed that had been built against the cliffs. I take it that, in the first six months of the ranch's existence, the church people built the stock pens under Drigger's guidance. I think Jerry said they used scrap lumber from the original ranch house that used to stand in the valley.

We spent the morning clearing the weeds leaving only grass and trees. We shoveled dirt and rocks against the fence where the hogs had tried to root underneath. But as the morning melted away, we began to tire. We had cleared all the outside area, but Drigger seemed to grow impatient as the morning wore on, and with his impatience, he began to call us girls and fags. It strikes me that he's supposed to keep at us (which makes sense when I think about my days in boot camp in the army). It's a technique that keeps the trainees both disoriented and afraid, but I also think Drigger enjoys his role.

As it grew hotter toward noon, when even our shadows slipped under our feet to cool off, Larry began to sweat profusely. He is extremely overweight and, forgive the allusion, he sweats like a hog. His hands grew greasy and several times his hoe slipped, causing him to lose his balance. Besides his profuse sweating, Larry stood all wrong, jiggling and jerking on the end of the hoe with his legs so far apart he couldn't get traction. He worked harder than Donald or I did, yet accomplished little, except to become the focus of Drigger's anger.

Drigger watched him for awhile without saying anything, but I could tell that Larry's performance was making him angry. So, several times, he took Larry by the shoulder. "Look, kid, you're standing like a woman. Do like this." He took Larry's hoe, handling it easily. "You're not throwing your shoulders behind it!" Each time he handed back Larry's hoe, Larry nodded, wheezing, sweating, grunting, and each time he went back to hacking. Finally, he dropped his hoe and this time, when he clumsily squatted to retrieve it, he stepped on the blade, causing the handle to whack him hard across the mouth. The blood spurted out (the allusion that came to mind, this time, was bleeding like a stuck pig); he backed away, rubbing his sweaty palms across his face, smearing his cheek with blood. Drigger stuck his shovel into the ground and wiped his hands on the back of his pants.

Then he grabbed Larry by both shoulders and, like a Marine drill sergeant, screamed into his face. "You beat all, you fat pig! You pervert! You know that!"

"I just dropped it!" Larry whined.

"I don't care!" Drigger whined back. "I don't want to see you drop nothing again."

"My hands sweat!" Larry protested. He tried to show them to Drigger, but Drigger knocked them away.

Larry's sides were heaving as he stared dumbfounded at the foreman. "It's too hot," he said. "I can't take the heat. I'm hungry. I'm getting dizzy." He did look as if he was about to pass out, but I didn't know whether it was from the heat or the fear that seemed to ooze from his skin.

"I don't care!" Drigger whined, again. "I've got a job to do and, like it or not, you're stuck."

In response, Larry picked up his hoe and began hacking at the weeds.

Drigger grabbed the hoe and threw it. "Did I say you could work?"

Larry looked at me as if for help. "Well—"

"Well nothin'!" Drigger shouted. "You go get us some water out of the Jeep." When Larry was loping away, Drigger turned on us. "Lucky for the rest of you fags, it's lunch time. You breathe a word of this to anyone and I'll make Hell seem like Heaven."

Other than pissing me off, this was the sort of treatment I expected. Maybe it doesn't have it's place in a religious environment, or shouldn't, except I just thought of it as army style and let it go. I was tired and relieved, and I intended to give Larry a few pointers after lunch, maybe take him aside and tell him that Drigger was putting on an act and to grin and bear it. Of course, I didn't think Drigger was acting one bit. Unlike the tightly coiled drilled sergeants in the Army, who could get into your face and scream as if they hated your guts one minute, they could turn pleasant the next moment, and you knew (if you hadn't lost your head at the screaming) that it was a well-controlled act on their parts, to deliberately disorient and frighten the trainee. Not so with Drigger. He stared slit-eyed as Larry carried the jug of water from one recruit to the next, following the poor kid with his eyes, watching for any mistake, I guess. It made me uneasy to watch Drigger watch Larry.

But even if I had wanted to complain that Drigger was getting mean without reason, who was I going to tell? *Probably Charlie*, I thought to myself, as Larry carried the jug back to the Jeep.

* * *

At lunch, I couldn't shake Jerry long enough to get Larry aside and give him my advice about Drigger, and Larry's S&M took him off through the chow hall before I had a chance to say anything to him, anyway.

The chow hall filled with recruits, and unlike the silence from the first day from the older recruits, now that we had been paired with our S&Ms, lunch was noisy, as each new recruit and his S&M got more acquainted—that is, acquainted according to some sort of script, because as I listened, I heard "Christian Speak" as the S&Ms asked their recruits to tell them stories of their "brokenness."

—*"path Satan led me down…filled with addiction to drugs and sex."*
—*"Was that when the Light shed in the darkness by the Son led you…"*
—*"tried to be faithful to my girl friend…"*
—*"couldn't stop the masturba—"*
"Brother, call it self-abuse, for in Christ we cease the language that offends."

—"Kelly?"

I looked at Brother Jerry, who was seated across from me, and I guess he'd asked a question. "I'm sorry, Brother Jerry," I said, "What did you ask?"

"Your sin," he said. "Ask forgiveness as you take the nourishment offered here in this holy place."

I was confused. I held a spoonful of watery soup to my lips, looking into it for a single chunk of anything remotely nourishing. "Praise God for this food," I said. "Your bounty and love nourishes me, as I pray for Thee to forgive my sin."

It went on like that for at least half an hour, and I tuned out the words that swirled around me from all over the chow hall, looking from one table to the next, where every head was shaved down to the moles and pimples on the scalps of every recruit. Some faces stood out, and I could see the dark, liquid eyes of a recruit of Mediterranean extraction, or admire the clean, well formed chin and sharply defined Adam's apple of another recruit. Even Jerry's apparent Nordic background was pleasant to look at, which is why I could put up with his Christian speak and endless coaching in the ways of the Lord during our repast. *Man, I don't think I'll ever be able to talk like this…*

After lunch, Larry settled into the Jeep like a sack of feed. "How am I going to make it?" he asked me.

"Just don't let that guy get to you," I said. "Just tough it out."

Then Drigger came out of the chow hall picking his teeth. He squinted toward us, then pulled on his cowboy hat and patted his stomach. I resented that gesture, since the foremen are fed at a table by themselves and get real food. He came over to us and slapped Larry on the shoulder, "Ready?"

Larry jumped turning around to see that it was Drigger. His face went through a serious of quick expressions—all of them betraying fear. "I guess so," Larry said to him, drying his mouth with his hand, then turning to Jerry and me, as soon as Drigger passed to the front of the Jeep. "But I wish I could've had some meat. I'm starving and I have a headache."

Jerry looked at Larry with sympathy and that made me like him a little better for a moment. "If you do the Lord's work…"

I shut him out of my mind and turned away. *Good old Jerry*, I thought with distaste. Then I looked at Larry's rolls of fat. "It wouldn't be a good idea for them to feed us a big lunch, anyway," I said. "It'd make you feel too heavy in this heat."

* * *

We worked in the hog pens, emptying large barrels of sour corn mash into the feeding troughs, which were fifty-five gallon drums that had been cut down the middle (most likely cut with a blow torch) from top to bottom, then laid on their sides and supported by old railroad ties. The mud around the troughs was slick and black and gave off an acrid stench. Larry slipped to his knees carrying a bucket of mash. He tried pulling himself up and his efforts made sucking noises. I helped him up, but he fell again. In the slimy mud, his fall seemed to happen in slow motion and ended in a grunt.

"Get up," Drigger said. "Act like a man!"

Larry waved for breath.

"If you weren't a sissy, you'd get up," Drigger said, more forcefully.

It was a challenge Larry wasn't equal to accepting. He just lay in the mud, heaving.

I tried to help him up, but Drigger shook his head and pointed at me. "You, fag, back off."

"Is that part of your job?" I asked, "to give this kid such a hard time?" Then, without waiting for an answer, I helped Larry to his feet. The strain on my own body was tremendous, and I nearly went down into the slime with Larry. But I managed to get him up and propped against the fence.

Drigger spat. "My *job* is to make men out of you women. You got anything against that, you talk to the Reverend Rafferty."

"Just give the kid a chance, then, " I said.

Meanwhile, Jerry, Donald, and the other two S&Ms continued to work, but there were mixtures of revulsion and humor on their faces—exactly the same confusion of sympathy and cruelty I'd often seen in boot camp when one of the basic trainees was fucking up.

"Hose him down, fag," Drigger said to me. "Since you're his girlfriend. Over there with the rest of the hogs."

Larry walked slowly around the feeding trough. He grabbed onto its side, stepping sideways. The pigs grunted and moved around him, rubbing against his legs. Their movement seemed to scare him, and he stopped, waiting for them to move away.

"Get over to the fence. Now!" Drigger shouted.

"The pigs'll bite!" Larry said, his voice high-pitched and on the verge of hysteria.

Drigger snorted. "Yeah, they'll bite. But if you don't *move*, they'll EAT YOU UP!"

Larry hurried, then, doing his jiggling sidestep. His back was to me and I thought of *Animal Farm*, at the end of the story, when all the other farm animals are outside the farmhouse looking in at the pigs and the humans, unable to distinguish one from the other. Covered from head to foot in pig slime, Larry was unfortunately a perfect example of that writer's imagery.

He gripped the fence, and I turned the hose on him. It tore at my heart to treat the kid so roughly, but I told myself that, at least, he wouldn't have to smell like a pig and the water was cold enough to cool him off. When I finished, I dropped the hose back into the water trough and turned to Drigger. "Done."

Drigger ignored me and turned to Larry. "Now you get back to the yard and tell Josh I said you're finished for the day."

* * *

When we got in from work that afternoon, we headed for the showers, but before we were permitted to take them, there was an unscheduled assembly, which gave it an air of importance as we gathered outside the chapel.

The whole farm of recruits, S&Ms, foremen, and other staff were assembled. Rafferty was dressed in his puke-green suit and carried a Bible. When we were all settled and the whispers among us had died down, he smiled broadly and brought Larry outdoors. With the Bible in one hand and gripping Larry's shoulder with the other, he said, "I know you're all wondering what has happened to this poor, wretched soul."

And I'll just bet you're going to tell us, I thought, barely able to keep from breaking ranks and taking Larry away from the crowd. The poor kid was sobbing and fighting to stop. He was still wearing his filthy clothes, still sweating, his busted lip purple and swollen. He ducked his head at the noisy whispers snaking through the crowd.

When we settled down again, Rafferty gave a sermon, the details of which I've forgotten, except the point was that Jesus takes us sinners just as we are. He ended with, "This poor young man's fall was only into the mud, but think on it as being mired in the mud of this world."

What I thought was that Larry was like a baby with a dirty diaper and Rafferty was like a cruel mother who wants to humiliate her child for something that couldn't be helped.

Finally, Rafferty stepped away from Larry and smiled cheerfully at us. "Larry has come to us from your 'gay' world." He looked at us, shaking his head. "Doesn't look very 'gay' though, does he? Just look! He is obese, obviously, to hide his real hunger. He eats as well to satisfy a longing he could not satisfy until now. The manifestations of his iniquitous living are visible in his body. Just as all sin really is manifest. It shows, brothers. And it stinks. Therefore, how right and good it is that Larry has come to this place that God has set aside for us in his Infinite Wisdom and Mercy. Praise Gawud!" he shouted.

"Praise Him!" one of the S&Ms shouted.

"Praise His Holy Name!" another said.

And then everyone began to chant, until a high wailing broke through our midst, as Paul Romaine began to sing…

* * *

There's more about Larry. But I'm just not up to putting it all down. I'm tired and hungry and, like Larry, I have a headache—a real eye-ball popper. I feel sick, too, that Larry was made a bad example of, and pissed at myself for not quitting, today. But it looks like the fun has just begun.

K. O'K.

V

Learning to Love Oneself and What is a Man

Lion's Mouth
Saturday, June 20

    Charlie Hays is such a nice man, and I think the more he is committed to helping me, the more he's helping himself, and the more enthusiastic he is in what I'm trying to do here. He's shy, however, so I can barely get him to talk to me here at the ranch. He might be afraid of blowing my cover or something, but he's the only one I can trust, and sometimes I feel like I'm going to explode. Everything I know about Charlie, I found out a few weeks ago when we met. He says he had a pretty restricted childhood, has never been to many places besides Carlsbad, except for his stint in the Navy during the Vietnam war.

    It's a wonder how he and I ever managed to discover the other was gay, and then how I was able to trust him enough to ask him to keep my journal entries. After all, he is a member of the Assembly of God Almighty in Carlsbad.

    I met Charlie Hays by accident at a garage where I was working in Carlsbad, waiting for my slot at the ranch to open. This garage doesn't depend on the automobile trade at all, although they dabble in it. Their specialty is tractors and farm equipment. One day, Charlie came in with a John Deere. He's the kind of guy who likes to watch the mechanics work on his equipment. Although he's shy, once we got better acquainted, he began to seek me out at the garage.

At that point in our acquaintance, I don't think either of us thought the other was gay, but we enjoyed talking to each other while I worked on the cars and pickups (and sometimes the farm equipment) and he asked questions or we traded information about mechanic work. He's easy going when he gets to know you, easy to talk to about trivial things, and even for his age of fifty plus, easy on the eyes. I wouldn't describe him as cute, or even handsome, but he has a very pleasant face and kind, penetrating blue eyes. I was attracted to him—not necessarily in a sexual way—but I thought he was sincere and nice looking. He must've found me attractive in a way, too, because after a few weeks he invited me out for a drink after the garage was closed. That's when I began to suspect that there was more to his interest in me than my ability at the garage; and I was even more certain when he came to the garage all the time, whether or not he had equipment there to be repaired. Eventually, he made no pretense about why he came in; he'd ask for me as soon as he walked in the door.

Being the coy devil I am and quite practiced at coming out to someone gracefully, I eventually told him I was going to be attending the retreat—this over steak at the local K-bob's. At first I claimed I was going there to be cured, to diffuse the news that I was gay. I thought if he was going to freak out on me, he'd instantly see I wasn't a threat to him, if I'd been wrong about his interest in me.

Coincidentally, or maybe just because it's a smaller world in a small town, he just happened to be a member of the church affiliated with Rafferty's program. He took my "confession" in stride and downright seemed to brighten when I told him about myself, which confirmed my suspicions about him, although it was a few more days before he said it.

After awhile, I told him what my real purpose was. He agreed to help me gather information. I know this all sounds incredible, but then, gay people have a tendency to protect each other, at least those who are lonely and are relieved to meet one of their own. Charlie must've been excruciatingly lonely to jump at the chance to work at the ranch, though, since the program was established to cure the homosexuals who gathered there. I can't imagine living fifty years and never knowing other gay men! I don't want to be condescending about Charlie, but this whole business happening right under his nose must be changing his life in a way only the truly lonely can appreciate.

Anyway, we became fast friends and, finally, a week or so before I entered the program, Charlie confessed that he was still a virgin. It took a gallon of booze and a couple of packs of cigarettes (his consumption) for me to convince him that we should "do it." I ought to call it "making love," because it was Charlie's first time; and even though I needed the physical contact, and did like Charlie, it wasn't out of love that I did it. I wasn't challenged by the fact that he was a virgin, either. I just couldn't imagine living half a damned century without ever knowing the intimacy of another man's body. Shall I describe what we did, how he shook, and how he came all over us, several times? I don't think so. But when we were done, I stroked him, wouldn't let him get dressed as he wanted to, like he was going through a fire drill. Then, in the wee morning hours, he began to cry and sobbed himself to sleep in my arms. The next morning, he woke up and seemed as happy and refreshed as a teenager.

There's more about Charlie, but I think I better stick to the program. What follows is another installment about the ranch.

* * *

Step No. 6: Love and accept yourself.

All right. But if that's so, then why does this place give such strong daily doses of guilt?

It's the weekend, again. Week two is over. And I feel lucky to have worked with Michael. He's fun, even in a place like this. On Monday, the 15th, four of us followed Les Hunter out to the building site. He's the foreman on the carpentry projects, an exact opposite of Alton Drigger. Les is likable, about forty, has a small build that's swallowed up by his baggy shirts and khaki pants. But his clothes hide his strength. You can't tell about that until he's worked alongside you all day. That's also why he's likable; he works with us and cares whether we're doing a good job and enjoying the work.

When we stepped inside the foundation area to what would be the barracks, Les handed us empty nail aprons, gloves, claw hammers, and he gave Michael a crow bar. Then he showed us how to use our tools, even showed us a few tricks we could use with them to make our jobs easier. On Monday, we were tearing the wooden framing away from the foundation, now that the concrete has set.

"Take the nails out, then work the board free," Les told us. With the claw of his hammer, he caught a nail head by its throat and bent it out of the wood. In a couple of seconds, he had removed the nails from one of the boards. "Then, kid," he pointed to Michael, "You stick the crow bar in between the board and the concrete and push the board away from the foundation. It's safest, I'd say, to push away from your body."

He took Michael's bar and quickly worked the frame board away. He jerked the long board up and carried it over to a small stack of lumber. "Put them here, according to their width and length. And be sure to put your nails in your aprons," he said, clapping a couple of the guys on the back. It sounded simple enough. We watched Les a couple more times. "This work's pretty easy, but in this heat, you need to drink aplenty water. Rest when you feel like it."

I've already described Michael as effeminate. But Michael is more masculine, macho, than you'd guess by the way he acts. He just lacks that sense of himself. In public—even out here among newly fetched Christian influence—Michael plays a queen's role. He plays it; he knows he is playing. But he surprised me by the end of Monday, when we were shaving. He stood next to me at the mirror.

"It's been nice working hasn't it?" He said.

I asked what he meant.

"Well, actually, hon, I don't know," he said, sliding a safety razor up his neck, then flicking the foam into the sink. "I'm just excited. Last week, I cleaned the chow hall. You know, my typical scullery maid routine. I was just domestic Michael."

I didn't mean to, but I laughed—not that I was laughing at him, but that's how he took it.

He punched me in the stomach, and his well-placed blow surprised me. "But why are you excited?" I asked, recovering.

He slid the razor up his neck and tapped it against the wash basin. "I joined this program to learn how to be more like other guys. I'm so wild about straight looking men! Last week, I was disappointed, because I was assigned scullery duty in the chow hall. This week, I'm assigned to carpentry, but I'm still disappointed. Except for being called a man's job, the work is easier than working in the cafeteria!"

"So why do you like it?"

"Don't you get it?" he said, rinsing his face and looking at me in the mirror.

"No."

"I expected to feel sort of different—like a man feels when he's doing man's work. But I felt like myself."

"You're saying you're not a man?"

Michael didn't answer.

"Or you don't feel like a man?"

Michael dried his face, then leaned over close to me. "I want to know what it feels like to be a man, to know I am masculine—to smell like a man, maybe."

I laughed again and this time so did he.

"You didn't have to come to a place like this, Mike, to be a man, you know."

"Yes I did. Because I think I need a miracle, and they claim they can produce it."

"That's why you came?"

"Yes. Of course!" Michael said, sounding irritated.

I suspected that what he said sounded as hollow to him as it did to me.

"These others have each experienced something strong, don't you think?" he asked, after a moment.

"Yes," I said. "It's obvious."

"Well, it's what I want, too."

For a moment, I was disappointed, then I mentally kicked myself. After all, that's why I was supposed to be here as well; maybe not trying to become more masculine, but trying to become something different. "Is it just becoming a man that you want? Or is it the Christian thing, bec—"

"Kelly, honestly, hon!" Michael said, frowning. I listened for a hint of humor in his sharp tone, but found nothing. I looked at him in the mirror, and he was frowning back at me. "It's a whole range of things…" he trailed off looking around. Most of the others were already out the door, but one of the S&Ms and a new recruit were not ten feet away, picking up towels, bringing out bucket and mops—part of the cleanup crew for the afternoon. But the S&M looked away quickly when I caught his eye in the mirror.

"Let's go," I said, quietly, slightly nodding my head in the direction of the two guys.

We sauntered toward the door after dropping our shaving kits in the locker near the showers.

When we stepped outdoors, the late afternoon sunlight was still burning, glancing off the metal of a Jeep's flat glass windshield right into my eyes, and when I looked at Michael, his face was a silhouette, then it cleared, as my eyes adjusted to the light.

"They were listening to us," Michael said as he raised a hand to shade his eyes from the sun, turning toward the east, heading for the chow hall. Over his shoulder he said: "And you were sounding funny in there, about the religious thing."

Michael was right, I had dropped my guard. "It's just I've never been too much on religion, myself, Mike."

"Then why are *you* here?"

I pulled up next to him and lowered my voice. "A lot of different reasons," I said. "And maybe they're not any better than yours."

Again, Michael frowned. "Well, I bet you've never been called a sissy, have you?"

"Well, no. I—"

"Then you can't really tell me that's not a very good reason to come to a place like this, can you?"

"You should have joined the army, Michael, if you wanted to get a dose of testosterone."

We were fast approaching the chow hall, and again getting within earshot of a few other recruits and S&Ms. Michael put a hand on my arm and pulled me to a stop. "I thought about that, too," he said. He shook his head. "But I was afraid of going in the army."

"Afraid?"

"That the other guys would be mean or something. I needed to find a way to be more masculine first."

"But why? I think you're fine just the way you are. On some guys, the femininity thing seems forced. I've seen my share of queens, you know. But on you, it seems natural."

"See what I mean, Kelly? Even here, I'm different. And you just proved it. If I don't…you know…learn how to be a man…" he trailed off again, looking troubled.

We were quickly being left alone, as the others headed into the chow hall. And there on the front porch, clipboard in hand was Paul Romaine, looking straight at us. I hurried up and forced Michael to follow. As we came within earshot of the little chipmunk, I said, "so with the Lord's help, Michael, you will be renewed. Just keep walking in the spirit.

"A lovely evening the Lord has made, brother Paul," I said, as Michael and I passed by him and joined the others just inside the door. Then I leaned closer to Michael and whispered: "We'll talk in the tent, Michael. I can tell something is troubling you."

Michael nodded, then stepped up to the serving line, picking up a tray, turning deftly away from me, fighting to paste a smile on his lips I knew he didn't feel.

Ah, my sweet William, I thought. *Just like you, so many of these guys place all their hopes on Rafferty and people like him, only to be devastated when their hopes are ruined by the real truth.*

* * *

In the last few years, it seems, and increasing at an ever faster rate, incidents of violence against gays have continued to rise. After lights out in the tent, when I was forced to quit writing, I couldn't stop thinking of what Michael had told me earlier, once our supper had ended and we had walked back across the field to the tent, following our nightly Bible study and discussions. What was troubling Michael and had really made him decide to join Rafferty's program was his own violent incident. One had come to expect that teens out on the town and looking for something *fun* to do had discovered the relatively unpunishable sport of beating up fags.

Michael had been one of them. Along with one of his "sisters," who had not fared as well as Michael and still lay in a coma in one of Houston's hospitals for the indigent.

"It was over a year ago, now," Michael had told me. The tent was syrupy hot. Damned or not, I was down to my briefs, but Michael and the others who weren't already in bed were still dressed in Levi's and T-shirt. Beneath his shirt, Michael was mostly skin and bones, and his Levi's fit loosely on him; and so it was when he began his tale that I realized what an easy target he looked for roving packs of teens, even high school boys who were looking to prove their own tenuous masculinity.

"Rita and I were coming out of this bi-club one night," Michael continued. "We'd done the 'complete' woman thing that night, since cross-dressing is popular there. But it was one of those sticky humid nights, and at two in the morning our dresses were pasted on us. It'd been raining, too, which made it all the more humid, so Rita says, 'girl I'm stripping.' And that's exactly what she did, with cars passing by, sloshing water onto the sidewalk. She leans up against the building and strips down to her panties, bra, and high heels! We were drunk and laughing, heading to my car, when four guys came down the street. They were all young and cute and Rita was coked, and she started flirting with them.

"They were hooting at us, saying 'Ooh hot babes!' and stuff like that. We didn't mind, because that's exactly the kind of reaction we wanted. So they followed us for a little while, which we also didn't mind, telling Rita 'take it all off baby!' I guess thinking we were real women. I mean we both looked pretty good. And we had even taped ourselves up, you know, so nothing would spoil the effect. So, even in her panties, Rita looked like a woman, if you know what I mean.

"Anyway, she took the bate from the guys and said, 'you *really* want to see what Rita's got?'

"By now we were in the parking lot and I'd already got my keys out. So as soon as we were next to my car, Rita started putting on this strip show kind'a thing, walking in among the guys and dancing around. We were still thinking this is a hoot, and these are kids, like maybe high school age. So I joined her. First thing I did was rip off my wig…"

In the tent, it was hot, as it was in Michael's story, but in telling it, Michael shuddered, wrapping his arms around his shoulders. "Oh, Kelly. I shouldn't have ruined the effect that night. Because those boys really did think we were women. We could have teased them, then gotten in my car and got away. But as soon as my wig came off, one of the really cute guys, who'd been laughing, suddenly turned real mean looking.

"'You're both guys? You're fags!'

"And that's when they all started yelling. I'd never seen guys go from one extreme to the next so fast, and before I knew what was happening, they had Rita against the car and were ripping off her bra and panties. Got her stripped bare and were punching her. I tried to help, but got punched out myself. I guess I fought pretty hard, but like I keep telling you, fighting like a she-cat and not a guy. Lucky thing I had a gun in my purse, though, because when I started swinging it around, I knocked one kid in the head so hard he keeled over. I guess it scared the others, because they stopped punching Rita long enough for me to realize about the gun, which I pulled and fired right into the middle of those guys. I didn't care who I hit, but I guess I didn't hit any of them. That's all it took, though, and they took off.

"Rita was barely conscious when I got her into the car, but by the time we got to the hospital, she was convulsing or something, so bad that, as soon as the paramedic saw her, he flung the door open and called for help.

"I don't want to go on about this, Kelly. It's too painful. Except that was the last time Rita was conscious as far as I know. I've gone back to the hospital several times to see her, but she just lays there, you know? Just lays there and gets fed through the arm.

"So to make this short and sweet, that night I decided I just had to get myself together. Pump up, you know? I tried going to the gym, but those buff, brainless people picked me out as a fag soon enough and teased me and stuff. So I just kept doing my same old routine as a 'woman' in the clubs, but since that night, I just didn't feel into it any more.

"Eventually, I joined this program, and here I am."

* * *

At least now I know a little more about Michael, and what motivates him to come here and put himself through this torture. All I can say is I wish him luck. He just might get those muscles, and even get a more masculine looking body to boot—especially when he's assigned to work in the field with a hoe and shovel. But it'll take a lifetime for him to lose those effeminate gestures, I think. It will be kind of sad if he does. But if that's what he wants, I wish him the best.

* * *

On Tuesday the 16th, we began framing. The work was simple, but it did require accuracy. I asked Michael if the work disappointed him. He said it didn't. We got hot kneeling in the dirt measuring plates for the foundation. Step one was nothing more than drilling holes in long two-by-four planks to match the steel bolts sticking out of the concrete, then screwing nuts onto the bolts when the plates were laid in place. Les came along and tightened them with a wrench. But this job took time.

By that afternoon, I was sleepy because of the heat and because we'd had the same bland soup and stale bread for lunch we'd had almost every day.

Michael took off his T-shirt. "At least I can get a tan," he said, tossing it aside.

"I could use some water," I said, so Michael and I walked over to a pine tree where Les had set up some jugged water. We sat down on the tailgate of Les' pickup, under the shade. We were higher up than the chow hall and could look over it to the fields where another crew was irrigating. The water had spread across the field like liquid fingers and was visible from where we sat. Below and to the left, toward the west of the valley, was the chapel and the meeting house.

"It's kind of pretty up here," Michael said. "Things are coming along nice."

I agreed, thinking the work on the barracks was coming along well, but I was still worried about the crops, which had sprouted then just sat there.

"You're not tired of it?" I lay back into the bed of the pickup.

"No. If you mean the work. Not yet, anyway," Michael said. "Don't you think it's good—you know, being forced to do this?"

"Forced?"

"To get up early; to eat that specially blended food—"

"What are you talking about?? Specially blended for what?"

Michael lay back with me, laying one arm under his head. "Brother Alex says we're being fed a particular blend of powders and proteins that will cleanse our bodies of toxins."

That was bullshit, but I perked up my ears for more. "You don't think they're starving us?"

"Oh, hon, I've always eaten like a bird, so it doesn't bother me, and you don't think it could hurt some of the others like, Lar—"

Michael stopped at the sound of Rafferty shouting down below us in the barracks area.

We both sat up. Josh stood at the end of the building site. He was looking at us and talking to Les. Les turned to look at us, too, then pointed and said something to Josh. Josh walked over to where Michael had left his shirt. When he looked up again, he began walking rapidly toward us.

As usual, he was wearing a suit, with his neck choked into a necktie. By the time he got to us, he was red-faced. Glaring, he wiped the sweat from his eyes and threw the shirt at Michael. "Put in on, Mike."

Michael looked surprised. "Huh?"

"Put it on! Just put it on." Josh said. He looked back over his shoulder at Les and the other two recruits who appeared to be absorbed in their work.

"Les said you two were just taking a break, but from down there, it looked as though the two of you were getting into a compromising position, here. What's going on?"

"We were just resting, sir," Michael said. His voice shook a little and I hated the sound of his submission.

"It was my fault, Reverend Rafferty, Sir," I said, taking up Michael's tone. I thought we could use a little rest and some water. Brother Les said—"

"All right!" Rafferty said, snapping his jaws. "Just be aware of the example you set for the others. You are not to pair off out of the earshot of the others. You are not to remove any article of your clothing in the presence of others unless it is to shower or go to bed. And you are certainly not to lay together when you talk. Stay focused, both of you. Remember your old habits die hard."

I didn't say anything. Josh had hit that particular nail right on the head. I had been admiring Michael's flawless skin and the way his long waist looked so graceful as it disappeared into his Levi's.

"We were just talking," Michael said, his voice taking on an edge of anger at Rafferty's tongue lashing. "What's wrong with that?"

Rafferty looked heavenward, then shut his eyes against the glare of the sun. "Under the circumstances, so recently away from your homosexual life, and with your shirt off, wouldn't you say your thoughts may turn to abnormal interests? We're here to help you through them. Please do not put yourself in such compromising positions. That's all."

Michael slipped into his T-shirt. Now, standing with legs spread, he stared frankly at Rafferty. I think he was pissed enough to be defiant, but I was hoping he wouldn't rile the preacher any more than we had. "Thank you, sir. You're right." Michael said. I was relieved for Michael's sake.

That was Tuesday. The rest of the week, we worked hard. By Friday, we had the outside walls framed and Les gathered us inside. "Well boys, I think you've done good work. I hope the next crew catches on as quickly."

I asked Michael how he felt.

He considered this, and I knew it was a continuation of the conversation we'd had all week about what it means to be a man. Was it the work?

Of course not. "I've found muscles I didn't know about. And if I do much more of this, my figure won't fit into a size 16!"

I enjoyed that. I laughed loudly.

"And my nails!" He pretended disgust. He flipped his hands out like fans. "I used to pride myself on my nails. Now they're…they're positively masculine!"

"You're play acting, aren't you?"

"Yes," he said. "Is a man a man because he doesn't have pretty hands and feet? Or because he can't wear Jr. Miss sizes? If that's it, I'm enjoying the work!"

* * *

I don't know about this program. The religious rigmarole, the chapel services, the Caucasian gospel singing in the evenings after vespers—doesn't add up to a specific cure for homosexuality. I'm here in the tent, again, of course, where I do all of my writing. The bugs that love the light seem to be getting worse every night, and I sweat in this oppressive heat, unable to concentrate. Maybe the lack of protein in our food is getting to my brain, but I sincerely hope not. I've been paying closer attention to the food since Michael said what he did about it being something specially blended. Maybe they're at least putting salt peter in it.

I'm calling it a day, but tonight what I've written has made me smile a lot. I get tickled, as I did with Michael, thinking that "man's" work is something mysterious, something only a man can do. He seems convinced that he's a queen and that the cure for that is man's work, but he's as fit and able to do it as anyone else here. Yet, he's still trying to discover his miracle.

That rule—love and accept yourself—might lie at the root of Michael's problem with his masculine/feminine identity, yet it's precisely the opposite of self-acceptance that this program seems designed to bring out in kids like him. And if he does begin to feel more masculine, and if his body does rearrange some muscles and he likes the male figure he sees in the mirror, how on earth is that going to be good for curing him of his attraction to men?

When Rafferty made Michael put his shirt back on in the middle of the afternoon, it was a hint that he's trying to instill guilt in us. Yet, not more than an hour later, we had to get buck naked in the showers. Figure that one out!

More later, when I'm not so fuzzy headed.

K. O'K

VI

Rewards for Right-Thinking

Lion's Mouth
Sunday, June 21

    I've only been on the ranch for a little over two weeks and, just like boot camp, it seems like forever. Charlie Hays keeps my perspective from getting too telescoped into the ranch and the continual indoctrination that goes on here. I must admit with some—no, with great—trepidation that a brainwashing program like this is likely to turn even the strongest minds into mush. The heat doesn't help much, either. This is only the first day of summer and the temperatures are in the nineties.

    I wonder how well I blend in with the rest of the recruits, here. I am kind of like the over-30 guy in the gay bars; in today's youth-oriented gay culture, people above the age of twenty-one are getting a little long in the tooth. I'm thirty five. But I believe I look twenty five. But then, don't all queens say they look a decade or two younger than they are? Actually, I got carded in a straight bar in Carlsbad a few weeks ago, so I'm not just deluding myself.

    The fat, unfortunate kid, Larry, is probably the youngest of any of us. This must be a retreat similar to the one Paul Romaine found himself in, according to what Tom and Joel said when I visited them. I think Larry is a high school student—like one of those I've read about, where the parents actually have their gay teen kidnapped and shipped off to a mental hospital (in this case a psyche ward in the middle of nowhere). But the rest of the guys range in age from eighteen to maybe thirty. It's odd that the older ones (myself excluded) are the mousiest, the easiest prey, and the ones most willing, it seems, to report certain unchaste appearing actions to their S&M. When Michael and I were alone at Les Hunter's pickup last week, and Rafferty came running with Michael's shirt, I thought good old Les, himself, got nervous about it. But later, I began to suspect it was one of the new recruits and his S&M who were jealous of Michael and me. I must not forget I have to be inconspicuous. I sometimes get carried away in the heat of the moment. I keep forgetting that the name of the game here is conformity. As I said before, it reminds me a lot of boot camp.

There is one difference between boot camp in the army and this program, however. No one in the army even pretended to be polite; nor did they sugar coat the program in boot camp with Christ-like love and concern for our souls. That was the purview of the chaplain. Here, the true motives are sugar coated, and one often hears the phrase "love the sinner but hate the sin." At least the sadist, Alton Drigger, is more honest than that. His hatred is like bared fangs, out front for all to see and fear.

Paul Romaine's hatred, however, is not. He is one of the subjects of this installment.

* * *

Step No. 4: Admit homosexuality is a sin and confess it.

I've had an opportunity to observe another one of those hidden surprises about this valley, about this ranch. When I first described the dynamics of the groupings going on here, I thought there was *us* (the new recruits) and *them* (the S&Ms and the staff). but that's not so, not by a damned sight.

Paul Romaine is the leader of a hidden program going on here. I'm sure of it, although as yet, I have no real proof of this. I have observed that, among the first wave of recruits (the S&Ms), three or four of them are continually at Paul's side—and none of them is ever assigned to a work crew. Nor are they always at the ranch—that is, they're nowhere to be seen for a couple of hours at a time, although they may be in the area.

On one occasion, one of the new recruits, Donald (the Adonis), was missing from our afternoon crew. Later that night, he came into the chow hall with the rest of us, but I noticed he had a nasty bruise on the nape of his neck. I asked him about it, but he wouldn't tell me how it happened. The odd thing is, his eyes betrayed fear, and I'd never seen such fear (except for Larry's, which is constant) on anyone's face around here. Since then, I've noticed that he's grown subdued, jumps frequently when one of the privileged S&Ms or Paul passes by him.

I might have shrugged off that bruise and Donald's sudden jumpiness, but then it happened to someone else. Same kind of bruise, same kind of fear. Same kind of jumpiness around Paul and what I'm beginning to call his inner cadre of S&Ms.

I've noted that we all wear white T-shirts and Levi's. I neglected to mention that the staff and Paul wear ordinary clothing—or so I thought at first. But Paul's clothing is odd. I swear it's meant to be some sort of uniform. Nothing you'd notice at first, nothing necessarily uniform-ish about it, except that he wears his shirts buttoned all the way to the collar, is the only one around here who still wears a nametag. That in itself wouldn't have affected the sense I've gotten about his dress being a uniform, either, but I got a close look at his nametag tonight. He's got some sort of symbol on it which, at first, just appears to be a cross, but it's so small you have to practically be kissing his chest before you can make out the fact that the cross is as wide as it is tall and that on each of the tips of the cross, on the clockwise side, there are pronounced serifs, marks that could, with a little imagination, turn the cross into another well-known symbol.

I got close enough this evening to see the nametag by accident. After supper, we gather for evening devotionals, sit in small discussion groups for one segment of it, and it just so happened that Paul was sitting to my right. He keeps notes on the discussions. He was tapping his pencil on his clipboard and dropped the pencil. I leaned over to pick it up out of courtesy at the same time he did. We did a little dance of nodding forward to retrieve the pencil, realizing the other was doing the same thing, drawing back, then nodding forward, again, until it was determined which of us was going to get it, which finally fell to me. I took my time to straighten up, just so I could get a closer look at that nametag, and there it was as clear as a bell. The symbol is a swastika. Now *this* fits too perfectly with what Tom Allen-Reece said about the Paul Romaine he knew for them not to be the same person.

I noticed another strange and disgusting thing about Paul I haven't quite been able to assimilate into my impressions about him. Although we're supposed to be completely celibate while we're here, which includes not masturbating, I got close enough to him tonight to smell sex on him. I don't mean just that faint smell, which will go away with the daily bath, either. I mean he was reeking like a hustler after a full day's work.

Of course this fucking heat brings out odors in all of us. Paul's bodily curse might be that when he sweats, it mixes in some weird way with a perfectly atrocious kind of cologne; or maybe chipmunks, like dogs, smell raunchy when their coats get wet.

* * *

After the evening meal, we're supposed to stay in the chow hall to discuss Bible topics. The topics are assigned like home-study Bible courses might be. We are presented with predetermined questions. And they have a nifty way of getting us to search hard for those right-thinking answers that go with them. Since we've been living on gruel (goo for breakfast, bland soup and dry bread for lunch, and some kind of reconstituted mystery meat for dinner), it's difficult to concentrate on anything but the hunger. And that's what keeps us on our toes during the study groups in the evening: After a short discussion, a well-fed group leader, like Paul or Josh, or one of the more well-fed S&Ms, asks the questions. Then those of us who are starving try to interpret the discussion, searching for answers. Those of us who come up with particularly right-thinking answers are rewarded with food credits—blue poker chips we can take with us to our daily meals and cash in, say, for a glass of milk or a refill on a cup of coffee. When these discussions are over, you can see guys pocketing their take; then, at night, you can see them recounting, over and over, to make sure they might have earned enough for a piece of sausage the next morning.

This system has been especially effective on the fat kid, Larry, who trembles on the edge of his seat every night during discussions to earn as many credits as he can. He's manic when, in the course of an evening, he earns three or four poker chips. It only takes ten, I think, for a piece of cake at lunch.

There is a pattern emerging from this nightly drilling that seems in perfect concert with the eighteen steps to salvation. While the entire group is moving continually down the list of steps, we're each being singled out by Josh to be tested on them. Let me be wildly paranoid, here, and imagine that those of us who *don't* earn the chips, and perhaps don't seem to be *hungry* for the credits are going to be focused on much more than those who *do* earn them. What form of concentration that will eventually take is beyond my imagination. But I have to face the fact that many ex-gay groups do not deliver on their promises to those who join them for salvation—much less a real cure. No doubt Rafferty and Romaine have been at this long enough to have discovered more effective methods.

The discussion, tonight, was on Step Number Four—confessing homosexuality as a sin. Our study also included discussion on the wages of that sin. An acceptable answer one might have given as a consequence of practicing homosexuality was that he should be shunned from his family. Although that's not in the Bible, it would get nods of approval from Josh or Paul, or one of the group leaders—but no food credit. As it turned out, of course, the best answer was the wages for the sin of homosexuality is death.

Although the Bible is our main authority, I've noticed there are creative ways to interpret it. We studied verses that described the sin and freely substituted "homosexual" where the Bible used terms like "effeminate" and "unnatural." In two weeks, we've probably gone through every verse in the Bible dealing with some angle of sexual perversion said to be homosexual, or caused by homosexuality.

Tonight, Larry, Michael, Brian, Paul Romaine, and I were studying together by the east window. The night was black and our reflections looked in at us like ghosts. Our reflections were multiplied by the number of panes so that we had quite a crowd in the glass. At one point, I felt Rafferty move up behind me. I looked at him in the reflection. He placed both hands on my shoulders. This is a favorite posture for him to take. Everyone else could see his face distinctly. I had been talking, so I spoke to his ghost in the window.

"I was about to say," I said, "that it's odd to think that getting sex leads to a lust for more and more sex." I looked directly at Rafferty's reflection, meaning to challenge him.

"Just a minute," he said. I saw in his reflection that particularly surprised expression he gets when someone doesn't give a pleasing answer, or says something that personally irks his system of beliefs. "The Bible teaches that having given up that which is natural for unnatural affection, the homosexual is given over to a reprobate mind."

His hands pressed down on me. I pushed ahead, anyway. "But it's like eating a big meal. Once you get full, the last thing you want is to eat, again."

"Right!" Rafferty barked. "But when you digest that—"

"No." I said. "I meant that we only eat three meals a day, at best. We have sex even less often."

At that definite contradiction, the ghosts' faces in the windows froze. I didn't look at anyone, just kept my eyes on the window. Some of the other recruits looked above my head at Rafferty. Their faces were fearful, and Larry was fidgeting so violently, I thought he was going to pee his pants. But Rafferty ignored them all, staring at me in the glass, as I stared at his reflection.

"Ah!" Rafferty said. There were cool spots on my shoulders where his hands had been. "You miss the point. Satan is lurking nearby, son. Can you not feel that it is this dark One, causing you to disagree? The reprobate mind is like a child with candy. The child will eat it until he vomits. The tendency for moderation is gone. And a homosexual mind is reprobate, isn't it, Brother Kelly?"

I looked at his reflection, but didn't say anything—couldn't even think for a moment with that remark about Satan, as if this were part of the Church Lady's show on SNL. Meanwhile, Larry was gyrating on the edge of his chair, with his hand raised, his face contorted, trying to get attention.

"Isn't it?" Rafferty repeated, bringing his hands back down on my shoulders, this time with grinding weight.

The chipmunk shot me a glance. I remembered the bruises on the necks of some of the recruits. "Oh, yeah. I see what you mean." I agreed with him quickly. I deadpanned my expression.

"So what is the answer?" Romaine asked, looking around the circle, bypassing Larry.

"I know! I know!" Larry said loudly.

"What is it, my boy?" Rafferty said, his reflection grinning affably at Larry.

"The homosexual mind is reprobate."

"That's true," Rafferty said, "but what exactly does that *mean*, son?"

Larry looked panicked, then triumph glazed his eyes. "All reason, all decency is sub— subject— subjugated to the sin."

When Paul doled out two blue chips to Larry's fat outstretched hands, he gripped them like they were gold. There were tears of gratitude in his eyes.

Rafferty's ghost grinned and floated away, deeper into the reflection, deeper into the night outside.

I looked at the reflection of the other guys in our circle, and finally turned to watch Rafferty leaning on another recruit, and another. The pattern. You do not disagree.

All around the room, the faces of all of us were serious—a tone that has been set from the moment we arrived. We're engaged in a deadly serious enterprise, here, and none of us will escape the loving cure that has been planned for us.

It's the pattern of pressure I expected from the beginning, even when I didn't really know what to expect. It was deadly effective on my William, and so it is on most of these others, I'm afraid. The peer pressure is strongly established—the sort of pressure that our biblical search for the truth about homosexuality produces. The thing we've *had* to know from the beginning is that Bible thumpers have a preoccupation with the gloomy side of life—what a historian once aptly described as the Puritan preoccupation and lurking suspicion that someone, somewhere is having fun, what Cotton Mather of Colonial America meant to convey with his sermon, "Sinners in the Hands of an Angry God."

God's plan for us homosexuals—hence Rafferty's plan and the goal of all Christians, Muslims, Jews, and like-minded ilk that want to cure our homosexuality—is that we be "cured" or we die. That's the strongest reason I can see for giving in to the conversion therapy.

I caught Paul looking at me. His was the only smile in the room. His eyes were glassy with hatred. "Shall we close with a prayer to our loving heavenly Father?" he asked. Then he swiveled his head around and looked directly at me. "Step number five, Brother Kelly O'Kelley, is 'Face and accept your basic anger problem.' Are you ready to do that?"

Reminded suddenly of the inexplicable bruises on the necks of some of the other recruits, and curious to know what sub-program the chipmunk and his cadre were running, I said, "Sure, Brother Paul. Your place or mine?"

That bastard actually licked his lips. "I'll let you know when the time comes."

* * *

Some of us who were trained as medics in the army were sent to Shepherd Air Force Base in Wichita Falls, Texas. Why this was necessary, only that mysterious inner circle in Army Command knows. But right after boot camp, when our technical school training was decided upon, I was sent to that Air Force school, rather than to an Army facility.

Part of our training was to go on bivouac in a dry river bed near Lawton, Oklahoma. For one week, we lived in tents large enough to hold forty men. These tents at Lion's Mouth are exactly the same kind. In heat such as we have during the day, the tent provides a little relief from the sun. Being open at both ends, the air can circulate easily. The sides of the tent don't touch the ground, either, so there is continual airflow at the bottom. Since cool air sinks, it comes into the tent at ground level and pushes the hot air to the "ceiling," which is at least twelve feet high. So during the day, at least, being inside can be preferable to being outdoors when the sun is out and strikes the desert like a hammer on an anvil.

At night, however, when the air cools off, the heat that collected in the tent during the day is trapped. When it is cool outdoors, being inside the tent can feel like being in warm syrup. Add the twelve naked light bulbs, strung from one end of the tent to the other, at a hundred and fifty watts each, and the heat can be overpowering.

It's like that now.

So I am, an hour before lights out, wearing only my briefs and dripping with sweat. Getting down to our underwear with the lights on is forbidden—too much naked flesh exposed for our reprobate minds to deal with—but I don't care. I look around the room. Our cots are spread out in this large area. Michael's cot is still closest to mine, but his back is to me. He's prone, one long arm bent at the elbow is supporting his head. He's writing a letter. Larry is off in a corner at the east end of the tent, his cot as close to the open flap as he can get without being called down by an S&M the next morning for blocking the path of his brothers. He's sitting with his back to everyone, staring out into the triangle of night that is visible to him. I have no idea what he could be doing, sitting in the middle of his cot, his face resting between his hands, staring into the night. Donald, the blond Adonis who had the bruise on the back of his neck is apparently asleep across the aisle from Larry.

The rest of the recruits about the tent are busy writing letters or reading the Bible. No one is speaking to anyone else. This is not only a quiet time at the ranch, it's the only free time each of us has to be alone—or as alone as any of us is allowed to get.

In comparison to the bivouac in Oklahoma in that tent, the silence in here is palpable. On bivouac, the hour before lights out was noisy. Free time in the army was not gloomy. Guys played cards, cursed and laughed, wrestled, slapped each other on the shoulders, or fought loudly. Here, except for the scratching of pens on paper, the turning of a page, or the sniffling of a runny nose, I can almost hear the thoughts of the recruits like a continuous whispering, or a sibilant stream of rushing water, washing over rocks. No one is happy.

In two weeks, we've gone over and back over the eighteen steps to salvation. Daily, we have been assaulted, even at work, with sermons and questioning, and continual focusing on our conversion. At the same time, we've moved only part way down the list. Each Sunday, we've gotten a day-long dose of Jesus as Savior (step one). Every minute of every day, we are constantly reminded that we must "be controlled by the Holy Spirit" (step two). This step has become a cliché. "The strength you need to work in the field, even when the sun is like a sword, will come from the Holy Spirit," so said an S&M one day. "I was drawn to ask you by the Holy Spirit, Brother (fill in question)..." has become the preface to many questions. Prayers end with step two being invoked..."and may we be continually controlled by the Holy Spirit," etc. A companion to this is "walk in the Spirit" (step three). God! None of us just walks around this fucking ranch, any more. We walk "in the Spirit." We bathe in the Spirit, breathe in the Spirit, piss and do number two in the Spirit, until I want to puke.

We fall all over ourselves in what is supposed to resemble casual conversation to "Admit homosexuality is a sin and confess it" (step four). It's the only topic of conversation.

Paul, the chipmunk Nazi, asked me tonight whether I was ready to take Step Number Five. Yes I am. I freely "admit and accept that I have a basic anger problem," which is more than I can say for many of the other recruits. They seem to have gotten past that step, and have gone straight for the others—which basically translate as follows:

Seven: Learn to control your mind. Translation: Don't think for yourself.

Nine: Stop homosexual acts. Translation: Don't you dare even think how nice it would feel to make love with another guy tonight.

Ten: Avoid homosexual hangouts and friends. Translation: Shut out pleasant memories of gay friends back where we came from, beyond this ranch.

Fifteen: Give check-up privileges to one or more of your intimate, "new" Christian friends. Translation: Tell Rafferty, one of the foremen, or Paul when someone is doing something we don't like.

* * *

The more normal Christian steps in our eighteen, like loving and accepting oneself, being a people helper—these are sorely lacking in our daily routines, it seems to me.

There's Larry, his back to all of us, looking dejected, staring, hunched down. He's the one I hear crying every night. There's Donald, bruises on his fair neck, fear on his face, silent now. I suspect that Paul and his cadre have done something to him and Leo (a pretty faced kid with a bruised neck in the cot next to Donald). There's Sidney—a skinny, pimpled youth (or pox-scarred thirty year old, it's hard to tell)—closer to me, who seems to be soul-dead already. He stands out from everyone only by his nervous tick and his damn-near six-foot-six frame. I say "soul-dead" facetiously, because the program just isn't fazing him as far as I can tell. He constantly gets erections in the shower, and his cot squeaks at night in that tell-tale rhythm of the incessant masturbator and abuser of himself. I'm wondering when Paul or Josh will hear of his reprobate mind and decide to take action. Remembering the smell of sex on Paul, I think maybe Sidney has already come to Paul's attention. I just wonder how it is that horny Sidney ever decided to STOP HOMOSEXUAL ACTS. He certainly hasn't stopped his homosexual thoughts. Then, there are the nondescript others I share this tent with—those most easily succumbing to the program, who give the right answers at night, who have already become committed to their salvation. Most likely these are the ones for whom religion itself is most important and always has been, because that's how they were raised. Prior to entering this program, I bet they played the most mind games about their unwanted attraction to other men; and I'll bet the ranch that once they leave here, they will lead unremarkable lives, full of secret shame, but will outwardly hang onto the lie that they are successfully converted ex-gays.

My heart palpitates. The sweat oozes from my skin. I've seen enough of this place, felt enough of the shame and guilt and fear from the others to know what William must have gone through. I WANT OUT. But what am I going to do about it? Who will record the methods of this program if I leave?

My heart stops at a weird thought. *Could I leave, even if I wanted to—even if Charlie were willing to help me?* I'll have to discuss such a possibility with him.

* * *

There's something giving way within me about this place. All of a sudden, I'm spooked in this hot, syrupy tent, spooked until the hair has risen on the back of my neck. I still have *sixteen* weeks to go.

K. O'K

VII
Punishment for Wrong-Thinking

Lion's Mouth
Monday, June 22

On the day the fat kid, Larry, fell into the hog pen, Josh Rafferty used him as an example for the rest of us. He said Larry's very obesity was his sin made manifest. I just thought Larry was fat because he ate too much and probably had very bad eating habits. Paired with the fact that Larry probably *has* been unhappy with his homosexuality, he turned to food. But after all, when any of us discovers we're gay, we must wrestle with the hatred society has for us; and for many of us, it becomes a struggle with our own self-hatred. Maybe Larry's craving for food is a kind of lust, but is it evil? Is Satan in the potato salad, urging Larry to go for seconds, or residing in the fifth doughnut? That's bullshit. Larry is fat because he eats too much. Because Rafferty made that an issue, the rest of us have been made even more aware of it.

Every afternoon after work, all of us recruits and S&Ms have to shower together. Of course, none of the staff showers with us, but one of them is always there to supervise (in the event, I suppose, that our homosexuality drives us to copulate in the shower). Today, it was Paul Romaine, fully dressed, clipboard in hand. I wonder if he takes notes, because I saw him jotting things down a few times. To be cynical, I think it's probably something like: "Michael has a nice cock for an effeminate fag...Brian needs to shave his nuts...Sidney's dong would choke a horse..." Who *knows* what goes on in that snotty head of his? None of the other staff takes notes while we're showering!

At any rate, even our showering has become a form of brainwashing—this one to instill guilt in us, I think. If we're here to be cured of our attraction to members of the same sex, what better way to rub salt in the wound than to have us shower together? At the same time that we *want* to see one another's bodies, we are also made to be ashamed of that desire. It's the perfect attraction-repulsion recipe to make us feel guilty.

Guilt Stew

> Take 20—30 naked, sweaty young men, place in large room where the odor of sweat, cologne, and desire mingle with Zest. Add water. Stir in one fat boy with repulsive rolls of body fat, one six-foot-six boy with a foot-long dong that stays half hard, and 16 or so downright cute bubble butts. Sprinkle all with the notion that homosexuality is a sin, add liberal dollops of guilt and let entire mixture simmer for twenty minutes. Serve with Hellfire and Brimstone.

The shower facilities are in back of the gymnasium, set up much like a high school P.E. facility. We all undress in a big room lined with lockers for our clothing; then we shower under communal shower heads, where we must stand within two feet of each other while we're naked. (There sure is a lot of looking heavenward in this place.) Eye contact, alone, is grounds for suspicion that we're not pure of thought, so we are afraid to look at one another. I guess each of us is afraid of the other seeing a hint of that old desire in the other—and of having that desire reported to Rafferty.

A long time ago, when I was in high school P.E., I managed to keep my dick in hand—er—from getting out of hand. Oh, it tingled in the shower room, for sure, but never became embarrassingly erect. Here at this cure camp, it doesn't even tingle—mainly because I'm turned off to guys who are turned off to themselves. Add to that fat Larry, whose body fairly jiggles as he hurries from the lockers to the shower stall and my dick tries to crawl into my abdomen. Being made newly aware of Larry's fat, I think the rest of us have similar lack of penile reactions. The anxiety factor, alone, for the rest of the recruits who really are here trying to get over their homosexuality, is enough to keep most of our dicks down.

That is, except for Sidney's. It thrives on anxiety. Today, his long member was particularly troublesome, if not magnificent. No sooner had we stripped out of our T-shirts and Levi's than everyone (although looking heavenward) became aware that Sidney's foot-long dong was standing at attention. Room was made for him under the showers, too. We even huddled near Larry for protection, lest Sidney's one-eyed god began spitting at us. That is, except for Leo. His eyes seemed to grow too tired to stay plastered on the ceiling, and several times they fell toward Sidney and, especially toward Sidney, Jr.

Beyond the steamy mist of the showers, Paul Romaine sat on one of the benches, clipboard resting on crossed legs. I was standing in such a way that I could see him from the corners of my eyes. When Sidney's dick hardened, Paul's pen scratched the pad. When Sidney's dick stayed hard, Paul's pen scratched harder. When the rest of us finished showering and hurried to the lockers, where we dried off and got dressed, Leo stayed behind with Sidney. They lingered. Sidney dropped the soap. Leo picked it up for him. When he left the shower a moment later, I noticed that Leo, as well, had the hint of an erection, although his face was respectably red.

Paul must have noticed because, when Leo came out of the shower, I heard Paul's pen scratching again. In fact, that annoying rhythmic scratching was the only sound in the room—except of course for the fleshy slap of Sidney's recalcitrant member on his abdomen as he flew across the room and strangled it into his Levi's.

* * *

At supper, Sidney was put into the "hot seat." Any person in the room can ask the person in the hot seat anything. It goes on during the entire meal.

The opening volley was begun by none other than Paul. "The Holy Spirit has directed me to ask, Brother Sidney, why you are here at Lion's Mouth."

"To be delivered from my homosexual desires," Sidney said.

"And of the steps toward salvation, Brother," Paul sneered, "which steps would you say you have accomplished?"

Sidney cleared his throat and went down the list. "I've accepted Jesus as my savior. I try to be continually controlled by the Holy Spirit. I walk in the Spirit. I know homosexuality is a sin. I—"

"The Holy Spirit has directed me to ask, Brother Sidney, if you spill your seed." This came from one of the S&Ms whom I've identified as one of Paul's inner cadre.

The questioning continued in that vein all through supper. It came out in near graphic terms that Sidney masturbates every night. Who didn't know that? It was pointed out that Sidney is usually erect. Who could fail to miss that, either?

He was reduced to tears, to stammering. "When…when I was a kid…when I was scared…I got hard—uh—got erections. They just happen. I can't help it. I know they're wrong. I hate them. I can't help it."

I think I should leave Sidney, here. I think I've got an idea what Sidney's basic problem is. He's a heterosexual, trapped in a homosexual body. How else could one explain his strong desire to change and his body's continual contradiction to that desire?

* * *

Tuesday, June 23

Paul was in the showers with us again, clipboard in hand. Sidney's cock refused to be cowed. Leo lingered. Paul scratched on his notepad.

I suspect that this troublesome cock has Josh "stumped." He conferred in private with Sidney after our supper tonight. Whatever was said hasn't stopped that rhythmic squeaking in our tent. In fact, it's harder and more rhythmic than ever. Poor Sidney. If something doesn't give within him soon…

Poor Leo, too. As I said, he's one of the pretty ones. He's also one of the guys who has had a bruise on the back of his neck. Tonight, it was his turn in the hot seat.

I don't know how much longer it will take for everyone—myself included—to succumb to the continual brainwashing. Hell, I don't really notice much difference, any more, between us "new" recruits and those first wave recruits I've been calling S&Ms. At first, there was a distinct difference between us and them. The S&Ms were like robots, the walking dead—as if they weren't really here for a cure of homosexuality at all; at first, I even thought that *maybe* they were pretending to be troubled homosexuals like the rest of us, but were actually well trained brown-shirts in the art of brainwashing. But we're into week three of our own indoctrination, and most of the guys I arrived with are indistinguishable from the S&Ms.

Luckily, there are still a few of us who exhibit real personalities, whose eyes are not glittering chunks of glass, but our numbers are dwindling. There are still a few of us whose faces betray fear and not that eerie pasted on smile of the enlightened. Among those of us who are still "alive" are Brian, a cute chunky kid (from Louisiana, I believe), Donald, the blond with the bruised neck and, of course Larry, Michael, and me.

Although Larry has been lucky in the past couple of weeks, he seems never to have forgotten his humiliation in front of the whole ranch. He also seems incapable of controlling his voracious appetite. Not only does he trade favors with some of the others for some of their food credits—like making their beds, giving them some of his paper and loaning them postage stamps—he cashes in his poker chips for anything that will provide the most bulk in the way of food. And he begs from others when he thinks none of the staff, Paul, or Rafferty is aware of him in the chow hall.

I haven't been able to find out much about most of the other guys, like where they come from, what brought them here, or why they felt the need to seek such a cure. It's not permitted to speak of our past amongst ourselves. Michael and I have just been lucky to have gotten away with it so far. At first, when we were paired off, the S&Ms had a list of such questions. But those have gone by the wayside, as we've gone over and over the eighteen steps. "Avoiding homosexual hangouts and friends" includes not talking about the past. Recalling those days, which would include our homosexual past, might cause us to be homesick for what now might seem the good old days. The object, here, is to keep us focused on the present, to keep us "involved in a Bible-centered church" (Step eleven); to make us "vigorously seek Christian companionship" (Step thirteen)—that's us, here at the ranch, the staff, and Rafferty. He's a real friend. His love for us underwhelms me. "Finding one or more intimate new friends" has been taken care of by our daily pairing with the S&Ms.

My first intimate new friend, Jerry, is still paired with me occasionally, as he has been this week. But I've stopped playing with his head, because I suspect that he gives interesting little reports to Rafferty and Paul about me. Step number fifteen is "Give check-up privileges to one or more of these new friends." Jerry was unsuccessful in gaining my trust, so now he's taken to sitting in with me when we're about to write letters home.

"Who are you writing to so much?" he asked last night.

"My mother," I said. "But it's ironic, Jerry."

"Ironic?" Jerry asked, actually taking me seriously, evidenced by the pouty turn of those luscious lips.

"Yeah. When I was a kid, I resented how smothering she was. She wouldn't let me play with boys who were too rough. She wouldn't let me wear rugged clothes, kept me in dress slacks in grade school when all the other boys were wearing Levi's. I hated that, too. But the irony is, now, I can't seem to do without her advice. I so want her to approve of me. I've told her to watch for a nice girl for me when I get out."

"I understand," Jerry said. "I was…interested in your writing. You seem to do so much more than anyone else."

"That's because I want to be a writer, Jerry. Practice. Practice. Practice. The Spirit has moved me to write, you know."

He beamed, and I shot him the mental finger.

* * *

Wednesday, June 24—a day of reckoning

The nightly routine changes on Wednesdays. Right after work, all the regular staff are let go. Supper on Wednesdays is usually sandwiches and real ham and cheese and milk, and all the coffee we want to drink. During the rest of the week, you can see the guys counting on Wednesday nights. Sandwiches might sound rather dull to anyone used to considering them a snack, but we've come to consider them as luscious as T-bones and baked potatoes. There isn't any K.P. duty, either; instead, we usually gather in the chapel for a sermon and prayers in a little more religious setting. But tonight, our routine was changed even more.

I should have known something was different when we headed for the showers; both Paul and Josh Rafferty came into the locker room. That made me nervous as hell. It also made me want to giggle. Could it be that Sidney's little-league baseball bat was gaining a reputation that even Rafferty, himself, wanted to see? I understand that even a heterosexual man can be induced to gawk at a truly magnificent specimen of manhood.

Everyone else seemed doubly nervous as well. I drew the unlucky company of Larry, whose bulk seemed to jiggle and dance even worse. Why that kid gravitates toward me is beyond my comprehension. I'm practically the only one he'll talk to. And if we're not talking, he just hovers near me. Poor kid, maybe he thinks I'll protect him. Around Rafferty, he's particularly nervous. When Larry saw him enter the shower room, his breath became shallow and wheezy as he peeled off his sweat-sticky Levi's; he almost tripped and fell once he wrestled his body out of his clothing, trotting across the floor with his towel wrapped around his middle, covering about as much area as others might accomplish with a wash cloth.

The other recruits and the S&Ms were more subdued, too, with Rafferty in the room. Heaven was now directly over their heads, causing them to look ridiculous keeping them cocked at such an uncomfortable angle. I almost burst out laughing as Rafferty was compelled to look up at the ceiling to see what everyone was looking at. I kept my eyes neutral, focused somewhere near the wall above the heads of Paul and Rafferty, so I could see what they were up to. It didn't bode well.

The show Rafferty had come to see began when Sidney slid nervously out of his clothes. His anxiety was especially evident by his splotchy skin; his acne appeared even worse against his pasty-white face. But his cock was more than happy to make its presence known. You could almost feel the heat rising from it, as it began to flex and grow. Paul licked his lips. Rafferty leaned forward. Sidney's cock leaped for the ceiling and preceded him with magnificence into the shower.

We scattered like nervous hens. I chose a shower head near the door to the showers so I could see Rafferty. Paul was gesticulating with his hands, licking his lips, tapping his clipboard; Rafferty nodded as he peered into the shower facility.

As on previous nights, Leo was the only one who could NOT keep his eyes off Sidney's dick, and tonight, his own smaller member, couldn't control itself. Leo just turned redder and redder, his member grew harder and harder.

One by one, as we finished our showers, we came out, passed by Rafferty, who was now standing right outside the showers, frowning and fuming, and got dressed as quickly as we could. Paul dismissed us with an irritated wave of his hand. "Get out as soon as you can. Make yourselves sandwiches and be prepared for Chapel Service in twenty minutes."

Normally, even suppers on Wednesdays are at least an hour. It is one of the most pleasant times of the day, to eat, then sit on the porch for awhile as the sun sinks beyond Lion's Mouth Canyon, sometimes lighting up its walls and the hills around the valley with a blood-red brilliance. It is also then, I assume, that someone named the canyon Lion's Mouth because, at a particular angle at this time of day, it does remind one of looking down the throat of some man-eating beast. Tonight, there was no relaxing on the porch of the chow hall to enjoy the waning sunlight before our Wednesday night sermon. We barely had time to choke down our food. We all seemed to share the feeling that something awful was about to happen. My mouth was dry, and I almost gagged as I hurried out of the chow hall, trying to swallow bits of bread that clung to my throat, as I joined the others on the way to the chapel.

A half-hour after our showers we filed into the chapel. Its changed appearance so shocked some of us that there was much whispering, among both the recruits and the S&Ms. I noticed that of Paul's inner cadre, there were some tightly reined grins. The chapel had been converted (with some amount of bad taste, I might add) into what was, immediately apparent, meant to be a funeral parlor. Gone was the gaily colored banner behind the podium which declares, "GOD is LOVE." Instead, there was a black curtain with a new banner whose words sent a thrill of fear down my back. Some overeager zealot had cut out in large wavy letters the message:

"The Death of the Spirit"

In front of the podium was a simple, crudely built, coffin. The sight of it scared me, as a literal interpretation of the message behind it, but it was all the more frightening because it was larger than any I had ever seen and was painted a flat black.

No amount of contemplation could give me a clue as to what was about to happen. Michael was sitting on the hard, backless bench to my right; Larry was sitting to my left. And from either side of me, it was clear that they were as frightened as I was. Their breaths were shallow like mine. Michael was whispering a litany more to himself than to anyone else, but I could hear him distinctly: "Oh girl, Mary, what it heaven's name. Oh girl, Mary..." Larry was wheezing and rocking to and fro rubbing his sweaty palms on his Levi's. I wanted to take both their hands, as much to comfort me as to comfort them. We were sitting about midways in the chapel, with mostly empty benches behind us. In front of us were mingled recruits and S&Ms—indistinguishable at last. All of us were dressed in our clean white T-shirts, and it was an odd contrast to the front of the chapel that was mostly black, from the curtain behind the podium, to the black coffin, to the growing blackness of the high windows.

The effect was further subdued with only a single light in the ceiling shining onto the "stage" where the coffin was resting, shut, and silent. Absent from our numbers were Rafferty, Romaine, and Leo and Sidney. My guts told me that this funeral parlor had been set up for their benefit, but my mind refused to accept it.

After we'd sat there for what seemed an eternity, the chapel doors creaked open. I glanced quickly over my shoulder and caught sight of

Rafferty and Paul dressed in black suits, leading Sidney and Leo behind them. At first, I couldn't believe my eyes, but as they drew closer to the light at the front of the chapel, I and the rest of us gasped in unison. Sidney and Leo were both naked. Their hands were tied behind their backs, and they were walking so shakily they threatened to keel over.

Just as they began to swoon and Sidney fell forward onto one knee, Paul flicked his head and, from both sides, his four goons grabbed Sidney and Leo, dragging them the rest of the way to the podium. Before any of us could grasp what was happening, Rafferty opened the coffin to its dense black interior, and Paul, the goons, and a couple of volunteers from the front row, bodily picked up Leo and Sidney, holding them aloft at the foot of the stage.

If I had been in their situation, I think I would have struggled, but they didn't. There was no telling what sort of preparation they had gone through under the Reverend Rafferty's coaching prior to entering the chapel, but both of them seemed stunned, or drugged. Sidney, in fact, appeared to have fainted, his head lolling like a rag doll. Leo seemed to be conscious but completely void of will; and just when he was turned parallel to the coffin, his bladder let loose and he peed onto the stage, reminding me of the way a scared dog might urinate as its final act before being mauled by a pack of wolves.

In the next few moments, at Rafferty's direction, Sidney and Leo were placed into the coffin. The lid was lowered, and the final horror was the click of the padlock Paul put into a hook and hasp that had not been visible in the dim light.

Then Rafferty took his place behind the lectern.

The room had suddenly become tomblike as not even a breath was drawn.

"My children," Rafferty intoned. His voice had a sad quality to it that made me sick at his feigned sincerity. "For some time, we have been proceeding with this program. We opened our doors to you troubled souls in an effort to help you overcome your homosexual illness."

There was a rustling of troubled souls all over the chapel as we gazed in disbelief on the coffin and listened to Rafferty.

"Homosexuality sears the mind," Rafferty continued. "It causes one to reject the God-plane, diverts one away from the desire to have a wife and children. It IS a sin. But it is also an illness. An abomination to Gawud all Mighty. As we discovered not a few nights ago, the homosexual mind is reprobate."

Paul jumped to his feet. "Amen!" he shouted, making half of us jump at his sudden outburst.

"Amen!" shouted his goons as they stepped off the stage and joined him.

"Shout Amen!" Paul screamed. And some of the recruits and S&Ms jumped up and shouted as they were commanded.

Shit! I thought.

When silence followed, I heard sniffling. Michael was crying, shaking his head and whispering.

In front of me, Brian and Donald, two of the guys I'd noticed with bruises on their necks, had begun to blubber, and the entire chapel was filled with the discordant sounds of despair and horror and glee.

When the room seemed to rock with emotion, Rafferty shouted. "THE MIND OF THE HOMOSEXUAL IS REPROBATE! HIS HEART AND SOUL ARE DEAD!" Then he bowed his head, raised his arms to silence us and stepped from behind the podium, where he stood next to the coffin, letting his fingers play along its surface. "You might think," he said, his voice falling to a whisper, his tone sinking to one of despair, "you might think that because homosexuality IS an illness, that one who practices it would be forgiven. We do not put CANCER victims into prison. God does not throw them into Hell for *their* disease."

I lifted my eyes up, forced myself to look directly at this preacher who had caused my poor William to take his life. But I could not see a hint of real sadness or caring in that man's face.

"But Gawud *hates* homosexuality. He does not CARE that it is an illness. He will throw a homosexual into the lowest pit of Hell."

Larry began to gag, and I was afraid he would vomit, so I scooted closer to him and threw my arm around his shoulder, hoping Rafferty wouldn't notice.

"'Know ye not that the unrighteous shall NOT inherit the kingdom of God?'" Rafferty said in a stronger voice. "'Be not deceived,'" he said, his voice rising as he began to play with the rhythm of the scripture he was quoting. "Neither *forn*icators, nor *idol*aters, nor *adult*erers, nor e*ffem*inate, nor ABUSERS of themselves with mankind shall inherit the kingdom of GAWUD!

"'AND SUCH WERE SOME OF YOU!'"

He pointed like the figure of death over the audience. "In order to be saved you must Stop Homosexual Acts! If you do not, your soul will die! In the time of the Second Coming, you will wear the mark of the Beast of Hell! You will be a creature without a soul, unworthy of Eternal Life. That, my sons, is the wages of your sin!

"IT IS DEATH!"

"Death to the homosexual!" Paul shouted.

"Death!" echoed his entourage.

Rafferty wiped sweat from his brow and ran his fingers along the coffin lid. Then he leaned close to it. "Sidney Leech! Leo Smith! The wages of your sin is death. Do you hear me??"

Every eye was frozen in horror as we waited to hear something from within the coffin. But the silence was complete.

Not one of us protested outwardly. I lacked as much courage as the rest—or maybe even more, since I'm the different one here, the one supposed to be watching and listening. I was ashamed of myself as I have not been since I was a kid.

Rafferty continued to lean close to the coffin, his attention on its contents. "We have tried through persuasion and reason to reach you. We have begged you, prayed for you to control your mind. STOP

HOMOSEXUAL ACTS! We have involved you in a Bible-teaching church and daily Bible study. We have provided you with Christian love and intimate friends in Jesus. Yet *nothing* has penetrated into your foul, reprobate minds. Homosexuality is a sin. It is death. So now we bury you together. From the foulness of your breath mingling as you lay together in that dark, enclosed interior, from the stink of your soul-dead bodies you WILL know the imminent death of your spirit." He stood erect and faced us, then raised both arms in a supplicating gesture.

"GO! The rest of you. Think on this service. Pray with all your hearts and minds and souls for these two lying here, entwined as they so desired to be!"

* * *

We filed out of the chapel into the black night. I looked up at the brilliant stars in the moonless sky, and I knew there was no God. A cool breeze kissed my neck. But I was hot. Sweat trickled under my arms. I was angry as I stomped across the ground on the now familiar path, north toward the tents.

Footsteps sounded behind me. I recognized the sniffling as Michael's as he caught up with me and grabbed my left arm. "They'll let them out tonight, won't they?"

Wary that others were too close, I looked around. We had managed to outstrip the others. "I don't think so, Mike," I said. "I'm afraid they're going to be in there all night."

Michael didn't say anything as we continued walking across the fields. I could hear him breathing, as if he were struggling to draw in a breath. "But they're cramped in there! They'll go crazy! Kelly, it's not right. They can't do that!"

"Who's going to stop them? You saw how many guys were willing to help. Who are we going to tell?"

"You and Charlie are friends, Kelly. Tell him," Michael pleaded.

I stopped, shocked. "What d'you mean, Charlie and I are friends? He's one of the foremen."

Michael pushed me, then dropped his voice to a whisper. "Hon, it's obvious that Charlie is one of us. He's in love with you and don't you tell me you don't know it!"

My breath hurt as it struggled out of my lungs. "Does anyone else know? Is it that obvious?"

"Do you mean if any of the others…the guys who've been around longer than we have—"

"Anyone, Mike. Even the guys we came in with."

Michael let go of my arm. This time he looked around then quickened his pace. "Come on, Kelly. Hurry. People shouldn't hear us."

We picked up our pace and walked farther into the night. Another breeze came up, rustling the leaves of corn. It sent shivers down my back as I followed Michael, almost running, but trying not to seem anxious.

When we were safely out of earshot, Michael took my hand. I wanted to withdraw it, but the night was black and no one could see.

"You know what this place is?" he asked.

"Yes. It's a place where homosexuals like you and me come to get cured."

"Right, sweetie. But it's also an insane asylum. I regret the day I came."

"You do?

"Oh, come on, Kelly, so do you. You're not here to get cured."

My heart was beginning to pound. I felt lightheaded. "Is it that obvious?"

Michael squeezed my hand then let it go. "Don't worry, hon, I've worked with you long enough to know things the others may not. But you do let your anger show. You need to watch that."

"Are you friend or foe?"

"Don't insult me, Kelly. Just do me and the rest of us a favor. You tell Charlie Hays what happened, tonight. Things are getting too rough, here. You do know that Paul is snatching some of the others and doing things to them, and don't tell me you don't know that, either."

"I won't. I do know that people disappear for awhile and when they come back, they're scared, and they've been battered."

"Fucked is more like it," Michael said, and began to cry.

I threw caution to the wind and put my arm around his neck. "Mike, do you know what's happening to them?"

He pushed me away. "Don't do that. I might kiss you. I don't know exactly. Paul's hurting them, and probably raping them. Paul and some of his friends. The ones you don't usually see paired up with us. I was in the restroom the other day when that kid, Brian, came out of one of the stalls. He'd been in there for a long time, and I thought he was probably relieving some of his anxiety, the way some of the others do…you know?"

I nodded.

"Anyway, I went into the same stall he'd just come out of. He'd done a pretty good job of cleaning himself and flushing the evidence down the toilet. But there was still rectal blood in the bowl."

"Rectal blood?" I asked, disbelieving. "Are you sure he didn't have a nosebleed?"

In the dark, I could here Michael swallowing back a sob. "Why would you go into the toilet to take care of a nosebleed? Yeah, it was rectal bleeding. And you've seen those bruises on his neck. It doesn't take a rocket scientist to figure out what's going on."

"Do you know where Paul takes these guys?

In the dark, Michael pointed east. "There's a draw behind the pig pens. I've seen dust rising from one of the Jeeps. I don't think it's any of the foremen. I've been too afraid to follow them, but if you tell Charlie, he can go. He can find out. Can't you work up a pretext to talk to him? Please?"

We reached the tents before the rest of the guys caught up to us. We slipped into the tent, and the darkness grew solid. The lights are rigged to a box just inside the flap, but I didn't bend over to flip it on.

Neither did Michael. Without hesitating, once we were hidden from view, we slipped into each other's arms and kissed. It wasn't a kiss of longing, but one of seeking and giving comfort. Michael drew away first. "Thank you, Kelly." He bent over and flipped the switch.

The darkness receded to the corners of the tent. In that light our cots, lined up in two rows, beds made, footlockers before each one, reminded me more than ever of boot camp; I had to shake my head, recalling that once I had signed an oath declaring myself a soldier, I was bound to a set of military laws older than the Constitution of the United States. Although I was still a citizen, I had "voluntarily" suspended my civilian rights. Then, as now, I felt caught.

I had signed papers to get into this place, as well, "voluntarily" submitting myself to the Program, but I was damned if those papers were going to carry any force, whatsoever. The problem was to get away from here if need be or, if I stayed, to survive long enough to tell our story. I was convinced, now, that with the slightest twist, the symbolic death I had witnessed tonight could become real. Michael and I parted under the light and went to our cots.

When the others joined us a minute or so later, I took out my paper and pen and began writing, not wanting to miss a minute of time before lights out. Tomorrow, I decided, I would tell Charlie of Rafferty's cruel game of death.

**

My eyes are watering. My heart is finally calming down after the cruel scene in the chapel, although I doubt I can fall asleep. A few minutes ago, I decided I would go back to the chapel and let Sidney and Leo out of the coffin. But I had no sooner stepped outside the tent, when Paul Romaine grabbed my shoulder.

"I *thought* you'd be the one to make an attempt to release the soul-dead," he said.

"You mean Sidney and Leo? I'm the one who has to take care of my bodily functions, Brother Paul. The Spirit has moved me to do it now, before I foul my nest. But speaking of those two guys in the coffin, without their clothes on, in that tight, airless space—I think it is immeasurably cruel."

"There's always one in every group," Paul said, ignoring me. "One who won't face and accept his basic anger problem."

"What?"

"You heard me, Brother Kelly. We do this "death of the spirit" bit with each new group. It works wonders for those like Sidney and Leo who just can't stop lusting after each other. But it also reveals the strong ones in the audience, the ones, like you, who have anger problems. I told you I'd get back with you on this."

"So you did. But it'll have to wait. I'm going to take a leak."

Paul wasn't convinced I hadn't been on my way to the chapel, so I stayed near enough to the tent so he could hear my urine splashing.

* * *

So, here I am, the last one still up this night. It falls to me to turn out the lights. The others, including Michael, are silent as death—each in his own way, I suspect, are full of thoughts about Sidney and Leo, lying together in the coffin. I hope they can breathe. I hope that neither of them will be so freaked that they go crazy in that black box. I shudder at the hell Josh has put them in. I wonder who could have dreamed up such a cruel treatment.

Goodnight, Paul Romaine, you little fucking Nazi. I know you're still outside. I wonder if anyone else will attempt to sneak back to the chapel. I wonder how you can stay awake, Paul, to be the watchman—or do you have help?

* * *

June 25—another day of reckoning

As it happened, this week I was working under Charlie's supervision in the fields. Irrigation had been done by another crew the week before and now, with the ground drying out a little, we were walking up and down every row of that hundred acres, weeding the crops. It presented the perfect opportunity for Charlie and me to talk, without fear of being overheard.

I couldn't concentrate on the work, but neither could Charlie.

"Nobody told me about that coffin," he said. "I didn't know, until now, that they ever did that. You said Paul told you they do it each time? I can't believe that."

"That's what he said last night," I said. We were hoeing weeds, managing to stay ahead of the rest of the flock in the field. Behind us, we heard singing from the group. It made me want to scream. How could they even concentrate, knowing that two of their brothers were probably going nuts inside that black box?

"Well, I don't think the people in the church are aware of that little exercise, either," Charlie said, shaking his head.

"What I can't believe, Charlie, is that in almost a month none of the first recruits have said anything to anyone about the first time it occurred, or which one of the first wave of recruits were stuck in there."

"They're all scared as rabbits in the beam of a spotlight, Kelly. You ever been hunting rabbits?"

"You mean at night, from the back of a pickup? Yeah."

"Then you know what these kids are like. You get out into the desert and drive in amongst the bushes, flushing the rabbits out of their hiding places by making a lot of noise, banging on the cab, screaming, and they dart from one bush to another, not knowing what's happening. Then you bear down on them with the pickup, shining your spotlight on them. If they dart straight at you…Wham, you shine the light in their faces and they freeze, long enough for you to aim and pull the trigger."

Charlie was right. Even though I detested what had happened to Sidney and Leo, I was as frozen as the rest of the guys. It didn't do any good for me to rationalize that I would jeopardize myself by objecting—even though that's what I should've done.

"So, what do we do, Charlie?"

"You're not to do anything, Kelly. It's still a good idea for you to be doing what you set out to do, unless you've had enough. If you have, you just say so. But if you can stick it out, lay low. I'm going to pass the word around about this. I intend to be there when those two young men come out, today, too."

* * *

At noon, we assembled in the chapel for the opening of the coffin. Rafferty had excused the staff, using what excuse, I had no idea, but they were gone by noon, probably glad to get off the ranch in this incessant heat. They were asked to come back for supper, but until then, thank you very much, we could handle the work here. Now I know how this little exercise in cruelty is kept from the staff from the church in Carlsbad. It tells me not only of Rafferty's cruelty, but because he keeps it a secret from the rest of the staff, he *knows* it's cruel.

Charlie pretended to leave the ranch with the others, but as we were going into the chapel, I was gratified to see a plume of dust rising from the canyon. I felt much better when I sat down on the hard bench next to Michael, knowing that in a few minutes, Charlie would casually walk into the ceremonies.

Rafferty led us all in a prayer, the substance of which was that Sidney and Leo now be given a second chance, by the love of Jesus, to redeem themselves.

Paul stepped forward, head bowed at the solemnity of the occasion and removed the padlock.

The click was the only sound in the room, until the chapel door creaked open. I could not resist turning around to watch as Charlie and the black man, "Sharp" Jones, slipped in, pulling the door shut behind them. They stood just inside the entrance, arms folded across their chests. All heads turned, and Josh stepped off the podium. "Brother Hays. Brother Jones. You're not needed here. I thought—"

"We know what you thought, Josh," Charlie said, "but I didn't feel right, what with all the hoeing in the fields we've still got to do, so I wanted to see why you were having a meeting. And Sharp, here…he thought maybe he'd see what's so important to pull his crew off their jobs. So go right ahead and finish your little sermon. What we got, a funeral?"

Rafferty was visibly upset, but he regained his composure marvelously. He turned his back on his audience and opened the lid on the coffin. At first there was nothing—no sound, no movement. Then the smell of vomit and urine filled the chapel, and both Charlie and Sharp rushed from where they stood, bounding down the aisle to the coffin.

"Lord Almighty, Rev'rend. What you gone and done!" Sharp shouted, looking into the coffin and back at Rafferty. Then both Charlie and Sharp began pulling at Sidney and Leo. "You boys come out of there," Sharp said, lifting Leo, shaking him as he did so. "This boy's unconscious, Rev'rend! Don't you know you cain't shut people up in a box like this without them able to breathe!"

Rafferty tried to intervene. "This is just a demon—"

Charlie ignored him, elbowing backwards, just missing Rafferty's stomach. "Looks kinda' cruel," he said, pulling at Sydney. "How long these boys been in here?"

"Just a little while, Charlie, just long enough to make a point."

"Yep, I reckon, a long little while," Sharp said. He slapped Leo's face and stood him up. When Leo regained consciousness, he began screaming, filling the chapel with his horror. Sidney had come to and lurched on his own out of the coffin. His chest was covered with vomit, his face caked with it, like flaking skin.

Finally galvanized by the sight, some of the recruits and S&Ms came off the benches and surrounded Leo, helping him outside. Sidney continued to stand on his own, looking around bewildered, as if he were just waking up from a coma. Rafferty had slunk to the side, his head hung. Paul was whispering in his ear.

All looked to Charlie and Sharp. "They put 'em in there last night, Charlie," someone said. "While everybody was gone," someone else said. "Right after supper." The chorus of voices continued.

Sidney made it halfway down the aisle on his way outside when he stopped and shook his head. Then, before anyone realized what he was doing, he began pushing people away, ripping at their clothes. "Filth! Don't touch me!"

Paul tried to stop him, but Sidney back-handed the little chipmunk so hard he went sprawling. None of his inner cadre moved to help him.

Charlie followed Sidney outside, and I ran after them. Behind me, the rest of the crowd came, followed by Rafferty and Paul, holding a bloody nose. In the sunlight, on the stingy plot of grass in front of the Lion's Mouth Chapel, the assemblage looked weird. Two men (Rafferty and Paul) in black suits, Charlie and Sharp in Khaki, the rest of us in brilliant white T-shirts and Levi's—all looking sick, pasty faced, surrounding two naked men, one screaming, and the other with his inevitable, inscrutable erection.

Charlie led them to his Jeep. "Don't care what you think Reverend, I'm taking these two lads to Carlsbad. Don't care what the program is, here, they're leaving. And I'm gonna have a talk with the church. We've got some studying to do on this. Meanwhile, I'm leaving Sharp in charge."

When Charlie was gone, and his Jeep was hidden in a cloud of dust moving toward the tents on the north side of the valley, where I presumed he was going to get Leo and Sidney's things, I sighed with relief that, at least, neither of the guys had suffocated.

Sharp stood up straight and hulked his way over to Rafferty. There was a glint of anger in his eyes that made the rest of us part for him and made Paul move behind Rafferty. Rafferty didn't move, and I was reminded of Charlie's description of the rabbits caught in the spotlight.

"You, Rev'rend, you best get into your chapel and do some praying," Sharp said. Then he turned to us. "As for the rest of you," he said, tears brimming on his eyes as he looked at us, one by one, "I thinks y'all deserves a holiday."

* * *

Sunday, June 28

That was three days ago. I'm just now getting around to finishing up this installment. There's a lot more to write about. Like what happened when Charlie went to the church in Carlsbad, how Rafferty recovered himself. Some of it is good from where I sit. But then, Rafferty does have powers of persuasion. It's true that Sidney and Leo are gone from the ranch for good. But we're back in full swing.

Gee…This is only the end of week three of this eighteen-week program. Fifteen more weeks to go!

I could use a long, hot bath. I still feel filthy having witnessed what I have—and not having the courage to do much else besides write down what I saw.

K. O'K.

VIII
The Aftermath

Lion's Mouth
Tuesday, June 30

    I keep having to remind myself that most of the guys at this ranch chose to be here because they believe they can be cured of their homosexuality. I'm probably the only one who came with no intention whatsoever of getting cured. But then there's Larry, poor, fat Larry, who didn't want to come at all. His parents sent him. I also have to remind myself that once here, a truly committed patient (penitent), is more likely to put up with horrible treatment—all in the interest of getting "cured."
    I recall last Wednesday night. I was stumped by how willing Sidney was to submit himself to what Josh had planned with the coffin, even though he couldn't know he was going to be imprisoned in that dark hell for almost twenty four hours. That scared me, how willing he was to do as he was told, how he surrendered his will to Josh. But now I think I understand. Sidney didn't enjoy his erections in the showers, nor masturbating. He really did hate his homosexuality. He really did think it was a sin. And to him, Josh represented a hope for a cure. But rather than building on that trust, Rafferty betrayed him by entombing him in the coffin in the name of Christian *love*. I can't imagine how it felt to be in that coffin, getting vomited on, pissed on, and kept cramped

up with another human being, both of them fighting for breath (maybe even wishing the other would die so there would be more air), or being unable to pull his hand up to wipe the vomit from his face.

Rafferty tossed Leo to the same fate, even though Leo didn't enjoy his attraction to Sidney, either. He just couldn't help it—even when Rafferty was in the shower room to watch. It was something Leo had no control over. Yet Rafferty betrayed him, too. Didn't Rafferty get *his* eyes full? Wasn't Sidney's erect penis the whole *point* of his visit to the showers? For that matter, wouldn't a heterosexual man have a damned hard time avoiding a hard-on in the shower with a bunch of naked women? Ironically, a heterosexual man might even be condemned or suspected of being homosexual for *not* getting an erection in that situation.

Rafferty displayed no compassion for either Sidney or Leo. Neither chose what attracted them, yet he went on like an idiot about the reprobate mind and how it was their homosexuality that made them unworthy of even God's love.

Life goes on here. The program is still underway. But I'll bet the percentage of guys who are committed to it has dwindled to maybe eighty percent, or seventy percent or, in their heart of hearts, to even a smaller number.

Sidney and Leo were taken away from Rafferty, because the people in the church at Carlsbad do have compassion. But Rafferty lost more than that by the symbolic burial. He lost my friend Michael on Wednesday night. He lost the trust of several more of us. The spell of brainwashing was even broken on a few of the S&Ms. I've seen a few of the guys coming back to personal consciousness, whose eyes had formerly displayed the stares of the brainwashed. Before last Wednesday night, no matter what was said or done, they were unblinking, glassy-eyed with "enlightenment." The thing with the coffin did something to them; made them at least blink, their eyes shift. For awhile, there was *thinking* going on in their heads.

That's the good news.

The bad news is that Rafferty is still in charge of the program after a flurry of meetings between him and his staff and the church in Carlsbad and their people. I couldn't believe it when Charlie told me what had transpired in those meetings. I think I'll write about that later.

On the day the coffin was opened, Charlie took Sidney and Leo to Carlsbad, stopping by their tent long enough to get their belongings and, of course, to let them get dressed. He didn't come back to the ranch that night. He told me later that his brother kept the boys at his house.

The rest of the staff returned to the ranch that evening with much wringing of hands. The way they acted, I thought (hoped) the program was finished. The easygoing camaraderie between Rafferty and the staff was strained. Rafferty was made to sweat it out. As Sharp Jones had demanded, all work was suspended and, for one glorious afternoon and evening, so was the "program."

Paul and his cadre disappeared completely. Even though I had an idea where they had gone, I decided not to follow them to their hiding place east of the stock pens.

Michael and I went hiking. Our favorite place is the site where the barracks are being built. In three weeks, the wood-framed walls had been put up, and a few squares of plywood had been nailed to the corners of the building to support them. The interior framing is almost done. Michael and I walked through the barracks. He ran his hands along the studs. "It's neat to look at this," he said, smiling wistfully, "and realize I did some of it, like a real hunky construction worker!" We laughed about that, then took off beyond the barracks and climbed the hill to the south of the ranch, where a few pine trees grow.

Another surprise is that there's a little stream about a foot wide that trickles down the hill, then goes underground, forming a small pool with clear water. We were lucky that others didn't follow. It gave us a chance to talk freely.

I told Michael why I am here, what I had been doing. I told him about Charlie and me, our secret meetings to pass him my journal and getting to know each other.

"I'm angry at you," Michael said, smiling.

"You are? Why?"

"Because you led me on about wanting a cure. If I'd known—"

"You might have told on me, Mike. You, yourself, said this was your last chance to be cured. You said you were tired of being ill treated by people—even gay people. You seemed sincere and committed to what they were doing, right? So in the interest of your commitment to the program—"

"Right, hon. I might've squealed once upon a time; but now I'm glad you told me. Now I have a big, he-man protector." He laughed. His face is beautiful when he laughs. Hell, his face is beautiful when he's serious. He brought his hands up to his cheeks in that inimitable gesture of the effeminate gay, but it looked odd on him, now. At first, I couldn't see why that gesture, once looking so natural, now seemed forced. Then I knew. His wispy frame was giving way to muscles he'd never developed, especially in the upper arms, chest, and shoulders.

"At least you're getting one wish from this whole thing," I said.

"What?"

"Have you looked in the mirror lately?"

"Hon, I do it every day when I shave."

I leaned over. We were sitting side-by-side by the pool. "You're beginning to look butch," I whispered.

"I am? You're not teasing?"

I shook my head.

"Praise Gawud!" he shouted. "I is becomins a may-un! I is gettins de sex change ob de Lawud!"

We howled with laughter and hugged each other. God, how good it felt to have a man's arms around me, again! We kissed, one good male-to-male liplock that brought a tingle to my manhood. Then I drew away.

"But listen, Mike, are you going to continue with this program?"

Michael sobered up quickly. "Do you think it'll go on after today?"

"Maybe not, but if it does, how are you going to hold up? I mean are you still trying to overcome being gay?"

"Kelly, I was lonely. I lived in Houston in the biggest gay ghetto of the city, and I got so tired of the bar scene, the dancing, the drinking, the crack and coke—not that I was into that—but all my friends were. Or shall I say my sisters? And then what happened to Rita...that did it. When I read about this ministry, I went to the church group sponsoring it. There I saw such clean-cut men, hon, looking so wholesome, so pure, I knew they must have something I lacked. When I looked at myself in the mirror and saw this twenty-two year old queen with painted nails, I hoped for the first time in my life that there really was a program that could do something for me, something people in the gay world won't do—or can't do—to give me the incentive I needed to make some kind of change."

"So, you think it's working?"

"It is a miracle, Kelly, what is happening to my body. I like what I see in the mirror, how I feel at the end of the day. But I was confused about what it meant. Was this man they call Jesus actually working something within me that made me begin to change? Was it really that homosexuality, itself, drove me down the wrong path? At first, I thought so. But then, I began to wonder. Maybe it's just the attitude of the religious that makes the difference."

"Like what?"

"Like they have *the* answer. It's the attitude that says a person can make changes in his life. It's the real strength of religion, isn't it?"

"So, did it help you?"

Michael shook his head a little sadly, it seemed to me, but he squared his shoulders. "Nothing I've been through, here, has changed that thing inside me that says I like men. That religious stuff just goes in one ear, rattles around for a second in my head, then goes out the other. I tried to concentrate on it. I tried so hard to believe that day by day I was changing within, that I wouldn't feel attracted to the guys in the shower or, I wouldn't get that little thrill just being with other guys. But I do. I feel enriched when we're singing, listening to the voices of all these men, their clean-shaven faces looking so beautiful. It makes me feel happy just being among them. None of that has changed. I still wonder what it would feel like to kiss Brian and Alex and that little number, Donald. Do you know what I'm saying?"

"Yeah, Mike, you're a queer, faggot, homosexual pervert."

Michael laughed again. We kissed a little more deeply. "Yes, I am, Kelly, and right now that seems all right. I like being with you, and when we go back, I'm going to concentrate on that—that you've come here to write about this program. Someone has to know what happened to Sidney and Leo. I'll help you when I can. You have me as an ally. No matter what happens, okay?"

"Okay. Thanks."

* * *

We were relaxed when we got back to the rest of the people. We found out that, in our absence, the staff had returned and they had prepared a barbecue for everyone. That night, Les Hunter, the foreman in charge of carpentry, and a guy everyone at the ranch likes, including me (cynical Kelly), brought out a fiddle and played such wonderfully hokey country music that—had anyone been brave enough—we homosexuals would have danced with each other. No one was that relaxed. The guitarist from the S&M group of recruits joined Les as an accompanist. The crowd applauded and he cracked a smile that went beyond the bland smile of enlightenment I was used to seeing pasted on his face; I actually believed he was still human, rather than a Christian zombie.

That night, there was none of that "awe-inspiring" Caucasian gospel, either. We had become just a group of people enjoying the country setting, eating the appetite whetting barbecue and Pinto beans.

Rafferty didn't make his currently unpopular presence felt, either, preferring the company of whatever God he finds solace in, there in his chapel—praying no doubt for his hide. Nor did Paul and his inner cadre bring their fear-inspiring presence to the festivities.

Yet, in all that joy of being at a long-overdue recess, there was still an undertone of sadness. I could see it in the eyes of the recruits and the S&Ms. No one knew how Sidney or Leo was doing. The staff wasn't talking and, since Charlie wasn't there to tell me, I had no way of finding out.

Larry gravitated toward Michael and me. He sat on the grass with us while he ate barbecue—or rather, inhaled it.

I couldn't stand it, watching him stuff his face, hearing him grunt with satisfaction with each glob of beef that slid down his esophagus, into that mammoth belly. "Larry?" I said, finally. "Wouldn't it be easier on you, with all the work we do around here…wouldn't it make you feel better, if…" I paused, couldn't finish.

He looked at me with his round face smeared with barbecue sauce, his cheeks bulging. "Wha? Oo mea' eatin'? I'm hun'wy." He swallowed, then bit right in again without pausing for breath.

"But it's really bad for you, hon," Michael put in. "To eat that much stuff after being on the strict diet we've had. Can't you stop after one or two helpings?"

Larry began to look uncomfortable—not only because his Levi's were already stretched at the seams, not only because he was sprawled on the ground like a ton of Jell-O in a T-shirt, with his fat oozing from the neck and sleeves—he looked uncomfortable in the way he did when Josh had him in front of the chapel making us look at his obesity. He looked scared the way he did when Alton Drigger was in his face.

"I wouldn't be stuffing myself now, if they weren't starving us, if they had donuts and stuff for us when we went to bed. It's such a long time before breakfast, when the last thing you eat is supper—and that hardly a bite. At least now that this program is over, my parents will have to let me come home. And then I can have all I want."

Michael and I exchanged glances. I slid over closer to Larry and put my arm around as much of his shoulders as I could. Beneath my arm, his bulk felt even more massive than it looked. "I don't necessarily think it's over, Larry. What if it isn't? Wouldn't it be better to try to lose a little weight, to just eat what they serve? You'd get used to it. You'd—"

He began to quiver, to rock back and forth on the ground. "It can't go on! It can't! They almost killed Sidney…and…and…they'll kill us! I've got to get out! Why'd you say it might go on? It can't. I didn't want to come." He put both fat palms over his eyes and began to cry.

"But, hon, it might," Michael said. From the other side of Larry, he put his arm around the boy's shoulders. Our forearms touched each other on Larry's back. "But if you need help getting through it, Kelly and I are your friends, okay?"

"It ain't fair," Larry sobbed, then looked down at the bit of sandwich on his plate. He slapped it away, and it fell wetly into a clump of grass, where it looked like a glob of blood in the waning light. By morning, it would be covered with ants, more than ever resembling a rotting lump of flesh.

"Haven't you written to your parents telling them how unhappy you are?" I asked. "Surely if they knew—"

"They read our letters, Kelly. You know that. I tell my parents I'm okay, because that's what they want to hear and, besides, that's all Josh will let me say."

"Well, if that's the case, and you find you've gotta stay here, wouldn't it be better, to try a little harder to overcome some of the things that—"

"You don't know nothing about the things I have to get over, Kelly. None of you do. You don't know what my home life was like, either, or how my parents found out that I'm homosexual. They belong to the Assembly of God in Fort Worth, Texas. They collected money for Rafferty's program last year."

"But why did they do that? Did they already know about you? Did you tell them?"

"They caught me in the tool shed having sex with the man from next door. He's a member of our church. He got me started when I was just a kid. He used to be a Sunday School teacher in our church. He told me if I snitched, he'd kill Mom and Dad. I never did. We'd been having sex for years."

"How awful!" Michael said. "Oh, hon, didn't your parents bother to find out if that man was forcing you, or even if you were gay or not?"

Larry cried softly. "I don't know what I am. When I'd get horny, I'd seek him out, so I must be, huh? They caught me sucking him off in the tool shed last year. He tried to blame everything on me, but they wouldn't hear it. I tried to tell them he'd been doing things to me for a long time. They didn't want to hear that, either. All they wanted to know was that I was going to Hell if I didn't get help. So, when this program came up, they shipped me off."

"What happened to your next door neighbor?" I asked, sickened at the thought of what he'd put Larry through.

Larry looked from me to Michael and back again at me. In the dusky light, the whites of his eyes were visible, while the shadow of his forehead seemed huge and misshapen, like a beast undergoing a change. He sighed. "One Sunday morning, he walked out to the middle of the street just when the neighbors were leaving for church. He was naked and carrying a gun—a big one. I don't know what kind. But right there, in front of everyone, he shot himself in the head."

A moment later, Larry leaned forward and crawled away from us on his hands and knees. With his back to us, he leaned down, close to the ground, gagging and, before I could turn my face away, he vomited onto the grass.

It took all the strength I could muster to join Michael in helping Larry to his feet. It took maybe half an hour, but we finally managed to calm the kid down. Eventually, he looked at us and smiled. "Thanks. I never have had real friends like you two. I've wanted someone to hear that for a long time. I think I feel better. I like you guys. Thanks."

* * *

When the supper was over, when the musicians had tired and put their instruments away, Michael, Larry, and I followed the others to the tents. There was more mixing than before between us recruits and the S&Ms as we walked across the field. Some wall had been razed between us. There was no longer a feeling of "us" and "them." For the first time since I arrived here, I felt a real friendliness toward my S&M, Jerry.

The night was warm, the stars were out in force, and somebody looked up, shouting, "Hey! Did anyone see that shooting star?" Everyone looked heavenward. There was oohing and aahing at the sight of the universe above us, the gasp as another falling star streaked silently across the sky, then another. But no one mentioned God or heaven. That made me smile as I entered the tent behind Michael and Larry.

Their smiles were frozen—slowly, inexorably, their faces took on a look of horror. When I saw what they saw, my heart stopped, and it took me a second of sucking in to draw a breath. In that weird light from the naked string of lights, casting bright shadows over the room, I saw that the entire tent, its contents, and our personal belongs, had been ransacked. Letters, papers, books, clothing riffled through, then tossed onto the dirt floor. But that sight was minor to the real horror. Almost black and still glistening wetly, everywhere we looked on the walls of the tent were the messages: "Death to homosexuals!" and "Kill a Queer for Christ!" written in blood.

"We know who did this, don't we, Kelly?" Michael said, unconsciously taking my hand.

* * *

July 1, 1998

Now for the bad news. Josh Rafferty is still in charge. According to Charlie, on June 27 and 28, Rafferty met with the elders, deacons, and others in the church. They wanted to know why they should sponsor a group that would treat people as he had Sidney and Leo.

Charlie and I were in his Jeep, parked behind a cliff, in the bottom of a dry river bed. This was our secret meeting place. It's north of the tents, in the palm of the "hand" formed by hills and ridges. What appears to be one solid rise of ground north of the tents is really cut in two by a dry river bed. The entrance is at an angle from the tents, so that no one, in or near them, can see where a person goes into the hill.

We met there this morning, after Rafferty called everyone to the chapel, where he announced with great pleasure that the program would continue. "We have reorganized," Rafferty told us, "to account for and be humbled by my mistake in judgment. I am humbled by it and so, in the interest of reminding us all to never let our ministry make the same mistake again, we will keep the coffin on display in the compound."

I couldn't believe it. A reminder? Us having to pass that coffin every day on our way from the chow hall to the showers? It would be more like a threat, an imminent thunder storm over the valley.

Charlie was behind the steering wheel. There was no top on the Jeep, but there was a roll bar, which Charlie clung to as he told me what had happened at the meetings. "The Reverend Rafferty begged for his job, is what happened," Charlie said, shifting his weight and leaning forward, hugging the steering wheel. "He humbled himself. Told the elders it was a mistake, like he said this morning to you. He asked them if one mistake should stop the whole program, then said they could approve his whatchacallit…agenda…each week."

"And I'll just bet the church people decided Rafferty ought to make those decisions by himself," I said, angry, not only at the situation, but even at Charlie, just because he was the one relating the story. "Didn't you tell them, Charlie, how awful Sidney and Leo had been treated? It wasn't just one fucking mistake. It's happened before!"

Charlie looked directly at me, then shook his head. "There was a split in the church leadership, Kelly. I told them what I'd seen. But some didn't think what he'd done to Sidney and Leo was drastic at all. Others wanted to stop the program. One elder wanted to put someone else in charge and continue. But in the end, the Reverend won. He convinced them that he'd expel those like Sidney, if they couldn't...you know...restrain themselves and get rid of those not committed to their own cure."

"In other words, he can get rid of us," I said, "if he can't brainwash us, or if we embarrass him."

"I reckon that's so," Charlie said.

I thought of the condition of my locker, of the blood on the walls of the tent, with its gruesome messages of death. I thought of Sidney and Leo. I thought of Michael and Larry, or Jerry, but mainly I thought of Paul and his inner cadre of S&Ms. They had trashed our tents, gone through our personal belongings looking for something. In mine, they wouldn't have found anything out of the ordinary—at least that night. Who knows what they expected to find? Maybe Paul was angry because he didn't find anything bad in our lockers, and so he trashed our belongings.

The blood came from a pig that had been butchered for the chow hall. When Les Hunter and Alton Drigger investigated the tent, they found a tub from the chow hall at the scene, behind the tents. There had been no effort made to hide it. There had been no effort, either, to discover the culprits.

"Did anything come of the pig's blood in our tent? Did the church, or Rafferty try to find who did it?" I was so angry, I was almost shouting and only calmed down when I saw I was taking it out on Charlie.

"Nothin' came of that, Kelly. Josh said there was no way to prove who did it. Then he went off on a tangent, talking about the homosexual mind being rep...rep..."

"Reprobate?"

"Yeah. That's the word he used. What does it mean?"

"It means a homosexual is so lost and fuzzy headed he can't know the truth."

Charlie's eyes dulled with sadness. "Well, that explains why the church hasn't tried to find the people who wrecked your tent, then. Josh said it was probably some angry recruits taking advantage of the time off that Sharp had given them."

"And they bought that?"

He shifted his weight, again, and was now turned in the seat toward me. He was wearing khaki pants and a khaki work shirt. He had an old felt hat clamped down on his head. He pulled it off by the brim and combed his fingers through his hair. "They did. They're still inclined to believe homosexuals can be cured. Most of 'em still want that." He shook his head. "I'm sorry, Kelly."

"Hey, it's not your fault," I said.

After a moment, he smiled sadly. "So here we are, Kelly, back to the grind. You gonna hold up?"

We talked for a little while longer; then, as easy as pie, we drove out of the riverbed, headed east under cover of a ridge of sandstone and emerged on the lower end of the field.

***

It's almost lights out. As usual I'm the last one up—except for Larry. Since finding out the program will continue, he's become even more withdrawn. He left the tent a few minutes ago. I think I hear him pacing back and forth out back, between the tents and the hills. Remembering my meeting in the dark with Paul Romaine the night I was going to let Sidney and Leo out of the coffin, I shudder to think what Paul might do to Larry if he catches him.

Well, I can't worry about that tonight. I think I'll continue being the under-cover agent.

K. O'K

IX

Watch for Dust Rising in the East

Lion's Mouth
Thursday, July 2

    I think I've finally been able to put together an insider's view of the Lion's Mouth Christian Ranch. From what I've read about the Branch Davidians—or even that Jim Jones cult of the 70s, this place is rather like them. While Rafferty's mission may not be world conquest, it is control over people. I might have believed his heart was in the right place, although misguided. But I no longer think that. I believe he does not love the sinner but hate the sin. I believe he hates both. Rafferty's purpose is not to cure homosexuals at all. It is simply to punish and make life miserable for as many gay people as he can. He uses distorted images of gay people and uses our fears and shame to get us out of the daylight and back into the closet. That's *all* he wants and, as we gay people continue to stand up and, yes, stand *out*, there will be more Raffertys and Exodus Internationals, and religious fundamentalists trying to shove us back into our closets—or kill us.

    Rafferty lacks real compassion. This ministry is NOT compassionate! It's just a down-the-line cult.

        1) We're isolated.

2) We're starved. I believe our diet lacks protein, and having to earn those food credits is a psychological boot to our necks.
3) We're continually assaulted with one message: "We're sick and sinful and we ought to die."
4) We get up early and go to bed late and, in between, we work hard and are given very little rest, very little food, and very little privacy.
5) They prey on our weaknesses—our self-guilt (or shame), our doubts, our losses in life, our loneliness.
6) They keep us disoriented—as with the "death of the spirit" demonstration.

Maybe even ransacking our living quarters and smearing blood on the walls of the tent was planned to keep us disoriented. I doubt that even Paul would pull a stupid stunt like that when the program, itself, was being threatened because of that coffin bit and Rafferty's "death of the spirit" demonstration—unless it *was* part of a plan.

Can I really trust anybody, here? Rafferty betrayed people's trust. But what if he *intended* to do it, to further disorient us? Maybe the point of stirring up the entire group of recruits and S&Ms was to further upset us, mentally and emotionally. I could go on about this paranoia, but I've made my point. The longer I stay here, no matter how strong willed I might be, I just might lose my perspective.

One last thought: they say hostages often fall in love with their captors. The longer they are kept in captivity, the more likely this is to occur.

Maybe I'm too cynical for my own good.

Maybe I'm not cynical enough.

* * *

Friday, July 3

Week four is almost gone. But things are not "back to normal." In fact, there are major cracks in what once appeared as a seamless unity among us.

Although we are still paired off by one S&M to one recruit, there's not much difference between us any more. I used to think that all the S&Ms were convinced that homosexuality is a sin and that their brainwashing was complete. Not so. There are some of the new recruits who already outdo the S&Ms in swallowing the dogma, spouting it, and looking around for those who do not. The lines are drawn. Some believe unconditionally in this program—right or wrong. They have traded one addiction for another. Some want to believe in it because they hate themselves, like Michael did (or does). He was hoping to become a "man" by having his homosexuality cured. It is a pity for those recruits and S&Ms, like Michael, that this program is not powerful enough to really cure them, but only able to increase their shame and guilt over something they cannot change. An even greater pity is there's little compassion, here. The rest of us believe this program is as misguided and harmful as every other cure-the-homosexual method that has been used, from castration to lobotomy. The major unifying factor that still reigns supreme at the ranch is fear.

When I was in boot camp, I recall that, by the third or fourth week, one began to feel "comfortable" in the role, although still afraid, still preferring to be anywhere but in the military. By the fourth week, when we saw the new recruits arriving at the base, looking stupid in their civilian clothes and wild haircuts, we felt superior, like old hands at soldiering. Our fears had become chronic—kind of ingrained, second nature. The whole point of boot camp is to make a person jump without thought when a command is given. At least one aspect of that power over a trainee comes from ingrained fear. By the fourth week, we were able to cope with our fears, to call them "discipline." But those new guys, just stepping off the bus, were put in shock as soon as the yelling started. You could see it in their eyes. You could make them jump by saying "boo!"

It's the "insider's" power over the novice—that little bit of experience with the system, the knowledge of what to expect—that makes them feel superior to outsiders. That's what made the S&Ms appear to be different than we were. Their fears were already chronic. They already knew the kinds of things that could happen if they let down their guard, if they showed anger, if they disagreed with the program or with Rafferty or Romaine. Like the experienced basic trainee, they were able to scare us with their knowledge of the program, with their ability to spout the dogma of the eighteen steps.

But now, the fear is chronic in all of us, and the thing some of us fear most is being found out—afraid someone (an S&M or a new recruit) is going to realize that the cure is not working within us and report us to Rafferty. We know what punishment Rafferty is capable of. Sydney and Leo's fate is not far from our thoughts.

I thought Rafferty was ready and willing to let those men go who did not exhibit conformity or cure, like Sidney and Leo were let go. But that's not true.

Yesterday, Larry packed his bags and appeared in the chapel. He told Rafferty (according to Larry) that he wasn't being cured; that he hated it here and he wasn't going to get with the program. He said his mind was made up and so it was a waste of time for him to be here.

Rafferty didn't blink an eye, according to Larry. He just ordered him to take his bags back to the tent. As he was leaving the chapel, Rafferty supposedly said, "It's not up to you, son, to get with the program. In time, your being here will be sufficient to work God's will in you."

Larry brought this news to me. I haven't told him I'm not here to be cured, so he was taking a chance complaining to me. Besides, I do not feel I could trust him with that knowledge—especially since I'm smuggling stuff off the ranch. He would probably spill that information to anyone, if he thought it would help him get out of here.

In Larry's case, it just may be that Rafferty wants to keep him here because Larry's parents want it. Hell, they may even be paying Rafferty for his services. Maybe if Michael or I went to him and said we weren't going to get with the program, either, he might let us go, because he's not dealing with someone's parents.

Again, I'm too reluctant to test him on that. Aside from feeling that this place is just here to punish homosexuals, I want to see what happens. So I stay.

* * *

Saturday, July 4

It is almost lights out tonight, but I've got to finish this entry and get it to Charlie first thing tomorrow. From now on, I can't risk having someone find my journal entries. I'll have to let Charlie keep them each day. This is the first time I'm *really* afraid of getting caught writing this journal, in full view of the others. There is fear and suspicion all over the camp, tonight. Larry is sitting on the edge of his cot, rocking back and forth, crying, but no one cares to go to him. We can all hear his litany: "They let Michael go, why not me?" He's been singing it, crying it, and repeating it over and over for an hour.

It boils down to this: Michael's cot is empty. Michael is gone, and I certainly don't understand why it should have been him who was blamed for what happened and not that fucking chipmunk Nazi bastard.

How shall I tell about this, so that it makes sense?

I'll start with lunch, today, when Michael and I had a moment to talk.

Michael was with the livestock crew on the east end of the ranch. He was paired with an S&M by the name of Eugene. Before today, I hadn't paid much attention to Eugene, but because Michael was working with him, I wanted to know about him, so when Michael sat down next to me on the porch, while we were waiting for the crews to reassemble for the afternoon, I asked him.

"How's Eugene?"

Michael looked uneasy, glancing around at the other people on the porch, then leaned in close to me. "Eugene and Drigger are like this," he said, putting his middle and forefinger together and squeezing them with the other hand.

"Really?"

"Yeah, I think it takes a sadist to know one."

"Really?"

"Yeah, they make the work as hard as they can. Eugene keeps drilling me on the eighteen steps. Drigger steps in calling me faggot and girl."

"What about the others? How many are you working with?"

Michael's eyes narrowed. "I'm scared, Kelly. I'm working with Donald and Brian and their paired recruits."

"What's so scary about that?"

"Don't you remember what Brian and Donald have in common, besides the fact they they're living dolls?"

"The bruises!" I said, and felt a jolt of fear as well. "And what about the other two?"

"They're friendly with Paul, hon. He's been by in his Jeep several times in the last couple of days."

Before I could ask anything else, Eugene came out of the chow hall. He has eyebrows that grow together above the bridge of his nose. That's the thing one notices right away. Then one discovers that the eyes are little black beads, that the nose is sharp, like a hatchet, above a slit for a mouth. Not a friendly face.

Michael got up, stretched, turning casually away from Eugene, and looked directly at me. "Watch for dust rising in the east, Kelly. Walk in the Spirit. Become a people helper."

* * *

I was stumped by Michael's parting words as I went back to work on the barracks. But I knew he'd meant to convey something by them. He didn't talk like that.

After lunch, the sky becomes almost white, its blue color bleached by the sun. Temperatures soar in this desert, and the dry air becomes like a blast furnace. During lunch, our tools were stored in the shade, but they were still hot to the touch when I picked up my hammer and my nail apron. I was still replaying my conversation with Michael when I realized what he'd been trying to say. I broke out into a cold sweat and shivered in the heat. *"Watch for dust rising in the east,"* Michael had said. *"Become a people helper."*

He was working with Drigger and the living dolls, Brian and Donald, who had bruises on their necks—one of whom Michael had also thought had rectal bleeding. Michael's S&M, Eugene, was like stink on shit with Drigger, the sadist; and Paul had been hovering around that particular crew.

"Watch for dust rising in the east!"

I almost knocked Les Hunter down in my effort to get away. He grabbed my arm. "Son? Where are you going?"

"Les, I've got to talk to Charlie!" I said. "It really can't wait. Is it all right if I take off for about a half hour?"

Unlike any of the other foremen, except for Charlie Hays, Les is his own boss. He doesn't push, nor quote scripture, nor feel particularly beholden to Rafferty and his rules. "Do what you need to do, son. Just let me know, later, so's if anyone asks, I can tell 'em where you are."

"Thanks, Les, I will."

* * *

I took an easterly route away from the barracks, using the hill to the north to hide my lone movement from the people working in the valley below. Rafferty is usually ensconced in the chapel, out of the heat. The crew in the chow hall can't see outdoors in the direction I was heading, and I didn't care if Charlie's crew saw me. They were still hoeing weeds. From above them to the south, I could see they were just now arriving in the field. I looked for Charlie's Jeep and didn't see it.

I peered eastward, but from my location couldn't see the stock pens at all. Nor could I see beyond the pens, east, where Michael had said he was sure Paul and his cadre go when they disappear. I looked toward the floor of the valley, scanning the compound for Paul's Jeep. He was climbing into it at the chow hall. Even from this distance, his form was unmistakable in his civilian clothing. Three recruits, or S&Ms, dressed in T-shirts and Levi's were climbing into the Jeep as well. But I couldn't tell if they were Paul's personal crew, the cadre. I assumed they were, since everyone else was now back at work.

But where was Charlie?

I continued walking east above the valley, hidden by the hill. When it played out about a quarter mile from the barracks, I had to dart from Yucca to Mesquite, to Juniper, hiding as best I could from prying eyes from the valley below. A lone figure on the ranch is highly suspect, and I didn't want to be stopped in my progress, until I could get close enough to the stock pens to make sure Michael and the crew were there.

North of me was the remaining part of the field. The crew was still back toward the west, about middle ways. Charlie's Jeep was crawling along the north side of the field, heading west, away from me! To catch him, I would have to go straight down from where I knelt, exposing myself to view; then I would have to walk westward, then northward. But Paul's Jeep was now moving in a straight line eastward toward the stock pens. He would arrive there before I could possibly get to Charlie.

In the pit of my stomach, I knew where Paul was headed. I knew the guys in the Jeep with him were the cadre. I knew Michael had been put with that particular work crew, under that particular foreman, and paired with Eugene for a reason. Since Paul is the one who makes up the work roster, I realized that Michael really was in danger, but I had no idea what kind, only that he might appear in the chow hall that night, full of fear, withdrawn, with bruises on his neck. But I couldn't prove any of it. I couldn't go to Les without proof of something. I wouldn't go to Rafferty. And Charlie was out of reach.

I made my decision and began running eastward, almost tripping over large rocks, almost falling into cactus, slipping on rocky ledges. My progress was hampered by the growing viciousness of the landscape. But I ran and fell and got up and ran, until I was scraped and bruised and sweating.

When I reached a place above the stock pens, I lay down on the hot sand on a ridge overlooking the area. I was about two hundred feet south of the crew, but in the dry, clear air, I could hear them talking as if they were within a few feet of me.

Other than Drigger's nasty stream of hateful words, the sharp barks from Eugene, the mumbled replies from Michael, Donald, and Brian, everything appeared normal. I lay down on the sand and tried to catch my breath. I looked to my left, toward the west and saw Paul's Jeep getting closer. He didn't appear to be in any great rush, although his progress would soon bring him to the stock pens.

I couldn't act until I knew what they were going to do. I waited, lying with my face an inch above the sand, my fingers barely reaching over the ridge of the cliff I was hiding on. I cocked my head to the right and, with my eyes, followed a path I could take that would bring me down and behind the stock pens, able to stay out of view. I could make it in about a minute, I calculated, but I felt paralyzed. What would I do once I got there—challenge everyone to a fight?

I waited.

Paul's Jeep had crawled to a stop about a quarter of a mile to the west. I wished uselessly for a pair of binoculars. From their distance, they looked like ants. There was movement around the Jeep as they got out, but I couldn't tell if they were looking back west, or east toward the stock pens.

I peered west, but my view was blurred by the shimmer of heat waves rising from the floor of the valley. From this distance, the tents looked as if they were going up in silver flames. My back was being broiled from the sunlight. I was getting dizzy from the heat, and my stomach ached from hunger from the sparse lunch we'd been fed, the contents of my belly spoiling in the heat.

"Ought'a be here any minute," came to me on the clear air. I jerked my head forward and cautiously peered over the ledge. Drigger had walked away from the crew and was standing with his back to them, just below me, looking west under his hand. He was talking to himself, but from the crew, I saw Eugene looking expectantly in his direction.

The rest of the crew, including Michael, Brian, Donald, and their two S&Ms continued to work. They were shoveling manure from the cow pens into the back of a trailer. Even from where I was, I could smell the cow shit.

I could smell the odor from my armpits, too, and taste the sweat from my face. I wondered how I'd gotten myself into such a mess. I wished I'd known Paul was going to dick around. From what Drigger had just said, I knew something was supposed to happen. But what?

Paul's Jeep began moving toward the stock pens, again, this time at a more rapid clip. I watched its progress, feeling like an Apache, looking for a chance to attack a wagon train. I wished I at least had a bow and arrows. When Paul's Jeep stopped again, it was only a hundred yards or so from the stock pens, still hidden from the crew there, but visible to me, since I was above the whole scene. Now I could make out the oval of Paul's face and those of his cadre as they once more got out of the Jeep. They were looking back west. They were watching for something—*or checking to make sure they aren't being followed*, I thought.

Maybe Charlie? I peered west again, but still saw nothing. I heard footsteps behind me, all of a sudden, and was too late to move, when a hand fell on my shoulder.

* * *

I almost shit my pants until I turned around and saw that it was Charlie. He hit the dirt as soundlessly as a cat as he lay down beside me.

"Char—"

"Shhhh!" he whispered. "Paul knows I'm trying to follow him," he said, into my ear. "I ditched the Jeep awhile ago, and he's still trying to figure out what happened."

I turned my head slightly and spoke lowly into the sand. "But how did you know anything was up?"

"I didn't. I went to see Les about a part I wanted him to get for me when he went to town. He said you'd left with the devil on your hind legs. He told me which direction you went."

"But why were you following Paul?"

Charlie chuckled. It made my ear tickle. "I wasn't, until he started looking suspicious. So I decided to see what'd happen if I did follow. He began acting even funnier. You'd told me you thought it was him who destroyed the tent, and Drigger's always seemed strange. It don't take no college education, does it, to figure somethin's up when it smells like shit around here? Les told me you looked scared, so here I am."

My heart was pounding inside my chest, but I was suddenly relieved. Now there were two of us, and Charlie's position as a foreman might help.

I almost stood up, relieved. "Let's go, then, and be down at the stock pens when—"

"You're not going anywhere, just yet," Charlie said. "I figure if I catch Paul up to something, it'd be better if he doesn't know you're involved."

"But—"

"But nothing, Kelly. You'd blow your cover." Charlie laid his arm across my back, then laid his head on the back of my neck. "Look west," he said.

Paul was coming now at a fast pace, dust funneling into the air, his Jeep jouncing along, almost comically. I wanted to laugh. I wasn't nearly as scared as I had been.

When he pulled up next to Drigger, he said, "Let's go. Get Michael and follow us. Bring Eugene with you, but leave the others so it'll look normal in case anybody shows up."

"Like who?" Drigger spat.

Paul turned around in the seat and looked back over his shoulder. "I thought Charlie Hays was following me there for awhile…" He paused, still peering toward the west. When he turned around again, he reached under the seat and brought up something shiny, handing it to Drigger.

"Handcuffs?" Drigger said, then dangled them in front of Paul's face, grinning. "Michael ain't got the strength to get away. I don't need these."

"Just do it the way we always do, Al. I don't want his hands free."

Our position on the cliff above the area allowed us a view that was denied the work crew. Most of the crew was working, anyway, and hadn't been paying much attention to Paul's arrival. Except for Michael's S&M, Eugene. He'd been glancing toward Drigger and Paul, and when Paul drove the Jeep past him, Eugene began moving closer to Michael.

I wanted to scream out to Michael about what I'd just heard, but he was, bless him, shoveling manure into the trailer, unaware that Eugene was coming up behind him. When Eugene was within three feet of Michael, he turned to look in Drigger's direction. Drigger was too far away from Eugene to say anything that wouldn't be overheard, but he raised both arms above his head alternately cupping each wrist with thumb and forefinger. Eugene nodded; then quick as a cat pouncing, he grabbed Michael's upper arms from behind.

There was a scuffle as Michael tried to break loose, but Eugene's grip was too much, and Michael finally sagged against him, what little fight he'd had suddenly gone. As I watched, horrified at the sudden violent turn at the stock pens, I turned to Charlie.

"Come on, Charlie! We've got to get—"

Charlie clamped a hand over my mouth. "No," he whispered. "We'll follow."

I turned back to the scene knowing that Charlie was right, but angry anyway that we couldn't just yell down at the crew to help Michael. But they continued to work. Their complacency reminded me of sheep that went on grazing after one of their number has been hauled off by a wolf. Brian and Donald and their two S&Ms had to know what was about to happen to Michael, yet they didn't even watch; and for that moment, I hated the four of them worse than I did Paul and Drigger.

When Drigger pulled his Jeep up next to Eugene and Michael, I couldn't watch, either, because I was sliding backwards away from the edge of the cliff, getting ready to follow them. When his Jeep headed east into a rise of ground where Paul and his cadre had just gone, Charlie got up on his knees in full view of the boys at the pens.

"Keep south as you work your way eastward," he said. "Walk upright, Kelly, but keep a lookout for Paul and Drigger. If they even glance in your direction, hit the dirt."

"What are you gonna do?"

"I'm going to visit with the boys down at the pens for a minute or two to let Paul and Drigger dig themselves in a little deeper. If I surprise them too soon, they'll stop, and we won't know what they had planned, right?"

"I know what they've got planned, Charlie."

Charlie shook his head. "You can't prove a thing, with what you've seen."

"I guess, Charlie, but what do you want me to do when I find out where they've gone?"

"Just watch them and see what they're doing. And if anything happens I can't handle, you skeedaddle back to Les Hunter and bring him and Rafferty with you, you understand?"

I nodded, then watched Charlie slide down the hill in full view of Donald and Brian and the two S&Ms. They looked in our direction, but didn't notice me as I slid backward, completely out of sight and began walking east.

Down and to my left, I could hear the Jeeps grinding around in low gear. Every once in a while, they came into view, moving slowly over terrain that looked like the moon, barren and pocked with holes, ridges, and drifts of sand. I came to a place where the land just stopped at the edge of a cliff. I knelt down and almost jumped in surprise; not more than twenty feet directly below me, the two Jeeps had stopped in an area about fifty feet across, enclosed on three sides by cliffs like the one I was on. The entrance to this area was from the west, from where they'd just come. I looked back and down and, just rounding the curve on foot, Charlie was sneaking along, following the Jeep tracks. I hoped he wouldn't stumble into view. I wanted to motion him to stop, but he did instinctively, listening.

I turned back to the Jeeps. Paul and his group were out of theirs. Drigger killed the engine on his; then he and Eugene pulled Michael out. Michael was handcuffed with his hands in front of him, for which I was grateful, as roughly as he was being handled. He was also complacent which, given his situation, I was glad of. I'm sure that, had he put up a struggle, he would have been beaten.

"Strip him," Paul ordered. At this, Michael tried to resist, which only caused Eugene to laugh. Drigger picked Michael up bodily, and Eugene knelt in front of them, fumbling at Michael's belt. "We're gonna teach you, faggot." He jerked Michael's belt open "Cleanse you of your sinful ways." He ripped the buttons open on Michael's Levi's, pulling down his pants and underwear together. He knocked Michael's sneakers off; then grasping the pants at the bottoms, as Drigger held Michael off the ground, Eugene pulled them off.

Paul undressed a little ways off, almost modestly, taking time to neatly fold his clothing and place them on the seat of the Jeep. While he was busy with this, his cadre were attending him. One of them pulled a bundle from the Jeep and laid it open on the ground. From where I was, I couldn't see everything, except for a few items. One of them was what looked like a cop's nightstick, and my stomach contracted.

When Paul was fully naked, one of his cadre handed him something, and Paul fumbled at his genitals, and I felt sick. The little Nazi was putting on a cock ring! I would have shouted to distract him, when I saw Charlie edging his way along the inside of the cliff face, almost in full view of the small group by the Jeeps, but no one looked in his direction.

He stopped, again, to wait a little longer, and I turned back to the group. Michael's cuffed wrists were now bound with a length of leather, which was then strapped to the roll bar of Drigger's Jeep. His ankles were strapped separately with leather, and Eugene kicked his legs apart, then tied each foot to one of the wheels. Michael's head was bowed, eerily silent. Paul rounded the Jeep, his dick visible from where I sat. It was swollen and red, like an uncooked tube of pepperoni, and looked like the blood would burst from it, from the restraint of the cock ring.

Drigger came up behind Michael, grabbing him roughly by the scruff of the neck, and one of the other cadre members came up with a jar in his hand, which he dipped into and began smearing Michael's butt. It was then that I saw how each of the other recruits had gotten bruises to the back of their necks and also then that I saw the truth of Michael's suspicion that Brian had been suffering rectal bleeding. When the cadre member was finished, he stepped aside, allowing Paul access to Michael's naked backside. But just when Paul was pushing against Michael's anus with the night stick, Charlie stepped away from the cliff face and cleared his throat.

Everyone turned in his direction.

"I can't see too well without my glasses," Charlie said, in a voice so quiet and charged with anger that he commanded attention, "but looks to me like there's some God-damned perversion going on here the Reverend Rafferty might not like."

He was still thirty feet from the others when they suddenly leaped for the Jeeps. Michael was cut loose and, before Charlie could react, the Jeeps were careening in two directions, almost hitting each other, as the drivers and the crews made their escape. Paul—naked as a jaybird, his face red as a tomato—was in the lead as Drigger followed him pell mell past Charlie out of their hideout. Michael was left in the dirt, and Charlie spun around, began to run after the Jeeps, then stopped, giving up his pursuit. He ran to Michael, who was just getting up from the ground and shakily pulling on his clothes.

When the Jeeps were gone, I scrambled down from the cliff and joined Charlie and Michael. "You all right?" I asked.

Michael burst into tears. "I thought I was going to get raped! I was afraid you didn't know!"

"That was close," Charlie said, trying to soothe Michael by patting his shoulder.

Michael jerked away. "It was too close! I feel like hitting somebody!"

Charlie stepped back from Michael with a mixed expression of sadness and hurt. "I wasn't going to let them finish, Michael, I just wanted to be sure they got themselves in deep enough, so there'd be no dispute about what happened here. I'm sorry."

Michael seemed to pull himself together, wiping his eyes and looking from me to Charlie. "I know now," he said. "But Charlie, I was so scared."

Charlie just nodded, then turned to me. "We better get back and tell Rafferty what went on here. But Kelly, you have to go back the way you came. Les isn't going to say anything to get you in trouble. It's..." he paused and looked at his watch, "about time for the crews to take a break. You be there when they do."

***

The rest of the afternoon was full of frustrations. After I left Charlie and Michael and returned to work, I knew no more than anyone else at the ranch, who hadn't seen what I had. From on top of the new barracks, where I helped nail on rafters, I eventually saw three Jeeps parked outside the chapel—Paul's, Drigger's, and Charlie's. But once those three men, along with Paul's three S&Ms, Eugene, and Michael entered the chapel, I saw nothing else all afternoon.

At the evening meal that night, we learned there had been two expulsions from the program—Michael and Eugene. They were already off the ranch, Rafferty explained, and headed back to their homes. "Once again, it is my sad duty to inform you that one of our staff has overstepped the bounds of the program. While it is understandable that we frail humans sometimes become overzealous in the Lord's work, it is inexcusable that we fail to show compassion for the sinners, while hating—even reviling—the sin."

I was stunned, seeing Paul Romaine at Rafferty's side. Hadn't Charlie told him what happened? Hadn't Michael also told him? Then I once again broke out into a cold sweat. In the meeting with Rafferty about the incident, Charlie and Michael had been outnumbered in their stories by three to one.

But then, why had Eugene been expelled if Rafferty believed Paul's side? I speculated all through the meal. Rafferty, no doubt, held a grudge against Charlie because of the coffin ceremony. There was no hot seat that night. Instead, Rafferty led us in an endless prayer—the rhythm of which caused some of the recruits to cry, some to shout, "Amen!" Then we were subjected to Caucasian gospel.

I almost cried as we were singing, thinking of Michael, and it seeming so long ago that I shared the sheet music with him while we sang. I would have directly assaulted Paul, questioned Rafferty until I was blue in the face, sought out Charlie—done anything to find out what had happened. But Charlie's warning to me to keep a low profile kept me in my seat.

***

There's nothing more I can do tonight. I'm still not sure that Charlie's right, that I should keep my mouth shut. There are now three empty cots in our tent. Larry continues to cry and sing-song his litany. At one point, he wailed so loudly that Paul Romaine, himself, came into our tent. He was downright *loving* to Larry. So concerned did he appear to be in his mission of "being a people helper," he didn't even glance my way. When he left, I thought I'd talk to Larry, but he had laid on the cot while Paul was "ministering" to him and had fallen asleep sucking his thumb.

* * *

Think I'll go take a piss. I'd just love for Paul to meet me in the dark, tonight! I miss Michael, already.

* * *

Sunday, July 5

Drigger suddenly took a vacation. Well, imagine that! We heard that from Rafferty this morning at breakfast, and I swear I felt a silent cheer go up from the room, although Rafferty seemed to be completely unaware of our jubilation.

"It isn't going to affect our wonderful work," he said to the crowd. "Charlie Hays has agreed to be the foreman at the stock pens, and his brother, David, will cover for him in the fields. With Gawud's help and with the guidance of the Holy Spirit, we will continue to move forward. Let us pray."

We prayed and went to work as if nothing had happened.

But as soon as he could, Charlie came to visit Les Hunter and me at the building site. The three of us took a hike up the hill to the south until we came to the pool of water.

Les and Charlie have apparently been friends for many years. Not only have they known each other in church, their mutual farming interests have kept them in touch. Together at the pool, they looked like two peas in a pod, both wearing khaki clothing, similar felt hats clamped down on their heads.

Their mutual trust and respect for each other made me feel relaxed as Charlie told Les what had happened the day before.

"But the Reverend Rafferty wouldn't believe you?" Les asked.

"Let's look at it this way," Charlie said, nodding at me, then returning his attention to Les. "Paul and Drigger and the others cooked up a version of the story that made Paul as much a victim as Michael. More of a victim because, according to Drigger, himself, while Eugene attacked Michael and tore his clothes off, it was Michael who had originally propositioned…" he turned to me, "you heard right…propositioned him."

"And got Paul's clothes off?" I asked, irritated, "and—" I stopped myself from mentioning the cock ring. "Come on, Charlie, even Rafferty wouldn't believe that!"

Charlie looked at me with hurt. "Kelly, I tried to give him my side of the story, and so did Michael. But Josh waved Michael's testimony off as being repro-whatchacallit, as he did Eugene's. Between Drigger and me it was equal on Josh's part as to whom he believed. But remember that Josh was already sore at me. Then there was Paul, sitting there crying, blubbering about almost being poisoned by the evil of homosexuality, thanking me…ME!…for coming just in time to break things up!"

"But surely Rafferty can't believe that when even you deny it!" I said. "And how did Paul explain how Michael had convinced him to drive his Jeep into the hide out?" I felt like punching something.

Charlie held up a hand. "Kelly, I wouldn't trust Josh as far as I could throw him. Maybe he doesn't believe their story, either, but he made his choice for his own reasons. I'm content that Michael is out of this thing. Aren't you? And beyond that, I think Josh is going to keep an eye on Paul himself. But with Drigger's testimony to contradict mine, he was put into a bind."

"As for me," Les said, "since I believe you and Kelly, I kinda think Kelly ought to step forward."

Neither Charlie nor I had told Les about what I was doing at the ranch to begin with, nor did Les know that Charlie is gay.

"I just want Kelly to stay out of trouble," Charlie said. "Maybe it would've worked a little different if Kelly had said he was there. But then Kelly, here, is also a homosexual," Charlie said. "Josh wouldn't no more believe him than he would Eugene or Michael."

Nothing of note has happened since the incident at the stock pens, for which I'm relieved. But I sure miss Michael. It feels very lonely around here, all of a sudden.

K. O'K

X
Cat Piss

Lion's Mouth Christian Ranch
Wednesday, July 8

There are a million things to do, here. Even with the expulsions of Michael and Eugene and the "deaths" of Sidney and Leo, there are still twenty-two young men, including myself, to do the work. There are fourteen original recruits (those I've been calling S&Ms). From now on, I think I'll just refer to everyone here as "recruits," since there's hardly a difference between them and us "new" recruits anymore. However, three of the old recruits are worthless as workers, since they belong to Paul's inner cadre.

God, I miss Michael! I feel very lonely here at night, once Charlie and the rest of the ranch staff is gone. Of course, Paul and Rafferty stay at the ranch. I wish they were gone as well. Paul sleeps in the other tent. Rafferty stays in a little apartment off the chapel. I guess he thinks of himself as "on call" twenty-four hours a day, in case he has to mend a broken soul in the middle of the night, him being our "spiritual" doctor and all.

I'm working with "Sharp" Jones this week. He's the black man in charge of maintenance, janitorial, and sanitation. He is also the guy who came with Charlie Hays on the day they opened the coffin to let Sidney and

Leo out. It was from his actions that day and his true Christian indignation at what had been done to Sidney and Leo that made me like him.

Anyway, the work I'm doing this week is what Michael referred to as "scullery" duty, since most of our work involves cleaning the kitchen and chow hall after each meal, doing the dishes, sweeping, mopping, and hauling the scraps out back, which is later picked up by the stock pen crew as slop for the hogs. We also clean and mop the showers, clean the toilets (they actually have flush toilets, here), and clean the chapel.

Six recruits work for "Sharp" Jones. The work is filthy only when we have to clean the chow hall after each meal. Some of the women and men from the church in Carlsbad do all the cooking. I don't know how they can look at themselves in the mirror with the slop they conjure up. I am mystified how Rafferty has been able to convince them that it's the Christian thing to feed the gruel they serve.

But I digress…

Sharp Jones is a friendly ex-Army sergeant. He likes to sit in the middle of the chow hall smoking a cigar while we're sweeping and mopping it. He'll point out places we need to mop, again, tables that haven't been washed. In the toilets (there are three stalls and a row of urinals), he has two guys scrub the toilet bowls, two guys scrub the showers, and two guys sweep and mop and carry out what little trash accumulates there. Jones smokes his cigar and looks for dirty places in the restrooms that need to be cleaned.

He handles all the maintenance himself. Very little of it needs much work, anyway. The buildings are sensibly built and simply wired. There are men's and women's restrooms in the chow hall, but only a private one in Rafferty's apartment in the chapel, which only he uses and only Jones cleans. Like the rest of the foremen, Jones wears khaki clothing, but no hat. He prefers a cap, which is usually stuffed into the back of his pants, unless he is walking between buildings.

Jones sings to us all the time. No one resents the fact that he doesn't work with us on the sweeping, mopping, and such, because he has such a lovely voice. KP duty was never like this in the Army, where the black sergeants were the toughest SOBs one could encounter. Jones is a gentle, truly loving man. His voice and song (usually "Negro" spirituals or Black songs of protest) carry throughout the chow hall.

Today, Jones was singing when I was on my hands and knees, applying a coat of wax. He was singing one of those Negro spirituals, I guess, or maybe it was the cozy, oily quality of his voice that brought the tears to my eyes. But suddenly, I just broke down and started bawling like a baby. I couldn't stop.

I worked as best I could, keeping my back to the others and to Jones. My face was hot with embarrassment, my eyes stinging with tears, when he caught me. Immediately, he took me outdoors, out back of the chow hall. Behind it there's a shed where they store the trash barrels, prepare the slop for the hogs, and keep tools and cleaning supplies. Between the shed and chow hall is a typical behind-the-restaurant place that draws flies and has that alley odor of rancid meat and cooking grease. He took me to his pickup, which was parked behind the shed. We got in the cab, and he opens the glove compartment, pulls out a bottle of Jack Daniels and makes me take a couple of slugs. Whatever was in that bottle (definitely not Jack Daniels) brought renewed tears to my eyes, made me cough and gag, and in a minute, he was laughing and I was laughing with tears continuing to stream down my face. He hadn't yet said a word, but just kept his "sharp" eyes on me.

When my crying and laughing fit was over, he says, "Kelly, I've been watchin' you and studyin' on you since you been here. You don't know it, cause I don't show it. I've been waitin' for that Romaine fella to assign you to my crew. I been waitin' for you to explode, you so angry."

That angered me. "I don't keep it hidden."

He took the bottle from me, tilted it, took a slug, and smacked his lips with enjoyment. He tilted the bottle at me. "You take one more good swig of my home brew."

I did. This time it went down smoothly, warming my throat and burning my stomach.

Then he took the bottle and put it back in the glove compartment. As he was raising up, he kissed my cheek. "Jesus loves you, boy, and don't want you to be angry."

"I know," I said, feeling disappointed in him. Not that he wasn't kind and trying to help. I appreciated that. But he was spouting the same theme. I felt a sermon coming on that would end with some message that anything is possible through Christ. Christ! I was getting tired of hearing that. I hadn't been crying for the reason he must've thought.

"No, you don't know that Jesus loves you, son. Neither does that som-bitch Rafferty. Nor that Romaine fella. This place has a mighty wrong feeling to it."

"Yeah, I know it does, Sharp. You saw how they treated Sidney and Leo." I wanted to tell him about Michael, but decided against it. "They don't feed us any better than they do the hogs, either."

"You know it," Sharp said, shaking his head and looking straight into my eyes. "That's what makes you angry, ain't it?"

"What?"

"The way they treat you."

I nodded.

"But there be more to it, ain't there?"

"What d'you mean?" I asked. I could've sat in Sharp's pickup all afternoon, spilling my guts. I wanted to so badly.

"This here prog'm ain't Christian. I don't be carin' what they say down at the chu'ch, neither. It ain't got Jesus in it. That's what. Your kind ain't gon' be changed by what they do here."

"I know, Sharp...Can I have a little more of your cat piss?"

Sharp grinned, showing a mouth full of yellow teeth. "Go ahead, son."

This time I took a couple of gulps, then passed the bottle to Sharp. He looked at me with the bottle held to his lips, took a long swig, capped it and laid it on the seat between us. "Why you here? You ain't here gettin no cure."

"Why else would I be here?"

He laughed, his voice deep and throaty and wonderfully oily. "Cause you crazy."

Fuck it, I thought. I was going to spend the afternoon in his pickup, drinking his home brew. "I had a lover…" I began. "His name was William…"

* * *

July 9, 10, and 11

Nothing out of the ordinary has been happening here in the last week. God, it seems like Michael has been gone a long time. We've settled into what seems the long, hot summer. Because of scullery duty, I haven't been getting out into the heat very much. But part of my duties this week have been to "police" the compound. That's a term the Army used for keeping us busy when they didn't have anything else for us to do. It involves going around with a tin can, paper sack, or other container and picking up trash, cigarette butts, whatever speck of trash we can find around the chapel, the chow hall, and the middle building.

This week has brought me near the coffin so often it has become an accusation, sitting out between the chapel and the showers, accusing me of going along with the cruelty because I won't reveal myself and my purpose, here. Talk about creating a wrong feeling, as Sharp said the other day. It's like a funeral procession, frozen in time. They've even built a little dais to set the coffin on. It will weather and rot, and fall apart, eventually, but for right now, it still has the power to remind me of that horrible night Leo and Sydney were entombed within it.

Outdoors, it looks even larger than it did in the chapel. Having to pick up trash around it, I've gotten a real close look at it. I'd say Frankenstein's monster could lie prone in it. A seven-foot Dracula would find it ample. Its flat-black color makes it absorb all the sunlight around it.

One enters the aura of its power about six feet from it. It frightens me in broad daylight.

It sets there as a reminder to Rafferty's mistake? Not so. It's a continuous threat. It has that particular shape that has always had the power to evoke the image of death. It has six sides in the shape of an angular sarcophagus—wide at the head and narrow at the bottom. It is raised off the ground about four feet and, standing next to it, one has the urge to lift the lid.

At dusk, the dying sunlight gives it a gloomy aura. Its blackness darkens. On the way to the chow hall from the showers, we give it a wide berth. Conversation drops to a whisper when we get close to it. After dark, it becomes an abyss, a blank spot in the scenery where no light is reflected. I can imagine that, after dark, if one were to open it, the coffin would be an entrance to the bowels of the earth.

*　*　*

We grow restless in the heat. The tent walls are hot to the touch. With every breath, our nostrils sting with the chemical sweat the tent gives off; the bloody messages of death give off their own odor, as well. With the lights on, it's even hotter. My T-shirt sticks to my back. The band of my Levi's are wet from the sweat that has trickled down my back. The moths flutter around the lights, hundreds of them, swooping into our faces. None of us can sleep. It's after midnight. Lights are going off any minute.

I hear more crying. Since Michael was expelled, others seem to feel lonely. But whether or not it's because Michael is gone, might be my own emotional feelings. But something has changed in the way the recruits interact. There's more crying, more chances are taken to pair off, to talk in low whispers in small groups. One goes outside more now that the nights are unforgiving in their heat. Once the lights are off, I can lay awake and listen to the footsteps. The soft crunch of shoes on the sand is loud after lights out.

I imagine the recruits in the tent next door are also restless, but do any of them dare to leave the tent without Paul Romaine's approval? Do they dare to pair off, to make friendships that have nothing to do with the program? Although we are not allowed to talk in pairs unless Paul has approved it, we are doing it more and more as the restlessness grows, as we wait for the long night to end and the next day to begin and be over and begin, again.

I've noticed that after dark, Larry gets up. His cot is next to one of the tent flaps. I can see his shadowy bulk fill the doorway as he leaves. Even though it is dark outdoors, it appears like the night under a full moon when one is inside the tent. During the night, I can see shapes moving back and forth in front of the flap. I know when Larry comes back, near dawn, as his shape is so much larger than the others. His cot groans when he lays down on it, again.

I wonder what he does in the middle of the night outside.

Ever since Michael left, Larry has become a crier. He cries and smiles through red eyes and laughs emotionally, full of choking sounds, like a hebephrenic. He laughs only when he cries. He cries and laughs at nothing, throwing up his hands while he's eating, and begins crying. Others say nothing, but they look worried when he sits next to them in the chow hall, like little old ladies in bus stations who grip their purses to their chests as they sit and listen to bus-station derelicts who hang around them. Others look at Larry with pity, but don't move to talk to him.

Whatever is happening to him is on everyone's mind, although no one speaks of him. Like Larry, it seems that some of the other kids need help, now, too. But I'm afraid of making another friend, like I had with Michael. So I am really of no help to anyone.

As the coffin reminds me every day, there is death here. It is the death of our selves. It is the death of conviction of self, replaced by mistrust of self; replaced by trust only of the approval of others. As Sharp

Jones observed, there is a wrongness about this place. Most of the recruits are not questioners any longer. They simply do what they are told to do, without question, without showing emotion whatsoever.

Those, like Donald and Brian, whom Paul got to as he tried to with Michael, are more fearful of doing something wrong than the others. I haven't spoken to either of them since the day Michael was taken right in front of them and they just went on working. But they have gotten my attention. There's a growing similarity between them that's hard to describe. They're sharing something that is not discernible to me—either some sense of shared pain they suffered at the hands of Romaine (Michael's observations about one of them suffering from rectal bleeding comes to me continually); or some sense of attachment to each other that, were we out of this place, I might call it a relationship. But I just don't know.

We're being slowly ground down to nothing but sweaty bodies. Except at night when the lights are out and then, like Larry, we rise from our beds like wraiths and walk in the sand around the tents.

***

Well, I think I've depressed myself. If things don't move along, I think I will scream. I just might start something, rather than let this slow-motion death reduce me to a shell of my former cynical self. Thank God for guys like Charlie, Les, and Sharp Jones. Whenever Sharp sees me, now that I have confessed my reason for being here, now that I have told him about William and his suicide, he takes a minute to pull me aside. "You want my cat piss, you know where it is. You hold up. You make it."

K. O'K.

XI
Storm Coming

Lion's Mouth
Sunday, July 12

    This week, I've been assigned to Charlie Hays, who is currently foreman of the stock pens. My paired recruit is Jerry. We are working with Donald, Brian, and their two paired recruits, Tom and Richard, who have been invisible to me—that is, I've never taken notice of them before, have never been paired with either of them, nor have I noticed them apart from the herd.

    It's hard to believe Michael has already been gone eight days. What happened to him out here is still fresh in my mind. That day, as today, Donald and Brian were here as well, but I don't remember whom they were paired with. My focus was on Michael and Eugene and Alton Drigger.

    I've noticed that Paul's method for choosing the work details doesn't have much to do with the work. I haven't worked at the stock pens since Larry fell into the mud; Brian and Donald are here after only one week of working elsewhere. I've also noticed that Brian and Donald are usually in the same work crew. I wonder if that is because it prevents them from talking to others about what Paul did to them. They were the ones he and Drigger raped and bruised. I'm assuming that's what happened, because of what I saw Paul attempting to do to Michael. Leo was the only other person I'd noticed who had the bruise before Michael. I wish I could remember if Leo usually worked with Brian and Donald as well. I wish I'd discovered the bruises on others—not that I want anyone to have gone through the pain, but I wish I knew if Paul got to anyone else. That might tell me who, in this group of twenty two recruits, has reason to be afraid.

It's obvious as I work with Brian and Donald that they are afraid. I feel resentment toward them for not lifting a finger to help Michael the other day, but I do understand that fear can paralyze. I think of myself and realize I'm often paralyzed by it, as well.

Realizing that, I tried and failed, today, to engage them in any conversation whatsoever about themselves. Charlie was unable to get them to talk, either—except for something having to do with the program. I was miffed at that, since Charlie was the one who took Sidney and Leo off the ranch. But that doesn't seem to matter to them. They still do not trust anyone. They only talk to each other, and I wonder if they've both been raped with the nightstick by Paul.

I wanted to ask them (out of anger) if Paul fucked them with his cock, too, or if he just jerked off. I wonder a lot about Paul Romaine and his motives. And I wonder just how much of his activities Josh Rafferty really knows about.

I tried and failed to engage Tom or Richard in conversation, too. Only Jerry seemed interested in talking at all; but it was *that* talk, *Christian-speak*, spouting his clichés, saying ludicrous things like, "Slop the Hogs for the Lord, guys!" I was mostly embarrassed for him, but I wonder if he talks that way out of a fear of his own—that if he doesn't stay with the program, doesn't repeat the steps like a broken record, his commitment to his own cure might dissolve like ice chips on a hot griddle. It might be that working with such damned good-looking guys like Donald and Brian, he has to block out all thought but the program.

As a matter of fact, I find all the guys in this work crew lovely to look at, and it strikes me, too, that the guys Paul raped with the nightstick are the best looking ones at the ranch—Michael included. Hmmm.

I tried to get far enough away from Jerry to talk with Charlie; that didn't work. Jerry stuck close to me as he is supposed to do.

That makes me wonder yet again why Josh Rafferty chose to believe Paul and Alton Drigger's story instead of Charlie and Michael's. If there was even a hint that Paul was raping the recruits, it seems to me Rafferty would have looked long and hard at those accusations, since the purported purpose of this program is to cure homosexuality, to stop it. Unless, of course, that's NOT the purpose.

Even though I would hope that someone who hated being homosexual could find a "cure," I'm afraid it's just not possible—especially with programs such as Rafferty's. It didn't help William. For awhile, he basked in the afterglow of his "born-again" experience; he had such idealistic plans of starting his life over as a heterosexual man; but it all went sour so quickly for him. So damned wrong. So it's all the more cruel, if Rafferty knows he cannot cure homosexuality, for him to continue as if he could—with the sermons, the Bible studies, the fellowshipping. It is beyond cruelty to offer hope with one hand, while demonstrating, not his love but his hatred, with the other. I am more convinced than ever that the purpose of this place is to build the fear and guilt and nothing else in these gay people in order to convince them to STOP HOMOSEXUAL ACTS.

As we were leaving for lunch, Charlie passed by me out of earshot of the others. "Meet me east of the pens when we come back," he said.

How we would accomplish that, I didn't know, but after lunch, when we were back, Charlie pulled the keys out of his pocket and threw them to Jerry. "You know how to drive a stick?"

Jerry nodded.

"I forgot the water jug. See Sharp Jones. He'll fill'er up."

When Jerry was a cloud of dust to the west of us, Charlie told the other four recruits to clean the milking area in the cow shed. Then he motioned to me to follow him.

The cliffs begin just east of the pens. The fences are built parallel to one face of the cliffs, and there is a narrow path one can follow to the first branching cliff that runs east. This is where Paul had frequently taken his Jeep when he was about his business of rape. We took the path on foot and noticed how often the Jeeps had come this way. There were already ruts, and it turned my stomach to think of Paul getting his own weird satisfaction from all the docile sheep on the ranch. From the look of the trail, he was getting his kicks regularly.

As we walked along, with the cliff to our right and a rocky hill to the left, I wondered, now that his hiding place was discovered, where or when Paul would re-establish his routine of raping the recruits.

Charlie stopped about a hundred yards along the path. He sat with his back to the cliff face and lit a cigarette. He offered the pack to me, but I declined.

"I wanted to give you this," he said, reaching into his pocket and drawing out a white envelope. My first thought was that it was a letter from my mother, since I had been sending her a few letters. I turned it over, noting the Carlsbad postmark.

"Open it!" Charlie said, smiling, anxious. "Let's see what Michael has to say."

I ripped the envelope open. "From Michael? I thought he was back in Houston!"

When I had smoothed out the letter, Charlie cocked his hat back and shut his eyes, and I sat down on his left, touching his shoulder with mine as I read aloud.

—

Carlsbad, New Mexico
July 8, 1998

Dear Kelly,
My dearest, dearest Kelly! By now you and Charlie are together in your hiding place, aren't you? I bet so. You two girls!

—

Charlie laughed. "Is that the way we're supposed to talk?"

"What d'you mean? Is *who* supposed to talk?"

"Us," Charlie said, looking down at the letter in my hand. "You know, people like us…" he trailed off.

I looked at his face, heard him swallow. Then it hit me. "Oh, you mean us gay people?"

He nodded, looking away from me. I felt embarrassed for his shyness. I leaned into his shoulder, felt it trembling slightly. "Well, you have to admit Michael has his own style," I said. "It's kind of a mark of what we call queens, to call each other girls. But you should just be yourself, Charlie."

He turned his face back to me, smiling shyly. "But is it…what we're supposed to like?"

I couldn't believe the naiveté of his questions, but I realized how isolated he'd been. "On Michael, it flows naturally, Charlie. But if you suddenly started talking like that, I think it'd sound forced. Besides, you're what we call *butch*." I was going to explain the butch/fem dichotomy in the gay world, but he tapped my knee.

"Never mind, Kelly. Just go on with Michael's letter."

—

I wanted to write you, Kelly, to tell you how sorry I am we didn't get Paul. And now I'm no longer there to be your sister (or brother, if you prefer) in crime.

It was too too weird, the day I got expelled from the program. I'm sooo relieved. You don't know how much into that place my head was. I didn't know how captive I was until I suddenly found myself walking along the streets in Houston in my old neighborhood just thirty-six hours after having my clothing stripped off in the desert of New Mexico.

It was weird, too, that trip from the ranch into Carlsbad. It was Charlie and me and Eugene Baker in that Jeep. I was so mad I could spit. Eugene was a total ass-hole creep, son-of-a-bitch, bastard, saying how Satan was in me and Charlie, how he was doing the Lord's work, was part of the Lord's army. He said he knew, because Paul had said so. Paul had claimed he was like Christ, taking the suffering and pain upon his own body, the humiliation.

"For what, sweetie," I said. "It hurts him to stick a dildo up people's asses?"

"You don't get it," Eugene said, and grinned. "You and Charlie think you're so smart. You don't know the half of it."

I told him I don't want to know. All I wanted was to get on with my life, that I was lucky Charlie happened along that day. I wasn't about to let him know you were there, too. They (meaning Paul and his others) don't need to know you're onto them.

"I'll tell you anyway," Eugene says. "Because I want you to know how stupid you are."

"You want me to know, too, you little fucker?" Charlie says.

We were all getting pissed. But even I could've handled Eugene as mad as I was at him. Besides, if I got nothing else from the program, Kelly, it was a sense of my potential as a man. A "butch" man...wow.

There was an appreciative chuckle from Charlie when I read the word "butch," and I smiled as I continued to read.

"Yeah, I want you to know, Charlie Hays. You country seed," Eugene says.

Well, Kelly, it turns out that Paul and five or six of the guys you call S&Ms—the recruits that were there when we arrived—are not recruits (like we were) at all. Sure they arrived on the ranch with the other recruits in the first batch, before we got there, but they all belong to a group that Paul had started somewhere in the south. Eugene said they call themselves "The Army for the Lord"—or something like that. It's hard to remember, because

Eugene rambled so much, said so many odd things. That's not important. But counting Eugene out, there are still five other guys at the ranch, besides Paul who belong to his group. They were plants.

Eugene claims that none of them is homosexual. I'd like to know what kind of straight men like to fuck other guys, however. I know about prisoners fucking each other because they can't have their women. But these guys came to the ranch with Paul, pretending to be like the others. They're all stuck in this Army for the Lord together. They say the pansy charismatics like Josh Rafferty aren't going far enough in the crusade to stop homosexuality.

The important thing is, Paul has been doing this for years! These same guys now at the ranch have been together in their little group for two or three years. Paul is the leader, the one who takes the pain and suffering, so they say, by being whipped after he has "fixed" a homosexual. You know what he means by fixing. He means ramming that stick up a guy's ass. While he's doing that, they whip Paul until he cums. Then they gather around him and masturbate onto his wounds. That's what Eugene says, anyway. But who can believe it? I mean Eugene calls it "masculine salve."

The trip got weirder, Kelly; the further Eugene got from the ranch, the nuttier he became. I doubt he'll be able to hold a job or have a life without Paul's guidance. You'll see what I mean...

You know how it's like twenty miles through the Guadalupe mountains before you come out on the plains? Then it's twenty or so more miles into Carlsbad? Well, as Eugene talked, he got horny. Right there in the Jeep, he stands up in the back, hanging onto the roll bar, pulls his Levi's down, and starts whacking off!

—

Charlie began to laugh. I looked at him, but couldn't see a thing funny. "This really happened? The way Michael says?"

"Just read the letter," Charlie said. "Hurry, though. I hear Jerry coming back."

—

Well, Charlie has enough, and he pulls onto the shoulder doing about fifty. Meantime, here's Eugene beating his meat and wiggling his ass in the wind, screaming something that sounds like Greek, or Chinese, and I figure he's speaking in tongues or something wild like that.

Charlie slams on the brakes and Eugene tumbles over the roll bar and his naked ass lands on the shift stick, just inches away from impaling him.

"Get out you miserable Bastard!" Charlie says. "Your ticket just ran out."

* * *

There was more to Michael's letter, but it sounded too weird to be true. Charlie was laughing hysterically, now, and I began to see a little of the humor, unable to imagine what a sight that must've been.

But as we walked back to the stock pens, I felt cold, like a knife slicing up my spine.

"Michael didn't say why he came back to Carlsbad," I said, folding the letter and handing it back to Charlie for safe keeping.

Charlie grinned at me. "Michael says he's going to stay long enough to see you through." I was relieved about that. But I was elated when Charlie told me that his brother, David, felt so badly about what was happening at the ranch, he decided to try to get to the bottom of things. "Michael is one of our witnesses," Charlie said. "You're another one. We might not be able to get the church interested in shutting down the ministry, because they're being paid a lot of money for renting out the ranch. In addition, each foreman gets five-hundred dollars a month to work at the ranch, besides getting our gasoline and expenses paid. The church also gets to keep the assets of the buildings and such after the ministry moves on. So, even though we may not be able to get rid of Rafferty's program, we're sure as hell going to get Paul Romaine and, because Eugene was so cooperative in spilling his guts to me, we're going to find and expel his entire group. We just might even press charges."

By the time we reached the stock pens, I was feeling great, but then I looked at Tom and Richard and wondered about them. Were they the plants Michael had mentioned?

* * *

Wednesday, July 15

I got up this morning feeling more energized than I have been in a couple of weeks. Part of it was having heard from Michael. But is was also a glorious morning, overcast, and a lot cooler than it has been. As tradition has it, we paired off with the guys from the next tent and began our walk across the fields, to the chow hall.

Jerry also seemed to be in a good mood. But his attitude began to irk me, immediately. "Oh, bless this day!" he said. "Isn't it wonderful the Lord brought us clouds?"

"Thermal pressures, highs and lows, brought us the clouds, Jerry."

He nodded, distracted. "You're not with the program, are you?"

"Moi?" I said, like Miss Piggie. "I'd like to know what I'm doing here, then."

"Then why are you always making fun?"

"Because it's the only fun I have, Jerry. Look at this place. Have you been happy with it, since *that* thing (I pointed across the field to the coffin, looking somber in the overcast sky) was put in the compound? Or even before, when Sidney and Leo were put into it?"

"That was a mistake," Jerry said. "Josh admitted it. It's a reminder of such things as being overzealous. In the Lord, we should have a maturity of manner, patience, forgiveness."

"But Paul Romaine said they'd used it before. Why didn't Josh think it was a mistake then? Huh? Was it because nobody from the church in Carlsbad caught him?"

"It wasn't bad, Kelly, the first time I saw it used. They only kept the guys in it a couple of hours, and it did remind us of the death of the spirit within us."

I wanted to scream. "The Holy Spirit has prompted me to ask, Brother Jerry, what did you think of Eugene and Michael being expelled?"

"I forgive them, Kelly. Is that why you're angry, because of what happened to Paul?"

"What happened to *Paul*?"

"Yes. Michael and Eugene tried to rape him, when he caught them committing—"

"What? Where did you hear that?"

"Why, from Tom, I think, you know the guy with Brian? Or was it Richard?"

"You sure it wasn't one of the other guys, one of the three guys Paul hangs around with?"

Jerry stopped in the middle of the field. He knelt down by a wide row bed, where squash had been planted. I continued to stand, leaning over his back. I made a quick examination of his neck. There was nothing there, no bruising. I liked the way his neck and shoulders looked from the back in the clean T-shirt he'd put on. His was the kind of skin that tans smoothly. His blond hair had a gleam to it. I wanted to caress his neck. "Are you sure you heard it from Tom or Richard?"

"Quite," Jerry said. "Looks like the squash is going to love this cooler weather." He stood up and looked around. "I've always lived in one city or another. The last one was OK City."

"Oklahoma City?"

"Right. That's where I lost my—That's where I came to the Lord. Anyway, you know, I think I'd like farming, or at least living in the country and raising a garden. I've never done this kind of work before. I enjoy working with the animals, too."

"You do?" I was relieved he was telling me a little bit about himself, that he could still carry on a normal conversation, without saying Lord this and Lord that.

He took a deep breath, and his chest swelled out in a beautifully masculine way—as Michael had once described the young Christians he met—in a wholesome-looking way. He was clean shaven. How he'd accomplished that since we usually shave in the afternoons, after we shower, I didn't know.

"You know how it smells in the country. I even enjoy that sweet cow manure and milk aroma in the cow shed when we're milking. Don't you?"

"I grew up on a farm, Jerry. I guess I used to notice the odors and things. But now I'm a mechanic. I'll probably die smelling like gasoline and grease."

"That stuff—grease and gasoline—stinks," he said. "You never can get it out from under your nails. Or your clothes."

"Maybe not, but the pay's good. Besides, I can do that kind of work, then go home in the evenings and write."

"Oh, yeah," he said, "You're going to be a writer. May the Holy Spirit empower you."

"May my intelligence and reason guide me."

"Nonono," he said, then stopped.

"What?"

"I was going to say that Reason is never enough."

"Oh, yeah. Right."

We continued our walk. Near the compound, the crowd of recruits and staff were gathering.

Paul was standing on the porch with his cadre. Although the three of them were dressed in Levi's and T-shirts, Paul was wearing slacks and a pull-over knit shirt. On his chest was his nametag with the swastika. I took a good look at the four of them, and you could see it, when you were looking for it—a kind of oneness. Their eyes locked on the same target, following one or other of the recruit pairs as they approached the porch. You could tell they were all listening with the same attention to the details of what was being said. Then I looked around for the other two, whom Michael said made up the five guys from Paul's group. Tom and Richard were practically marching Donald and Brian across the field at an angle, so that when they entered the porch, they came up on one end away from the rest of us.

Jerry began to move toward the entrance to the chow hall, but I hung back. At first, he didn't notice and had moved about ten feet ahead of me. Then he looked around and waited for me. But I wanted to hear, if I could, what was being said among Paul and his cadre, or among Brian, Donald, Tom, and Richard. I motioned for Jerry to wait. I continued to hang back as pair after pair entered the chow hall.

When it was only Jerry and me, Paul and his cadre, and the other four I'd been watching, Jerry became impatient and got behind me, pushing me into the chow hall ahead of him. I tried to hang back without appearing to be doing so deliberately, but it was no use. We were at the end of the serving line.

Paul and the others moved in behind me and Jerry. I didn't turn to look at them; then my attention was caught by Larry at the head of the line. He was standing with his back to the room, facing one of the servers, head on.

"I want six sausages!" he said. His voice was loud enough that the others stopped talking in the line and listened.

"But I've been instructed to give you only two, honey," the woman behind the counter said. She was holding Larry's plate out to him.

"But I've got enough food credits for SIX!" Larry protested, holding out his poker chips for all to see. "Haven't I?" He turned to the first guy in line, his voice had taken on that hebephrenic edge, again, on the verge of either bursting into tears or laughing. "Here, you count them!"

The recruit turned away.

Josh Rafferty was sitting on the far side of the chow hall, near the windows that looked east. Before him on the table was his Bible and scattered cards, part of his morning prayer, I thought. He stood up as Larry's voice grew louder. He began moving across the room, weaving quickly between tables, his neon blue jacket flapping.

Paul brushed past me, and I saw his eyes—flared, focused on the head of the line. He licked his lizard lips as he passed.

Rafferty reached over the counter and took the plate the server held. He set it on Larry's tray. "That's all you're going to get," he said.

"But I've earned the food credits!" Larry insisted, holding out a fist full. "I've earned them!"

"You're not using them wisely," Rafferty said, half-turning to the room so more of us could hear.

I think Rafferty must have counted on this reaction from Larry by cutting off his purchasing power with the poker chips.

"No!" Larry said. His poor fat frame jiggled with anger. He attempted to pick up his plate and hand it back to the server, but Rafferty pushed it down on his tray.

Larry pushed Josh, who backed away with a surprised expression; then, before anyone could register what happened, Larry had thrown the tray. His plate, glass, and food went all over the server.

Paul flicked his eyes, just his eyes, and I was bumped, knocked into Jerry as all three of his inner cadre bounded toward the front of the serving line and grabbed Larry. It took all three of them to hold him as he attempted to get away.

Recovered, Rafferty led the way out of the chow hall, looking over his shoulder. "Bring him to my office," he said.

When he and Larry were gone, along with Paul and his three goons, the rest of us began talking, filling the room with whispers. Laughter cracked over the crowd, and there was much shaking of heads.

Suddenly gone was the enthusiasm for the cool morning as we finally settled down to eat, each of us, I supposed, depressed at the scene, and Larry's further humiliation in front of everyone, being carted off like a criminal because he wanted to stuff his gullet. Paul and his three cadre members returned, picked up their meals and made their way to a table near the east windows. Then Rafferty came back, with his arm around Larry.

All eyes followed their movement to the serving line, where the woman had stood a few moments before with splotches of Larry's food on her blouse. She came out and, with worried eyes, listened as Larry spoke.

"I'm very sorry, Sister Joan," Larry said, his head hung, Rafferty gripping his shoulder. "The Holy Spirit has…has regained control of my mind, and I thank…thank…" he trailed off.

"And you thank, who, Larry, for leading you to recognize your what, Larry?"

"The Lord, my sin of lust. F-f-f-for food!" Larry said, then began to cry. "But I had the credits!"

Rafferty led us in a prayer about the bounty of the Lord. Afterwards, Larry was given no sausages, no pancakes, and his credits were used to buy what we would normally get—a glob of goo in the bottom of a bowl, with a little milk poured over the top of it.

He ate, hunched over, his eyes red from crying, his hands shaking with the palsy of the utterly starved. I had to turn my face away when, with three fingers clinched together, he mopped at his bowl, then sucked on his fingers. I pushed away a half-eaten plate of pancakes, which I had bought with my own food credits.

* * *

During the working hours of the morning, the clouds, which had been gray and pink in the rising of the sun, began to darken, and the air to carry the smell of rain in it. There was a west wind coming across the valley, whipping up tarpaulin flaps on a stack of hay, when the engine of a Jeep coming around the hill to the west came to our ears.

It was Paul, his three goons, and Larry.

My heart lurched at the sight of Paul. Then I wondered how he had the balls or the gall to show up at the stock pens—especially with him knowing Charlie was the foreman. Surely he wouldn't try anything again, so soon after being caught by Charlie.

But as he led Larry to us, I saw by the smile on his chipmunk face he was enjoying himself. He walked right up to Charlie, who had been twisting wire through the loops of the tarpaulin. Charlie stood at the haystack, waiting for Paul to walk up to him. I looked at Charlie's face and noticed a mixture of bemusement and curiosity there.

"Yes, Brother Paul? What do you want?"

Paul's own grin widened, his eyes sparkled with hatred. "Josh has charged me with the grave duty of showing Brother Larry, here, how he will look if he doesn't learn to give his appetite to the Lord."

"Give his what to who?" Charlie said, confounded at the words, their meaning obviously not registering. "You sure have a *queer* way of expressing yourself, Brother Paul."

At that remark, Paul's grin slammed shut. "Which *word* didn't you understand?"

Charlie turned his back on Paul and Larry. "Charge ahead," he said, into the stack of hay.

During the entire exchange, the rest of us stood with our mouths open, our eyes flicking from Charlie to Paul, skirting past Larry, who was crying, snot running down to his upper lip.

How much more the kid was going to be able to take, I couldn't imagine. I watched, feeling angry (and yes, paralyzed) as Paul pushed Larry toward the pig pens.

"These are called hogs, Brother Larry," he said, with a mocking, lilting tone. "They will devour anything you put before them, including meat, including their live young. Like tigers, they are carnivores. They will gorge themselves, Brother Larry, because they are the embodiment of the lust for food. Just like morbidly obese people, they can weigh five hundred pounds, even a thousand pounds, if they are allowed to gorge themselves. Then, all they can do is lay in the mud and grunt." Having said this, Paul snapped his fingers and one of his cadre opened a bucket.

Paul grabbed Larry's hands and shoved them into the bucket. "Take that rotten meat and throw it to the pigs," he said, "and watch."

Larry continued to cry, but didn't speak as he pulled out meat so rotten, a sudden death smell overpowered even the rank odor of the pig pens. He threw the meat into the pen, and the pigs gathered around it, fighting over it.

Paul continued to talk to Larry in lilting, insulting tones, and I caught Jerry's eyes. They were full of pity and shock. But he didn't say anything. None of us did. He turned away, and we continued to work as the wind grew stronger, the air cooler.

In the distance, beyond the mouth of the canyon, thunder sounded, far away, but its pounding rolled over the valley. *A storm is coming*, I thought to myself. I prayed for a good one, a virtual flood, that would wash down from all sides of the valley—through the throat of the Lion to the west, rush toward us from the north, where the "hand" and the "fingers" of the desolate hills would spill the water and wash away the tents, fall like the waters over the Niagara from the south cliffs. I prayed it would wash away the crops, send the pigs and cows floating away down a new river into the fissures of cliffs and canyons to the east.

I prayed that the Lion's Mouth Christian Ranch Chapel would be washed from its sandy ground and be dashed on the rocks and cliff faces that surround us.

But the storm held back. The sky darkened and noon came, and we went to lunch.

Larry was set off in a corner of the chow hall with Rafferty. His tray was brought to him. Again, the portions were small, and Larry once more shook as he ate, once again mopped his plate with his fingers, and cried.

* * *

The thunder grew closer as the afternoon progressed. At around two-thirty, the first pelting sheets of rain came without warning. The thunder shook the ground, and all seven of us piled into the Jeep. Without regard to the closeness of our bodies, we huddled together, laughing as Charlie drove us, splashing mud over the fenders onto our soaked T-shirts.

All over the ranch, in the gray slate of falling rain, Jeeps hurried hither and yon, finally gaining purpose and heading toward the chow hall. As they arrived one after another, the recruits flew off them and hurried onto the porch that looks out on the valley. The wind whipped the rain into our faces, and we were uniformly laughing and talking like happy boys, cuffing one another on the shoulders.

For awhile we talked and laughed, then our voices failed us as the intensity of the storm increased. Rivulets of running water formed in the compound, becoming streams in front of the porch where we stood. We watched fascinated by the desert storm as the streams became angry rushing rivers, carrying muddy water by us, full of debris. None of us went indoors, so fascinated were we by the display of the turbulent sky.

Through the sheets of water falling from the roof of the porch, the tents looked so far away, so vulnerable, I worried about my few possessions there, getting ruined, and I sighed with relief that my writing was safely away from the valley, except for the last few installments I'd been working on.

From the tents, my eyes swept toward the west and, as I scanned the compound, I saw that black coffin through the storm, pelted by the water from heaven. A crack of thunder pealed across the valley, the shock wave rolling toward me as I gazed at the coffin. BOOM! BOOM! BOOM! went the thunder, its power thudding into my chest.

I turned away from the awful sight of the coffin drenched by the rain; from the other end of the porch, I saw Paul's head swivel in my direction. I felt his eyes before they focused on me, past all the heads of the recruits between us.

He grinned and licked his lips.

*　*　*

I'm lying on my cot. It's amazingly dry, but the thin mattress has a wet feel to it from all the water that seems to have been absorbed by the interior atmosphere of this tent. It's cooler than it has been, but it's also perceptibly muggier in here and I can smell the pig's blood on the walls of the tent.

K. O'K.

XII
The Hot Seat

Carlsbad, New Mexico
July 13, 1998

Dear Kelly,

Now that I'm more settled in (I've got a kitchenette in the Pink Flamingo Motel), I'm able to write more sensibly to tell you more about what happened after I left the ranch.

God, I can't believe how free I feel!

As I told you, a day and a half after being expelled from the ranch, I was back in Houston, walking the same old streets I'd walked before I decided to go for the "cure." It was the same everywhere. The "girls" I'd left were the same. The bars were the same. The scene was the same. But I felt different. Something did change in me, Kelly, at the ranch.

Maybe it was just meeting you. Maybe it was seeing that no matter what work was thrown at me, I could handle it, you know? I think in the four endless weeks I was there, I gained twenty pounds. But I'm proud to say it went to my chest and arms. I've always had good legs—and I don't mean pretty, I mean strong. I've stopped shaving them, too, and under the arms. I've kept my hair short, too, since having it shaved off at the ranch.

I looked at myself in the mirror back in the hotel where I live in Houston. I didn't see "Miss Houston" anymore. I went to the storage where I kept my sequined gowns, my boas, my pumps, and wigs, and I put them on and paraded around my room in them. But I looked like a man in a dress! I had a wonderful laugh. I had an even more wonderful cry.

I took my female self by the hand and led her into my heart, and I said, "Honey, Michael will always remember you and think fondly of you, but it's time you let my male self out of the closet."

I think she understood, Kelly, because she wants a husband as much as I do.

Then I put those things back in storage, packed my bags and took them to the airport. I spent one more evening with my friends, my sisters, and told them I was moving to New Mexico for awhile. Some of them asked where New Mexico is, and I told them it was that big blank spot in their minds between Texas and Arizona.

So, here I am, in a dinky little town in the middle of nowhere, happier than I've been in a long time. The ranch did that for me, too, Kelly—gave me the incentive I needed to take control of the direction my life was taking—so there must be some good come of my experience there. But it didn't cure me of my homosexuality.

I see Charlie in the evenings. Hon, I hope you're not jealous, but he seems to need my company as much as I need his. We talk about you and he tells me what's going on there. He said you were curious what happened to Eugene Baker after we let her off on the side of the road in the Guadalupe mountains.

To be honest, Kelly, neither Charlie or I cared. That girl is sick. But as we were pulling away, I turned and watched his sick little naked butt get smaller and smaller. I think the whole experience of being thrown out on the side of the road in the middle of nowhere actually appealed to him. Or maybe he was trained by his Army for the Lord to survive in the wilderness.

Charlie is sure he managed to hitch-hike into Carlsbad and to make contact with Alton Drigger. Charlie says Drigger has quit the church, now that some of the members have heard and believed Charlie's version of what happened to me behind the stock pens.

Anyway, I've got a job, but neither as scullery maid, nor construction worker. But it's nice. I'm learning to build furniture at a little company on the highway out of Carlsbad on the way to White City. Charlie's loaned me a pickup. Can you believe me, the former Miss Houston, running about in a Toyota pickup truck? I've taken to wearing a cap, too! Hell, darling, I think I'll actually wear out a pair of Levi's. I don't know how long this testosterone rush will last, but I like it, Kelly.

I'm waiting for you! Don't think I mean in a romantic way, unless you do, and unless we date when you get out of hell. I don't want to rush anything with anybody, anymore. I just want to learn who I am and what I'm capable of doing. Well, I've said too much, and not enough. Please write! Charlie can give me your letters!

Hugs and Kisses,
Michael

* * *

Lion's Mouth Christian Ranch
July 15

It strikes me that if Paul Romaine wasn't here, throwing a wrench into the works, for many of the guys, the brainwashing of the ministry might have a stronger hold on them. And since he is raping the recruits, he's doing a lot of harm.

He is homosexual. Tom Allen-Reece is right. I would not call him *gay*, however. I wouldn't dignify his spiteful little nature by calling him that. I think he's the kind of person the Bible talks about, whom Rafferty says has a reprobate mind—not because he's a homosexual. Rather, it's because he hates being homosexual that clouds his mind and makes him vengeful.

He's about the weirdest sexual pervert I've ever met. It makes my skin crawl to think of those other guys who follow him, too—those I've been calling his cadre. How twisted their thinking is, participating in Paul's perversion and doing the things that Michael describes in his letter to me.

Anyway, if any dyed-in-the-wool homosexuality-hating Christians get a look at this writing about the ranch, they will no doubt point their fingers and say, "Aha! See! It IS homosexuality that causes all the problems." They would identify Paul as a homosexual and all his inner cadre, too, and they would say that, without him here, the ministry of Josh Rafferty could succeed in curing homosexuality.

Maybe it's because Paul feels guilty and filthy down to the depths of his soul that causes him to hate himself and, by extension, to hate homosexuality in others. Yet, that's the same guilt Rafferty is engendering in the young, impressionable minds of the other recruits. It was such guilt, I am sure that finally pushed my sweet William over the edge. He'd never felt very good about being gay; and when he went through Rafferty's program in Albuquerque, then failed to really get the cure he wanted, he must've felt even lower than ever about himself. So, if Rafferty is successful in instilling guilt in the other recruits, even if they don't commit suicide, it will twist and distort their thinking as it has Paul's. If, in their guilt, one of the recruits—like Jerry—continues to feel unworthy of Jesus' love, because in his heart he cannot stop having gay feelings, he will go through life emotionally crippled. His own guilt will not allow him to feel love for another man, but will destroy it. That would be tragic and would rob him of finding happiness where he most naturally could find it. Then, if his sexual urges lead him to "stray," he will *have to* call it lust and to think of it as sin, and he will redouble his efforts to punish himself—or, as in Paul's case, to punish others.

I would love to brush aside the hundreds of ex-gay programs operating right now in this country, but I can't. Rafferty and others like him are as far from true Christianity, today, as they were when Anita Bryant's "Save Our Children" campaign caught fire in Dade County, Florida, twenty years ago. She was among the first of the Twentieth Century religious fanatics to demonize gay people. The fact remains that the so-called Christ-loving churches have had two thousand years to get their Christian love in order, two THOUSAND years to understand and work through Christ's message. But they haven't been able to. I can't forget that it was the Christians who conducted the Crusades, slaughtering and killing all those who opposed them; it was the Christians who conducted the inquisitions, torturing and maiming even those of their own religion, since it fit their needs to instill fear in their people; it was the Christians (this time the Protestants) who conducted the Salem witch trials in Massachusetts, burning women at the stake and drowning them; and it was the Christians in Nazi Germany who not only allowed Hitler to murder millions of Jews, to consign to the lowest level of those camps, the homosexuals, but to be the participants; and it is the Christians in the United States, today, who continue to foment hatred, this time against us. Only constant vigilance and resistance will finally see an end to such ministries as Rafferty's.

* * *

Rafferty is beginning to look ragged. He must also be feeling the pressure of his job. He is probably also feeling the pressure the Assembly of God Almighty continues to put on him. Charlie and David Hays, Les Hunter, and Sharp Jones are telling the church leaders in Carlsbad that there's a lot of misery at the ranch.

Thus far, Rafferty's solution seems to be to subject us to even more brainwashing. We now get up at four-thirty a.m., instead of sunup. We gather sleepy-eyed into the chapel for a pre-meal devotional, replete with Caucasian gospel, prayer, and a mini-sermon. It's quite obvious that Rafferty has turned more to Paul for advice.

Paul's cadre sprinkles itself throughout the chapel. At Rafferty's fervently delivered sermons, they jump up and shout, "Praise God!" The rest of us have to do the same thing. Appearing to be depressed is not permitted. Being depressed is a sign that one is not right with the Lord, and if that is the case, a recruit can be assigned after-hour duties, like mopping the chow hall, even after the day crew has finished with it. Along with this extra duty, that recruit must recite the eighteen steps to salvation, or quote verbatim from the Bible those passages that refer to homosexuality. So we all try to go around with smiles of the Holy Spirit pasted on our faces, to act less tired than we are, and to do our crying in privacy.

"Jesus loves you," we say in passing one another as we go about our jobs. "Walk in the Spirit, Brother!" we say as we work in the fields. All is "glorious" or "heaven-sent," no matter whether it is a clear day, an extra helping at dinner, or the shits from some particularly disgusting concoction of soup. All has been planned by the Almighty, down to the smallest detail of our lives.

Following our religious services, we are herded out of the chapel and into the chow hall; along the way we continue to sing, our heads held high, our feet "stomping to the rhythm of the Holy Spirit."

Our portions at each meal have been cut, and now our food credits can buy back what had been a regular helping of gruel. It began with Larry and, after he appeared to be more docile, more willing to jump when someone said "boo," when he became more PLIABLE to the indwelling of the Holy Spirit, that is, Rafferty decided that cutting everyone else's portions of food was the ticket. No one objected when Larry's portions were cut, because everyone figured he could survive on the amounts he was given. Of course he could have, for awhile, but now that our own food has been reduced, it becomes obvious that reducing a person's intake of the amount of food he is used to does have a debilitating effect. The pancakes, orange juice, and even the eggs we used to be able to buy with our food credits are gone. What milk they get from the remaining milk cow is barely enough for cooking purposes. We are permitted to have as much water as we want, and only one cup of coffee.

Cutting our food has been effective. After breakfast, the work seems harder than ever.

It was so devastating—that thunderstorm. The corn was laid flat, and we had to get in there the next day and go through fifty acres of it propping it back up. Water had flooded into the valley from all directions, it being a natural recipient of mountain run off. We lost all our vegetables to the storm. In fact, half the acreage was washed clean away and collected on the east end of the ranch in one big lake. Only the alfalfa survived the deluge and, in fact, seems to have thrived.

The cow shed collapsed. We had three milk cows and three calves before the storm. The collapse killed one of the calves, and two of the milk cows ran off. We only managed to find one of them. By now, the other one has probably died of exposure.

You might say I got what I prayed for. I wanted the storm to wreak havoc on this place. What I didn't count on was the misery it would cause the recruits, besides myself. Rafferty delivered a sermon the day after the storm, praising God (?!) for His work and for burdening us with the opportunity to learn His Wisdom from the wreckage. I'm starting to wonder if Rafferty believes God speaks directly to him. I would suspect that it sounds quite similar to the sibilant hissing of Paul Romaine in his ear.

The church leadership in Carlsbad has apparently approved of cutting the food we eat, because it goes on.

Our biggest meal is still lunch. But with the reduced portions and types of food available for breakfast, it is not adequate. We don't get any vegetables at all, except for something that poses as green beans from gallon-size cans, with a few potatoes in them. "By His Wisdom," Rafferty says we were not meant to have fresh vegetables since He destroyed our own crop. "It is His message to us," Rafferty says, that there are still some of us who are not giving control over to the Holy Spirit that has brought the devastation to us at this time.

Finger pointing has begun in earnest. Many whisper that Larry is responsible, since he was punished repeatedly for his lust of food; and God, apparently, has decided the rest of us should suffer. Larry is more shunned than ever. The hot seat has become white-hot, now, for anyone sitting in it at our evening "meal." Supper is just one step above bread and water.

* * *

After the storm of the day before, we awoke to humidity in the predawn.

"Get up! Get up!" came the call as the guys from the other tent came into ours. The lights were switched on, and for a just a moment, I recalled another sensation from boot camp. After only a few days of being awakened at 4:30 a.m. in basic, all it took to get us up was for the lights to be switched on. Forty pairs of feet hit the floor instantly. A minute later we were dressed, including wearing our combat boots. Another minute and our beds were made, and a bare few seconds later, we were outside the barracks in formation and ready to march.

Here, there is not that great of a sense of urgency, but when the lights come on, seven of us get up immediately. Larry is the only one who has trouble with that early morning enthusiasm. It has to be infused in him by Paul Romaine, standing just inside our tent to slap the bottoms of Larry's feet with his clipboard. "Brother Larry, let the Holy Spirit have you. Up!" Paul says.

The morning after the storm, the rest of us were dressed and waiting outside with our paired recruits, when Larry finally came outside, Tom and Richard on either side of him. Larry looked stunned. His eyes were puffy from lack of sleep.

In the predawn, I could smell the water on the land. The rain had left the valley soaked, and the mud collected on our shoes in heavy globs as we walked across the fields. We could hardly see, but could feel the devastation. There was no rustling of corn leaves where there should have been.

The Hot Seat

The moon was already down, and we walked across the earth, feeling the moisture and the cold rise from it, without being able to see the ground, except for its blackness. In the east there wasn't the slightest hint of daybreak.

After being herded in and out of the chapel, in and out of the chow hall, we were all collected on the east end of the field. The sun was up by now. We looked across the field. The corn was flattened; where the vegetables had been, there was a sixty-foot wide gash of mud, silt, and standing water. Beyond that, the alfalfa was still standing. Some of us cried. Some of us stood with our mouths open. All of us were put to work in the fields.

By ten o'clock, the heat and the humidity from the wet ground was like a steam bath. The flies, gnats, mosquitoes, and other insects buzzed around our faces, sucking sweat from our eyes and ears. The mud got over our shoes, then on our Levi's. The sweat from our bodies made our clothing hug us, wet and hot. Bending to the ground to lift the corn stalks, kneeling to push mud around the roots, standing and moving to the next and bending and kneeling again, hour after hour, took its toll on us. By lunch we were exhausted, filthy, sweating, only to be met with a reduced meal, and less time to rest. Then it was back to the field and the heat and the insects.

By the time we were permitted to shower, all we wanted to do was sleep. But Paul, his inner cadre, and Rafferty had been resting all day, staying out of the heat. They were full of enthusiasm for us. We were like the living dead, stilted, fuzzy headed, weakened, and vulnerable.

That night at supper it was my turn in the hot seat. I'd been there earlier in the program, and had escaped easily by mouthing a few key phrases of praise and pertinent scripture. As I carried my tray to the center of the chow hall this time, I just wanted to go to sleep.

I set my tray on the table before me and yawned.

"Brother Kelly, the Holy Spirit has directed me to ask, are you angry?" I yawned and looked for the voice. It was Paul, looking fresh and perky. I wanted to throw my bowl of soup across the chow hall at him.

"No. I'm tired," I said.

"Is the strength of the Holy Spirit slack in you, then?" That question came from one of Paul's inner cadre members. At the moment, I couldn't even think of his name.

"No. I'm tired because I've been up since before dawn and I've worked about ten hours in the hot sun, in ninety percent humidity, with blood sucking insects all over my body, and worked on practically an empty stomach."

"You *sound* angry," Paul said. "The Holy Spirit has directed me to ask if you have been able to overcome Step Number Five on the road to salvation."

I yawned again. "Which one is that?"

"You don't know?" Rafferty asked, his voice rising with incredulity. "After all this time? We've been over these steps almost daily, son. Haven't you been concentrating? Haven't you been listening? Haven't you been reading? Haven't you been praying?"

The hot seat gives you a unique perspective. From the center of the room, you can look around and see recruits everywhere. While there are only twenty-two of us, you get the impression you're looking out on a sea of faces. You find the voice of the speaker a heartbeat or two after his question has died on his lips. This builds anticipation in the listeners.

Every face was turned toward me—even of those I suspected of not being with the program. Rafferty was on the opposite side of the room from Paul as I turned to answer his questions. I was itching to see Paul's face. I wanted to look him in the eye when I answered, but Josh was waiting for me to answer him.

"I've been here almost six weeks, Brother Josh. Like everyone else, I..." I paused, the lie forming on my lips. "I have daily been attempting like the child in the Lord that I am to overcome my worldly burdens." That sounded good to me, that wording, so I continued. "and we all know what burdens we carry as homosexuals, with minds that have been...that have been seared by Satan." *Yeah, that's it, Satan.* "Satan has visited me in the dark of the night, whispering unclean things to me, but I have fought, with the help of the Holy Ghost, and pushed against the Dark One. 'Be gone, Demon of Hell! I rebuke you!' I have said many nights. But he is clever, that One. I have fallen time and time again in my thoughts. And tonight, being tired and hungry, Brother Josh, I can't remember what steps on the road to salvation are my victories and which are my defeats."

"Amen!" Came a chorus of voices around the room. I took the opportunity to look at Paul. He was seething. I felt like laughing.

"Brother Kelly..." Paul said, then paused, waiting for the room to become quiet and for his voice to be heard. "The Holy Spirit has directed me to say that you are not being frank."

"What's your question, Brother Paul?"

"Have you faced and accepted your basic anger problem?"

"Yes."

"I don't believe you."

"What's your question?"

"Have you faced and accepted your basic anger problem?" he asked, again.

"Yes."

"I don't believe you."

"What's your ques—"

"Boys! Boys!" Rafferty said, from behind me. "That is quite enough. Brother Paul, if you can't accept Brother Kelly's answer, kindly rephrase your question, or move on, or allow others of us to ask ours."

"All right," Paul said. "Brother Kelly, the Holy Spirit has directed me to ask you to expound on your answer. If you have faced and accepted your basic anger problem, kindly let us know what that means."

My head was beginning to buzz. Although I was smart-mouthing my way through the hot seat, I was dead tired. I couldn't think. I took a sip of soup, took a slug of water from my glass. "I guess it means, Brother Paul, that I am angry, that I have continued to be angry. I face that anger and I accept it. What else am I supposed to do with that step?"

His eyes glittered. "You tell us."

I thought of Leo and Sidney, who had been entombed in the coffin and, for all I knew, had not been checked on at any time during almost twenty hours to see if they had smothered, or died of heart failure or shock; I thought of Michael who had almost been raped, who had, with the direct witness of one of the foremen and a man of the church in Carlsbad, gone to Rafferty with their story and were rebuked in favor of Paul Romaine; I thought of Brian and Donald and of all the recruits who had been raped by Paul; and I thought of William, my poor dead William, who had put his trust and hope in Rafferty, who had committed suicide rather than face the guilt and shame of having not been cured of his homosexuality. I thought of Larry's continual humiliation by both Paul and Rafferty, and I thought of the guilt and shame all of us were subjected to at this place. The anger that welled up within me gave me the strength to sit up straighter in the hot seat, to meet Paul's eyes, to stare at him. And the white-hot anger cleared my mind.

"I am angry about a whole host of wrongs that have been done to the recruits who have come to this place, who have put their trust and hope and even their physical well-being in your hands, Brother Paul. I do not think that entombing two live human beings in a coffin for almost twenty-four hours was done with Christian love as a motive. I am angry that Michael was expelled from the program, when it was not his fault. I've heard it said that he was the one who attempted to perform some sexual act on you, Brother Paul, and I don't believe that at all. I believe he was framed, so that the truly guilty in that incident could escape."

The silence in the room was palpable, as each person drew in an astonished breath, or dared not breathe at my direct assault. I even saw a few smiles.

I turned around and looked at Rafferty, and I saw a hint of satisfaction from his eyes. For an instant, I wondered if Rafferty had been waiting for someone to challenge Paul. But the moment passed; Rafferty said nothing.

The silence continued. Not a sound in the room interrupted my words. They hung, suspended in time, and I wondered if I had spoken at all, when Paul suddenly jumped up.

"You were not there!" he said. "You do not know the humiliation I was subjected to. So do NOT...Do not DARE to make accusations against me!"

A hissing, as from a steam pipe began to come from the room. At first it wasn't clear what was happening, but then I could see the parted lips of the recruits who, under their breaths, were hissing through their teeth. Paul looked around, like a puppet whose head is jerked by a palsied puppeteer, and the hissing stopped.

"We are all sorry for our mistake in judgment...in...in placing—"

The hissing came from his left, and he turned to see who was doing it, but it stopped, again. He looked distracted, but regained his posture of having been affronted. "An hour would have been sufficient, Brother Kelly, for the point to have been made with the 'death of the Spirit demonstration.' But your anger is out of all proportion to the act."

Hissing on his right. He flicked his eyes.

"And your anger about something you do not have the facts on, indicates a deeper seated rebellion within you. What about that?"

God, I wanted to smash his face. I wanted to blurt out the truth, that I had seen exactly what went on beyond the stock pens, that I had seen him preparing himself for the rape, using a cock ring to make himself hard. I wanted to tell him exactly what his method of rape entailed, but I couldn't reveal myself, not yet. Charlie had cautioned me on that. I still wanted to stay at this place long enough to finish him off once and for all. Behind me, Rafferty's silence (even through the hissing of some of the recruits and in letting me have my say) spoke volumes.

"About my deeper seated anger? You want me to tell you that?" I said. Then, without giving him a chance to take the lead in our dance of wills, I said, "I'm also angry that other recruits have been raped. That before Michael was expelled, there was more of that same kind of activity. I personally know that three other recruits were raped, brutalized to the point where one of them suffered rectal bleeding, and they were all so scared, Brother Paul, they wouldn't tell anyone."

"If they told no one, you CAN'T know that anyone was raped!" Paul screamed. "Does Satan put such thoughts in your head? Do you and Satan have a pact?"

The room was electrified with the shouting. I took time to look for Donald and Brian. They were crying. Brian was rising up out of his chair. He was shaking so violently, I thought he was having an epileptic seizure.

Paul apparently realized what was about o happen, as well; when Brian struggled to his feet, Paul flicked his eyes at Tom and Richard. We both knew that Brian was fighting against his paralyzing fear in standing up.

Tom and Richard were sitting next to him. "I think Brian's about to faint!" Tom said, grasping him around the shoulders. Brian struggled, until Tom's arms encircled him. His face clouded over, and he slumped against Tom's chest.

Rafferty had also risen and moved across the room. "Take him outdoors, boys. Let him rest. Brother Kelly is right. You've all had such a hard day, it might be best for us to call it quits for the night, get a good night's sleep. And may the Lord bless and keep you. Good night!"

* * *

That's all I can write. The lack of food, the predawn awakenings, the pre-breakfast services, the hot, muggy days, the shorter lunches, the hot seat, the Caucasian Gospel singing, the recruits rising after lights out and wandering around outdoors—all continue. Larry went out about an hour ago. I don't expect him in until well after everyone else has gone to sleep.

K. O'K

XIII
One Shall be Taken

Lion's Mouth
Monday, July 20

    Three things have happened in such close succession in the last few days, that I think the fabric of the ministry is unraveling. First, one of the recruits whom I was sure had been raped admitted it to me; second, Rafferty asked for my information on how I knew others had been raped (which means, I hope, that he's beginning to have serious doubts about Paul); and third, Larry is missing. With this sudden combination of problems, information, and doubts, I can't see how we can possibly fail, not only in bringing down Paul, but in causing the Assembly of God Almighty church in Carlsbad to have serious doubts about this ministry.

    After we got back to the tents following my turn in the hot seat, and after I did some writing, I fell into a very deep sleep; then sometime during the night, I began having a wet dream. It felt so real I woke up. The tent was dark, soundless, except for that particularly sensual sucking sound of a blow job. My wet dream was real, no dream at all. Someone, I couldn't tell who, was at work on my very erect and nearly exploding cock. God, it felt so good, I laid back and almost let myself come. Then I freaked, wondering who in the hell. I felt down there and found myself caressing some very nice, very naked, very busy shoulders.

I pulled him up to my face and, after getting a wonderfully wet and warm kiss, I held the guy's face. He didn't struggle. "Who have I got?" I whispered in the dark, "and what do you think you're doing to me?"

"Brian Donnelly. Kelly, I'll do you from now on if you'll just protect me!" he whispered. "Just please, protect me!"

I did want to protect him, but I wasn't sure from what, so I led him outside and away from the tents. He told me what I had already suspected, that he had been raped by Paul, and had since been continually raped by the rest of Paul's inner cadre. He said when I accused someone at the ranch of raping the recruits, he knew I was onto Paul and the others. He said he was going to support what I said by admitting that he had been raped, but Tom grabbed him, and by his touch conveyed the threat that if he opened his mouth, he was in trouble.

All right, so when we were outside in our bare chests and underwear, I couldn't forget what he'd been doing to me in my cot. I held that beautiful kid close and let him cry his eyes out, and before we went back to the tents, I kissed his luscious lips and held him. But I am honorable once I am fully awake. I told him not to breathe a word to anyone of his late-night visit to my cot and to carry on as usual, and I would try to think of a way to help him.

With the other two things that have happened, I feel certain that help is on the way for Brian and all the recruits. But now I have to backtrack so things make sense. Here goes.

* * *

Sunday, July 19

I am in the library, just after breakfast. There are south windows in this room. From my perspective, outdoors is just a burst of white light. All I can see is a bright, blinding light coming in through the windows. It burns out all the scenery beyond. In contrast, the library is cool and gloomy. I am relaxed, able to write for the first time, without looking over my shoulder. I'm doing it with Rafferty's permission; of course, he doesn't know I'm writing to outsiders. He thinks I'm writing answers to his questions: "How do you know three recruits were raped while in this program? Who are they? Why do you believe you are correct?"

These questions came in response to my being in the hot seat July 15 and making those very accusations. Rafferty was silent for a few days, but this morning, before church services took place, he called me into his office and said he'd been thinking about what I'd said. It was odd to sit down face-to-face with the man. I hadn't done that since I was in Albuquerque checking into this program. Back then, he looked and sounded confident—kind of like those bubbling personas of the evangelical talk show, the now indicted and imprisoned Jim (and Tammy) Bakker of the now extinct PTL Club, or Jimmy Swaggart, the now disgraced "John" of the street-walking industry. Back in Albuquerque, he had the shit-eating grin of Jerry Falwell and declared himself part of the "Moral Majority." He had even talked about other programs like his that were great successes, like Exodus International, begun in 1976 which, since that time, had freed hundreds of men from the homosexual lifestyle. But I wondered if there had been Williams in those programs, too—aside from the two co-founders who began this most successful ex-gay program, then ended up being lovers and one of its most powerful detractors.

"*Oh yes, son, we offer a cure for your homosexuality,*" Rafferty had assured me when I questioned him about it "*Through the indwelling of the Holy Spirit, you will come out of the darkness of your present life, even though you may not perceive it as such; you will come to realize what a deep, dark pit you are now in.*" That was back in the fall of 1997, in the cucumber cool of his Albuquerque office.

This morning, in the chapel at Lion's mouth, however, he didn't look so confident, or perky.

In Albuquerque, I had asked if through curing my homosexuality would I start to find members of the opposite sex appealing, would I be able to get married and live a normal life. He nodded with self-assurance, back then. *"All things are possible through Christ."*

This morning I asked him, "Do you think any of the guys here are being cured?"

He looked askance. He didn't like my question. He shifted in his chair and leaned across the desk, speaking softly. "If the recruit believes homosexuality is a sin, confesses it, allows the Holy Spirit to come into his life and control him, shuts out his homosexual thoughts, prays continually, fights temptation, focuses on religion, does not allow himself to backslide, and believes—yes, he will be delivered from a homosexual lifestyle."

"But will he become a *hetero*sexual?"

"He will at least find," Rafferty said, settling back in his chair and making a tent with his fingers, "that it is far better to live a celibate, single life than that of the unrepentant, practicing homosexual."

"That's what I thought, Josh."

"I see," he said. "But I didn't call you in here to discuss this ministry. I called you in to find out what you know about…ah…actual rapes on this ranch. That thought repels me and compels me to get to the bottom of this. I want to know what you know and how."

"I'll write it down," I said, and he agreed.

So here I am.

This development, Rafferty's sudden awakening from his blindness about the hanky panky going on under his nose, does not endear him to me in the least. I still think he's misguided, just as Exodus International is also misguided and no doubt deliberately misguiding. When Josh finally admitted that his true objective is for homosexuals to live celibate, Christian-centered lives, I was determined to bring down this whole ministry and expose this program for the malicious sham it is. It is abundantly clear that the ministry, from the start, knew it had very little chance of doing anything *for* homosexuals, other than getting them to feel guilty. Now it is clear what Rafferty wants: homosexual Christians are to give up their sexuality, pure and simple. They will not miraculously become straight.

***

July 20
Larry is missing. For several nights I'd observed Larry's behavior after lights out. He would get up in the middle of the night and wouldn't return until very close to lights on. That was a pattern he'd set several days before—or even weeks. So no one thought anything of it when he left last night. But when the recruits from the other tent came in, this morning, shouting us out of bed, they stopped and looked around.

"Where's Larry?" Paul asked the rest of us.

"He left last night," someone said.

"He does that," someone else said.

"Where does he go?" Paul asked.

We all pointed toward the northern tent wall.

"Well," Paul said, "carry on as usual."

***

It's now the evening of the first day since Larry disappeared. No one spent any time looking for him until sometime after lunch. All morning they said, *"He'll turn up."* But he didn't. By this afternoon, everyone was worried and the major question on everyone's lips was where Larry could be. We organized search parties. Some of us were to search the hills north of the tents where, each night, we heard his steps. But we were to search only so far, following any footprints until they played out. It was late afternoon, and we were to watch the sun. When it neared the horizon, we were to turn back. Others were instructed to do the same east of the valley, following any footprints they could; others were to search west of the valley beyond Lion's Mouth Canyon, and still others went south, into the rolling-away hills.

I was with Jerry and four other recruits, among them Brian and Donald, but not Tom or Richard. We entered the "hand" north of the tents. I was very familiar with the terrain, since it is where Charlie and I meet. Our Jeep tracks showed clearly for awhile, but when we passed the place where Charlie usually parks, there was nothing, not even footprints. So we turned back, and made another stab northward beginning from the "hand." We searched methodically, following every trail of footprints leading away from the valley.

As I've described the hand and the fingers of hills, one has to backtrack each time to get into the next valley formed by the hills. We backtracked toward the palm of the hand and into another valley, then another, until the sun threatened to set on us, and leave us in this hot, barren purgatory in the dark. We found only our own footprints, zigzagging snake and lizard trails, and grass so tough, you could slice your hands to ribbons on it.

The other search parties came back just as empty handed, tired, and as thirsty as we were. As we gathered in the chow hall to give our reports on what we found, Paul stood up and said he and his guys would take a Jeep and continue searching.

"We can camp out tonight and get a fresh start in the morning," he said.

By this time, Rafferty didn't care where the help came from. He had my written report fingering Paul and his cadre as a secret group inside the ministry, acting outside the ministry with one of their own, which included rape and torture. But he was so worried about Larry (or what he would have to tell the kid's parents) that he would have said, "Fine, fine," to the devil, as he said to Paul. "Just find him!"

Paul chose his usual three goons, plus Tom and Richard, for his search party. I was not surprised. They accounted for all five of his fellows in the

"Army for the Lord"—according to what Eugene had told Michael and Charlie. Donald and Brian were free from them for the night. I intended to find out as much about Paul and his cadre from these two recruits as I could. I wanted Charlie to be with me.

* * *

It's almost lights out on this first night that Larry has been missing. Larry was a nuisance sometimes, completely unable to play the game, here. He was also a horrible reminder to us of those poor people, gay or straight, who go through life crippled by things they seem unable to change—and I don't mean their innate desires or needs. I mean things that by a little will-power and a good self-concept (maybe?) they can change. Like overeating, overdrinking, smoking—acquired habits, I guess. If Larry has had a horrible home life, if his story about the man next door is true, what a burden of guilt he must have carried around with him. What an interesting specimen for Rafferty to work with—all that guilt to manipulate.

It's not really like me to invoke God into my mental states. I use that word, God, as a harmless expletive (like, "God, am I thirsty" or "God, is he cute!"), but tonight, I'm praying to God or Allah or Yahweh, or the verb to BE, that wherever Larry is out there, in those hundreds of square miles of desert and cliffs, amid the rattlesnakes and vermin, that he has found shelter, that he has found food, and that he'll show up here tomorrow.

I'll close for now and write a letter to Michael. Just knowing he's waiting for me to get out of this place has given me more strength. He mentioned romance in his letter. I don't know about that. But dating him, maybe, or just being around him for awhile might be quite nice.

* * *

Lion's Mouth Christian Ranch
July 20

Dear Michael,

Charlie has no doubt told you I'm delighted to get your sweet and wonderful letters. Just knowing you are in Carlsbad and not back there in Houston, helps me make it through each day.

So you're having a "testosterone rush?" That really cracked me up. But I can see you behind the steering wheel of a pickup truck. I really can, Mike. When I said you were beginning to look butch, I meant it. But please don't think your particular brand of being special comes from being fem or butch. Remember, it was the queens who first stood up for gay rights in that bar in New York City back in '69. It was the queens who launched our movement.

I thought the image of you taking your female side by the hand and walking her into your heart was very touching. I hope she is never forgotten. She was enjoyable to visit with here at this ranch—that is, when we had the time to talk.

Charlie will probably have told you that our obese charge, Larry, is missing tonight. Remember how he told us about his parents sending him here? Remember how he didn't even know whether or not he was homosexual? Michael, all he wanted to do was get away from here. He came against his will. Of course, I don't think anyone should voluntarily come to a place like this, either. But until gay people have made long strides to outstrip the prejudice and hatred against us—even our self-hatred—these places will flourish. We haven't been fighting back long enough, or hard enough to change things.

Thank you, Michael, for coming back to Carlsbad. I appreciate your waiting for me to get out more than I can express. I'm not the least jealous that you and Charlie are able to see each other at night. Can you imagine, Michael, being fifty years old and never having experienced a loving relationship? Can you imagine the years' long—no, decades' long—sense of utter isolation that Charlie must have gone through?

He is such a decent person, toughened by the years, yet almost childlike in his shyness. Would it be too much to ask, once this is over, to introduce him to gay people we know and respect? The three of us could go to Houston to visit your friends. I'm sure Charlie would get a good, long look at the "gay" world, there. We could also go to Common, New Mexico, where my friends Tom and Joel Allen-Reece live. You'd like them, too, Michael. They can show Charlie what is possible in a gay marriage.

As you say, you want a husband. So do I. I imagine Charlie wants the same. He would certainly make some man a wonderful mate, wouldn't he?

Well, my friend and partner in crime, I'm going to bed. Tomorrow is a big day. The disruption of the program because of Larry's disappearance should prove to bring other disruptions as well.

Your friend,
Kelly

XIV
Found

Lion's Mouth Christian Ranch
Wednesday, July 22

    Sometimes a brief encounter with a stranger can bring the most rapid and lasting changes in a person's life. The most obvious such example is an encounter with a mugger who, by force and threat, encourages you to increase his bottom line by handing him your wallet, or purse, or jewels. If the encounter turns violent, you can be killed (that's a pretty rapid and lasting change), or you can be maimed, or scarred—physically and emotionally.

    Sometimes coming upon a suffering human being can so capture your sympathy that it makes you stop on your way through life. You want to offer some kind of aid, or you suddenly make the alleviation of that suffering a goal, a cause.

    Or, a brief encounter with a stranger can ignite you into action. It can be the proverbial "last straw."

    When I got up this morning at seven a.m., there was no Paul, goons, or recruits from the next tent to rouse us at four-thirty in the morning. I thought immediately of Brian Donnelly and his late-night visit to my cot a few nights before. I had promised the kid I would try to help him. If I was going to do it, today was the day, since Paul and the five members of his "Army for the Lord" were all out together, searching the hills beyond our valley for Larry. It was also the day I decided to "come out of the closet," so to speak, as the spy I was, to be forthright, at last, and let the devil have his due. My time had come to take action and not be a passive observer.

My decision made, I meant to protect Brian from Tom and Richard, whom I suspected used him and Donald as their slaves. This form of abuse—and it *is* abuse, when the slaves are unwillingly put in that role—occurs often in prison. This place is a kind of prison, being isolated as it is.

With a fire of purpose and determination lit under me, I set out immediately to find Brian and was lucky enough to see him and Donald walking toward the chow hall. This morning, there had been no recruit-pairing, no work roster, no assignments. Things were certainly in disarray. But humans are creatures of habit. When I stepped out of the tent, all the recruits were on their way to the chow hall, including the recruits I used to call the S&Ms. But there was none of the purposeful movement across the field. Our head had been lopped off, speaking metaphorically, because Paul wasn't around to tell us what to do.

I was relieved, but I saw that some of the recruits were uncomfortable having to think for themselves. I didn't stop to suggest to anyone I passed that we ought to try to continue with the program, nor to suggest that it was all right for them to exhibit independent thinking, since things were so unsettled. All I cared about was catching up to Brian. I saw him and Donald together, about midway through the corn field.

By now, the corn stalks were waist high and seemed to have come out of their beaten and abused state. But I didn't care as I ran over them in my hurry to catch up with the two recruits.

"Wait!" I called, cupping my hands to my mouth. "Brian! Donald! I've got to talk to you!"

They both turned around. Brian saw who it was and pulled at Donald's shoulder. They stood still and waited for me to come up to them.

"Now's our chance, Brian," I said, when I reached them. "There's nobody around to hurt you, and there won't be, so please, tell me what's been done to you, and who did it."

This kid—whose warm kiss I still remembered, whose tears had run down my chest, who had softly whispered a plea for help in the middle of the night—made my throat ache as he smiled. His dark eyes filled with tears. "You really think it's all right?" he said, looking around.

Donald, the blond Adonis, put his hand on Brian's shoulder. "I think it is, Brian. I told you I saw Kelly on the ridge at the stock pens. I saw him and Charlie watching us when they took Michael. Didn't I? I told you. We can trust him."

"Thanks," I said to both of them. In the early morning sun, there was still the fresh, rose tint to the light. In it, their faces looked too young to be in a place like this. They looked too innocent to have thought they needed to go to Josh Rafferty for a cure. They looked too whole and beautiful in the light for me to even contemplate how they must have been hurt and soiled by Paul and his "Army for the Lord."

At first, they spoke haltingly, with shame. Paul always worked in the daylight, they said, so everyone on the ranch would be busy, and no one would be the wiser. It was easy for him to arrange to have anyone he wanted brought to him east of the stock pens. With Alton Drigger working there, with Paul making up the work roster, he could arrange things perfectly.

"But how many of you did he take there?"

They said they didn't know.

"Then how did you find out about each other's abuse?"

"He took us there together," Donald said. "He always paired us together in the work crew, except once, I think."

"Did Paul always use the night stick?"

"No," Brian said. "He slammed his fist into his palm. "That would have been preferable. We had to perform oral sex on them."

"On who?"

"Every one of them," Donald said. "Paul, Tom, Richard, Eugene, Drigger, and those three guys who were always with Paul—Mo, Joe, and Curly."

Brian laughed at that, but it was choked off with a sob. "We had to do every one of them, every day! I got so sick, I couldn't eat, I couldn't work, all I could think about every night was that Josh approved, so there was no one to turn to until you—"

"Wait!" I said. "Josh *approved*?"

"That's what Paul said, and Drigger," Brian said. "Drigger was working for the church in Carlsbad. They told us, 'just try going to Josh.'"

"And the proof is how close Paul is to Rafferty. You can see that," Donald added.

"Well, Rafferty is not involved in that," I told them. "Whatever else he may be, he's not a sexual sadist."

"How do you know that for sure, Kelly?"

"Because I believe that he is sincere. I believe that he truly hates homosexuality. I believe he just wants to stop it wherever he can. But I'm not telling you guys to go to him. He didn't believe Michael's version of what went on with Paul and Drigger that day out at the pens. So it's possible he might be reluctant to open his eyes, even now."

"Then what are we going to do?" Brian said. "Paul and the others will have to come back either way."

"Let them," I said. "We're going to turn this place upside down. I promise."

Our walk to the chow hall was filled with such ugliness, I had lost my appetite by the time we got there. I left Donald and Brian on the porch and went to find anyone I could from the church in Carlsbad. I found Les Hunter at a table with Sharp Jones. The smell of eggs and sausage almost made me puke when I walked in, but I helped myself to some coffee. There were a few recruits eating breakfast. I wondered at the casual atmosphere, the blindness of the others to what had been going on under all of our noses.

But it was clear from the very casual atmosphere that the program had been once again suspended.

"Where's Rafferty?" I asked Les, when I took my coffee to his table.

"Gone." Les said. "I think to the sheriff in Carlsbad, to see if they can't get a 'copter out here."

"You boys can't do the kind of search that's required. Not out there," Sharp said, indicating the harsh, sunlit desert beyond the windows of the chow hall. "Might as well sit yourself, son."

I did and took a sip of the coffee. Its bitter blackness cleared my head of the images of Brian and Donald. "Where's Charlie?"

"Why, he took Rafferty to town, son," Les said.

I was sorry that Charlie was not here, but I decided that Sharp and Les would understand what I was about to tell them, and that when Paul and his five soldiers showed up, they would keep them away from any of the recruits.

So I related the story that Donald and Brian had just told me. "Look, Les, you know I was there at the stock pens, the day they took Michael to rape him. You suggested I tell Rafferty that I was a witness. But Charlie thought it'd be better if I didn't. We didn't tell you why."

"And now you're gonna, I hope," Les said.

"I am. Les, I'm not here to get cured. I never was. I was here to see first hand what would go on in one of these ministries." I told Les about William, as I had told Sharp that day behind the chow hall. During this telling, I wasn't nearly the basket case I had been when I related my story to Sharp. But it was still difficult to keep tears from wetting my eyes and making them burn. Whether they could understand my grief as his lover, I don't know, but they could understand my anger. "Since the day I arrived," I continued, "I've been writing down everything I've seen."

"Like I said d'other day, son, that explains your lookin' different than the others," Sharp said. He grinned and tilted his cup toward me.

"What do you mean, different?"

"You stayed awake. Most of the others didn't. You get my meaning on that?"

I did. I talked to Les and Sharp about keeping an eye on Paul and his little army, specifically mentioning Brian and Donald.

"Son, we'd be glad to," Les said. "Me and Sharp and the rest of the staff. We won't let 'em get within spittin distance of any of the other boys."

I was relieved about that and went to tell Brian and Donald. The rest of the recruits had finally made it to the chow hall. I counted thirteen souls, what was left of the recruits who were really in the program. That discounted Larry, who was missing, and the five S&Ms who had turned out to be part of Paul's secret group at the ranch, and Brian and Donald.

They were still sitting on the porch, side-by-side where I'd left them.

"It's all set," I told them. "You guys don't have anything to worry about when Paul and his guys come back. You just stick close to Les and Sharp. I told them everything."

They looked up at me and smiled. They were holding hands.

"Now why don't you two get in there and get some real food for a change?"

"Maybe later," Donald said. He smiled sweetly at Brian. "We're enjoying what we're doing."

* * *

I was left, suddenly, with nothing to do. Charlie was gone. Rafferty was gone. There was no chance in hell of walking out in the desert by myself and finding Larry. But I stepped off the porch and, shading my eyes, looked toward the eastern horizon. Then I made a complete circle on the bare ground in front of the chow hall, as I had the day I arrived, beginning from the mountains rising away from me in the south, turning counter-clockwise, running my eyes along the bluffs and cliffs to the east, turning north, to the hand and its fingers and fissures of valleys, turning west, looking into the throat of the lion, its canyon walls lit from the sun, showing its narrow passage out of the valley.

Then, my eyes caught on the glint of the sun off the naked cross, making them water at the brightness. I looked down, and my eyes fell on the black coffin.

I suppose it was a futile gesture, maybe even comic to anyone who might see me doing it, but I had a score to settle with that thing. I don't know why it affected me and had gotten under my skin, but it did, that giant sarcophagus, sitting out here in the bright sunlight, absorbing the light. I couldn't let it exist a moment longer.

I ran to it, jumped up on the dais where it sat and, with one violent burst of adrenaline, pushed it off its stand. I watched it fall heavily to the ground and listened with satisfaction as wood splintered and the thing came apart.

* * *

The morning slipped away. The heat rose to such a knife-sharp edge, that everyone stayed indoors. Even there we sweated. Concerned members from the church in Carlsbad began to arrive. They introduced themselves to us, said how sorry they were to hear that one of us was missing. We told them as best we could what had happened.

Some of the recruits gravitated toward the women who came. The women had kind faces. They engaged the boys in conversations. Throughout the chow hall, there was a rising of spirits, of laughter. There were also those who cried at the genuine kindness of these people from the Assembly of God Almighty.

There was quite a crowd, it seemed. To an observer, like me, who had no interest in the ministry, I could have continued to take a cynical view of what I saw happening there. But I didn't. These people from the church, who had welcomed Josh Rafferty and his ministry to set up this ranch, were discovering that the recruits were miserable. Sharp may have done some talking on his own about his feelings that "there is a wrongness, here." I hoped he had. I could imagine him, a black man in a mostly white congregation, speaking his mind occasionally.

I could see, in the faces of the church people, that their intentions in sponsoring Rafferty's ministry had been good. There was love on their faces as they smiled and cried with the recruits, nodding their heads as the boys talked. I still considered their good intention cynically. As Christians often say, "Good intentions are not enough." or "The Road to Hell is paved with good intentions."

In the case of Lion's Mouth Christian Ranch, those good intentions had been ruined by the hell that had been created. It wasn't just because Paul Romaine and his army were able to come in here like wolves among sheep, gorging themselves on their prey. It was because the entire notion that homosexuality is something to be cured, that it is not only a sin, but a sickness, that made this place have a wrongness to it. Jesus says, do not look for the kingdom of heaven over there, or there, but within. The same thing might be said of hell.

If we gay people feel guilty and shamed by our emotional and sexual attraction to members of the same sex, we do not have to worry about *going* to hell after death. We live daily in a hell of our own making. Rafferty had almost admitted to me that the best a homosexual could hope for was to become a celibate, Bible-centered Christian. There was no hope for a gay person to suddenly turn straight, because even as blinded by his hatred of homosexuality as Rafferty is, he knows (whether he'll admit it or not) that homosexuality is not something a person has a choice in. The only choice he has is to give up his sexual, physical life. *Kind of like Charlie did*, I thought, *for fifty years*.

Where was Charlie, anyway? Surely it didn't take all morning to contact the sheriff. If the sheriff was going to provide a helicopter to search the area around the valley, Rafferty and Charlie didn't have to stay at the police station. So where were they?

* * *

Morning gave way to noon. The cooks and other people from the church decided to prepare a meal the recruits wouldn't forget. While they had approved of Rafferty's reducing the portion we were given with each meal, he had fudged his request in his presentation, telling the church elders he was cutting minimum portions from only one meal, while telling the staff at the ranch that the church leaders had agreed with his request to cut larger portions. When the staff and the church people compared information, they were shocked and dismayed.

I ate lunch, today, until I was stuffed and had to turn down the freshly baked apple pies that were set out on a long table in the middle of the chow hall. I was becoming worried about Charlie. I really wanted him to be here when Paul and the others got back. I didn't like the idea of trying to stand up to Paul by myself. If he could turn the tables to his benefit with Charlie and Michael contradicting him, he would surely be able to lie his way out of my own accusations. I wasn't sure at all that Brian and Donald would have the courage to tell the church people their stories.

Dejected, by a little after one o'clock, I sat out on the porch as hot as it was, determined to wait it out. Sweat ran into my eyes, down the back of my neck. The floor of the valley shimmered with heat waves. Again, the tents across the field looked like they were on fire. Where would Larry have gone? Which way? If he had been intent on getting back to Carlsbad, wouldn't he have taken the only known trail, through the throat of the lion? Probably not. Yesterday, we had discounted it, because someone had pointed out that it was a much longer route; heading that way meant going west first, then curving down the mountain road toward the south for about ten miles, then eventually curving back east.

But then, it didn't matter which direction anyone went. On foot, in that purgatory of heat and sand and rock, the elements and the sun would consume any but the most experienced hiker. There were a thousand pitfalls within shouting distance along the outer edges of the valley—cliffs, and bluffs, boxed-in-canyons, and the endlessness, one hill tumbling away after another, until the eye failed. It was an infinity of harshness.

Could anyone believe that Larry—poor, fat Larry, afraid of his own shadow, unable to withstand even the work involved in hoeing a few weeds for an hour or two—could anyone believe it was *that* Larry, who had taken off into that vastness in the middle of the night?

A cold, dead thought settled over me like a shroud. Why had Paul Romaine, of all people, volunteered himself and his cadre to conduct their own search? All of them. Why was it necessary for all six of them to take off in one Jeep? Besides being crowded, they would consume more water. Why hadn't they gotten a good night's sleep, and set out the next morning? And why, for God's sake, had they taken off heading east, beyond the stock pens? Until now, it had not registered as significant. Was it just because Paul was more familiar with the terrain east of the valley?

I shook my head, disgusted with my thoughts. They were turning to paranoia, again. But where was Charlie?

Finally, my question was answered. I turned my attention back to the throat of the Lion's Mouth Canyon and saw in the distance two clouds of dust. In the lead, one of the ranch Jeeps was bouncing up and down over the rough trail. Behind it, causing a lot more dust to boil from the ground was a pickup truck pulling some sort of trailer. I watched the progress of the two vehicles, until I recognized the face of the person in the Jeep. Looking ragged and wind-blown in the open air of the vehicle was Rafferty behind the wheel. He was red-faced and sweating, and looked for all he was worth, like shit. His grim face had the look of a man who had been sentenced to die.

As the pickup truck drew closer and came out of the cloud of dust left by the Jeep, I could only hope it was Charlie. But there were two people in the cab. I'd had enough waiting. As the vehicles drew near, I got up from the porch and jogged toward them, past the corner of the chow hall, past the overturned coffin, past the chapel, and stood on the side of the trail, waiting for the vehicles to arrive.

The Jeep zipped past, puffing my hair and tossing fine, powdered dirt into my face. The pickup pulled to a halt beside me, and I found myself staring into the open passenger-side window.

"Michael!"

"Kelly!" Michael said, getting out and throwing his arms around me. "We've had a hell of a morning trying to get things set."

Damn, Michael looked good. Two weeks or so had done a lot to the regrowth of his hair. The work here at the ranch...the move to Carlsbad from Houston...Something had reshaped him, the way he carried himself; something had made his arms feel different around me. I stepped back from him after we hugged to get a better look at him.

He smiled as my eyes made a quick survey of him, but he didn't say anything.

Charlie got out of the pickup and came around to us. "We had one long talk with Josh this morning, Kelly. That old fart is stubborn, blind, deaf, and doesn't want anything to jeopardize this ministry."

"Who cares," I said. "We've had one long morning with a lot of the people from the church, and there isn't much sympathy with this ministry, I can tell you that."

Charlie just laughed. "Then we had to track down the sheriff and had to convince him that we have a missing person out here. He kept trying to tell us that officially a person is not considered missing until forty-eight hours has passed; then they'll call in search and rescue. We told him if he waited that long the kid might die of exposure. It took him another damned hour, though, to get permission to use a helicopter from the National Guard. Unfortunately, it won't be until tomorrow before they can free one up, so I brought us some horses. Do you know how to ride?"

"Do they bite?" I asked, looking back doubtfully at the horse trailer at the three dark beasts inside.

Michael laughed and hugged me, again. I got the same thrill of feeling as before—something in Michael was changed. He was more present, physical...something, and I liked it. But his hug was quick.

Recovering, I glanced at Charlie, then back at Michael. "What are you doing here?" I said. "It's great to see you, but—"

"When I found out that Larry had run off, I thought if I could possibly help find him, I would," Michael said. "I feel so sorry for him, Kelly. That's all I can say. Besides, I'm quite a rider, and you'll need me along to keep you from falling on your ass into a cactus!"

"But what did Rafferty think of you coming along?" I asked, looking from Michael to Charlie.

"Thought you'd never ask, Charlie said. "It seems that I had me a visit with Drigger this morning, real polite, I was. But he agreed to change his story. Talked to Josh on his own. I guess you could say his conscience gave him a black eye."

"Charlie! You didn't?" I said, grinning.

He just winked. "At least now Josh knows what really happened to Michael. Josh said as soon as Paul and the rest of them come back, he's going to tend to a few things." Charlie looked around. There was a knot of people around Rafferty's Jeep—mostly staff and church people. Most of the recruits were gathered on the porch. "Guess nobody's heard nothing about Larry, huh?"

"Nope, and Paul and his goons aren't back yet," I said. "So as soon as you feel like it, we probably ought to get started."

"Fine," Charlie said. "I don't know where we should begin. Look at all that..." he said, gesturing vaguely off toward the north, then east.

"I know where to start," I said, remembering my thoughts, earlier. I shivered, although it was at least a hundred degrees out. "Charlie, what if Larry isn't missing at all? What if someone was well aware of his pattern of getting up in the middle of the night, and that same someone says to Larry that they'd take him out of the valley, in the

Jeep? Remember yesterday, when Paul took his entire group of goons out in the Jeep after we'd all returned empty handed?"

"Yes. I thought is was strange. But Larry was missing that morning. Looks to me like Paul was just trying to help."

"Well, what if the night before, Paul catches Larry outside the tent and *takes* him off the ranch. What if he tells Larry he's helping him get away. Larry wouldn't scream; he wouldn't make a sound. He would go willingly, follow Paul anywhere. They could have easily walked to the Jeeps in the compound and taken off without any of us hearing a thing."

"But why, Kelly. It doesn't make sense."

"Who *knows*, Charlie? Why did he rape the recruits? What sense is that? Why didn't he get his kicks in some gay bath somewhere? Why take such stupid chances of getting caught in a program like this? Why did he smear pig's blood all over our tent? Let's just say I'm paranoid. I can't stand to think what Paul would have in mind."

Charlie gazed out over the ranch, squinting into the blast of hot summer afternoon. He peered eastward. "You say they took off in that direction?"

"Right."

"Then we should do the same. See if we can't pick up and follow the Jeep tracks."

* * *

Charlie had outfitted the horses with saddles, canteens, binoculars, and rifles. In addition, Michael was carrying along a first aid kit, and Charlie was packing what looked like tent poles and a rolled up canvas tent. "Are we gong to camp out over night?" I asked in reference to it.

Charlie shook his head. "It's what my brother Dave and I use to pack out deer, when we go hunting. I thought if we needed to, and Larry was maybe injured…" he trailed off.

I nodded, and got awkwardly onto the back of my horse, thinking—*or dead*—but shook off such a thought. Who knew what we would find?

It was near two o'clock when we took off from the chow hall. Les Hunter came out carrying paper bags. "Made you some roast beef sandwiches, Charlie, for later. Thought you could use them." He handed them up to Charlie on the horse, and with a slap of the reins, Charlie took off.

Michael made a snicking sound and kicked his horse. It took off behind Charlie. I tried the sound in my mouth and kicked my horse; it lurched to a reluctant walk and, soon, I was falling behind. "Hey, Michael!" I yelled, "How do you get this thing to go?"

Michael turned around in the saddle and grinned. "You'll catch on. Just try different things."

Try different things. I leaned forward as far as I dared and spoke into the horse's ear. "C'mon giddy-yap, please." The horse moved at a funereal pace. From where I sat, I felt like I was going to topple off sideways and hoped the saddle was cinched tight. The horse's gait was uneven, awkward, and I had a new respect for riders who made it look as if they and the horse were one, sailing over hurdles, riding up and down embankments. Here I was traveling over the flat ground of the ranch, as if I were riding two or three separate horses, all trying to move off in different directions. My legs felt like they'd been split to my navel, and my ass was bouncing up and down with every step.

After awhile, I was able to settle into a respectable semblance of riding, rather than wrestling to stay on. The horse picked up his pace only after the other two horses were almost out of sight at the hill, before the stock pens.

When I arrived, Charlie and Michael were already maneuvering their horses around the pens and were disappearing into the steep canyon, where Paul had taken Michael.

"Gives me the creeps to come back here," Michael was saying as he disappeared completely into the wall of rock.

A few minutes later, after completely losing sight of Michael and Charlie, I entered the boxed-in area where Paul had done his dirty work and, there, Charlie was stopped, leaning expertly to one side of his horse. "Looks like they made a campfire here, the other night. Why do you suppose they got this far then stopped?"

Michael and I pulled up on our horses. Sure enough, someone had made a campfire. There were Jeep tracks and footprints over footprints, all around the area. The campfire had been meticulously built. Whoever had made it, had taken the time to bring large rocks and make a fire pit. There were unburned chunks of mesquite, white ash, the usual detritus of a fire. But Charlie got off his horse and poked around in the ashes with a stick, anyway.

"You looking for something?"

He shook his head. "Nah. But from the looks of it, they were here quite awhile. They must've fed the fire a lot of—"

He stopped talking so suddenly I looked around, thinking he'd heard something.

"What is it?" Michael asked, dismounting as well. He stood by Charlie as he began pushing the ashes around, clearing them off the middle of the pile.

A moment later, he knelt down and picked up a blackened object. It was so burnt, I couldn't tell what it was, until Charlie took out his pocket knife and began whittling away some of the black. "Unless I'm mistaken, guys, this here's the sole of a sneaker." He held it out. "That what you two make it out to be?"

I practically fell off the horse, trying to dismount, caught my foot in the stirrup and did a *Barney Fife, Deputy of Mayberry* trying to avoid falling on my ass. Neither Michael nor Charlie laughed, for which I was grateful, as I tried to recover from my clumsiness and join them.

Michael gasped and put one hand to his mouth. He stared at the charred object Charlie held out. "It is!" he said. "Charlie, I bet that's Larry's!"

Charlie banged the sole on a rock and then put it into a saddlebag. "I'd say we've got some serious questions to ask somebody. Y'all ready?"

* * *

I struggled back onto my horse with the agility of a cadaver, long after rigor mortis has set in. We moved off slowly in what appeared to be a completely boxed-in canyon, but as we neared the far eastern side, we came upon an almost imperceptible passage just barely large enough for a Jeep to travel through. Rock slides from the cliffs on either side had almost closed off the path that, years before, must have been larger. We came through that bottleneck, then into another boxed-in canyon, except for another narrow passage. We worked our way through several such canyons. The floor of each was almost solid rock, but every once in awhile, we saw Jeep tracks, and knew we were on the right path.

Above us, the cliffs seemed to hover, waiting to fall onto us. The sky was a pale blue in the heat of the afternoon. The wind moaned over the ledges. Vultures passed to and fro over us, lifted into the sky on shafts of hot air. In the canyons, it was gloomy, cast in early shadow. Occasionally, the passage widened and we came out on what appeared to be level ground. There, we had to move off in separate directions until one of us picked up the slightest indication of Jeep tracks on the almost solid rock ground. Then we moved into other canyons. Some cliffs were only twenty feet high, others fifty, and still others became mammoth, at least eleven hundred feet above us.

We scanned the ridges overhead for movement, using our binoculars. But there was nothing but the silent majesty of the rocky cliffs, the moaning of the wind, the *scree!* of the vultures.

We talked little, each of us absorbed in our own thoughts.

"Why do you suppose they burned the shoe?" Michael asked.

Neither Charlie nor I had an answer—or we didn't want to give voice to the only answer that made any sense: *They were burning the evidence.*

We had been on horseback for over an hour since leaving the camp fire, when we rode out of a canyon and onto higher ground. In every direction we looked, the lay of the land was the same as that we had just come out of, a moonscape of forbidding nothingness.

With one exception.

Against the side of a sandstone cliff was a shack, built out of rock. Its roof was beginning to sag, but it was still intact. "What's that, Charlie?" Michael asked, pointing toward it.

Charlie rode past me and cantered over to the shack. "They say prospectors used to work this area in the late eighteen hundreds looking for gold," he said. He dismounted and tied his horse to a stump of Juniper coming out of the sandstone. "Wouldn't hurt to take a look," he said. "If the others passed through here, they would've done the same…reckon?"

I thought we'd find Larry in the shack, or evidence he'd been kept there, but when Michael and I dismounted and had a look inside, we found nothing. It was a one-room building with a dirt floor and not a sign that anyone had been inside. No footprints, except our own. This lack of other footprints was suspicious, because it indicated that Paul knew Larry wouldn't be in there.

We were stumped as we mounted our horses again and picked up the trail of Jeep tracks. We were about to continue our pursuit of Paul and his cadre when, on the clear air, came the sound of a straining engine coming our way from the south. We looked in that direction and saw a curtain of dust rising.

"Tell you what," Charlie said, "Let's hide and get a look as they pass by. Maybe get an idea what's keeping those yahoos out here all damned day."

We agreed. I thought it was odd that the only trail we had been following was that of Paul's Jeep when we had found no evidence of Larry's trek this way (if he had left the valley under his own steam). If we had found Paul and the others, I was beginning to doubt that Larry would be with them. I kept wondering about the shoe in the campfire. I felt uneasy from the base of my skull to the base of my spine. Something was not right about our assumptions.

We barely had time to get behind the cliff to the west of the miner's shack, when the Jeep came into the area. From our location, we could see the occupants, but as long as they didn't look to their left, and into the shadows, they wouldn't see us.

They passed within twenty feet of us and I could see Paul's army was tired, sunburned, and grimly determined to get back to the ranch. Their heads lolled in unison over the ruts. Larry was not with them. I was both disappointed and relieved.

But my relief was short lived. Charlie had ridden ahead of the shack a little ways toward the north, then turned south, I guess, intent on seeing where Paul and his group had come from. By the time we caught up to him, he had dismounted and was holding something in his hand.

"Anybody recognize this?" he said, and held out a thing that chipped sunlight.

I dismounted reluctantly and took the thing. "It's Paul's swastika name tag!" I said, holding it in my hand. It felt dirty to the touch and I handed it back. "So, he must've lost it as they came through here. But that could have been on their way out here or back, looking for Larry."

"No," Michael said. He was still mounted on his horse about ten feet away from us. "The Jeep went through here," he said, pointing to the ground at his horse's feet, "not over there where you guys are. Paul was out of the Jeep for some reason."

The miner's shack was behind us. We had looked in it, but not around it. From where we were standing, now, when we looked back at the shack, just barely visible on its left side was a black slice out of the sandstone—a fissure in the side of the cliff, just large enough to walk through. The ground around the miner's shack was all weeds and, in bare places, hardpan dirt. A closer examination of the area around the shack revealed traces of footprints.

"They may have just been examining the place like we're doing," Michael said. He was now off his horse and joined Charlie and me outside the entrance to the fissure.

"Maybe," Charlie said, then stepped into the blackness. From his breast pocket he pulled out a lighter and flicked it. Like a huge beast hovering over us, his shadow danced on the walls of the cave. He turned with the lighter holding it up high. Above us, there was a crack in the ceiling, where water trickled down and, clinging to the walls, were bats. There was the slight odor of bat dung, but not nearly as strong as when one enters the Carlsbad Caverns in these same mountains.

"Ugh!" Michael said, holding his nose and coming reluctantly into the cave. "It looks empty."

It was, and there was no sign anyone had been in here. The cave was a dead end, too. Charlie lowered the lighter and was about to flick the lid over the wick, when just the slightest gleam of metal caught my eye. "Wait! Shine your lighter over there, lower," I pointed to the left, just inside the entrance.

"Aw hell," Charlie said. "I'll bet these are Larry's clothes."

Charlie carried the tightly wrapped bundle out into the sunlight and unwound the Levi's. A bloody T-shirt fell onto the ground.

The Levi's were also black with blood.

Michael began to cry. He took the clothing, carefully rolling it back up, as he made his way solemnly to his horse, and placed the clothing in his saddle bag. He came back to us wiping his eyes. "But where's Larry?"

* * *

The odd thing was, there was no blood at all around the area. We climbed the hill behind the miner's shack. Nothing. We looked in the miner's shack again, dusting the dirt around the entrance. There was not so much as a drop of blood anywhere, even though Larry's clothes were soaked.

Charlie took out Paul's name tag and tapped it in his palm. "We do know that Paul got out of the Jeep. Because of this name tag. And we can just bet he was present when the clothes were hidden inside the cave. Right? But we can't prove it. He may even be the one who put the clothes there, but we can't prove that, either. We can only say we found his name tag at the same site where we found Larry's clothing."

"And without a body there's no crime, right?" I asked.

"Kelly! Don't say 'body'. We don't know Larry's dead!"

"But there's blood on his clothes," I said.

"And they were hidden," Charlie added.

A very hot wind rushed through the canyons, rustling the grass and blasting our faces. The screech of a rodent, the clack of an insect sounded, then a dead silence descended. We looked for Jeep tracks or footprints, but found no more. We got back on our horses and, gauging the sun, figured we could spend another half-hour before we had to head back.

In all that stretch of time, we followed the Jeep tracks to the south, where Paul had just come from, keeping our eyes open for any sign, our ears perked up for the slightest human cry. We were about to turn back, when the *scree!* of a buzzard circling overhead came to us. Then we saw other buzzards looping in the air, some descending, rising back into the sky with carrion in their talons.

We turned in unison, toward the column of buzzards, circling, descending and, when we topped a hill, there at the bottom of a ravine was a lump of flesh, the form of a body, gashed open, blood glistening on entrails, and the stench of the rot hit us in the face.

"The other milk cow," I said. We all breathed a sigh of relief.

* * *

The afternoon was still hot when the sun began to set. We were approaching the stock pens, empty-handed, except for Larry's bloody clothing, Paul's name tag, and a burnt object that was probably one of Larry's shoes. None of us felt like talking, so dejected were we, feeling...what? Relieved we had not found Larry's body, which meant there was reason to hope? Yet feeling as if we'd failed, too.

I wanted to scream, thinking that Paul Romaine and his five stinking soldiers had committed murder, yet had the gall to go back to the ranch. But there was no way to prove that a murder had been committed. For all we knew the blood on the clothing could have come from an animal. Paul and his five freaks could have played a game of blood-splashing on Larry, from a pig or even from the rotting cow back in the ravine, and still have Larry hog-tied somewhere, naked, but very much alive.

We passed the wreckage of the cow shed. Very little reconstruction work had been done to return it to its previous state before the storm. It spoke of the recent nose dive in the program, that even the basic work around the ranch was not being taken care of. Thinking of that, I wondered aloud if the remaining milk cow had even been milked that day.

"Kelly, how can you even think of such a thing when, for all we know..." Michael trailed off, didn't finish.

"I can, Michael, because if she hasn't been milked, we need to at least let the calves in there with her, or her udder might burst. We can't forget our responsibility to any animal we keep domesticated."

"Michael laughed in spite of his heavy heart. "Get *her*, Charlie!"

Charlie smiled in response, but he hadn't yet spoken.

We rode past the pig pens. Earlier I hadn't even glanced in their direction. But I did now, remembering that Larry's fall had begun right here, with Alton Drigger only a few weeks ago. And now, Larry was probably dead. It didn't seem possible.

The pigs were rooting at something, pushing each other out of the way with their tight hog bodies, their snouts close to the ground, their grunts almost given voice, like lazy fat men. They were smacking busily, and biting into the slimy mud for more of what it was. *A garish white hand flopped out into view making me almost puke. My God! They dumped his body into the pig pen.*

I gagged trying to call to Charlie and Michael, who were riding on ahead. I couldn't stop staring at the pigs, rooting in the muck. One hog clenched hair and pulled. Larry's face appeared, or the lump of it appeared until the hog bit into his cheek and red blood—

I leaned over and vomited, and spurred my horse, galloping wildly, spittle flying from my mouth, ramming into Charlie's horse. "He's in the hog pen! The hog pen!" I screamed, then fell roughly, landing on my shoulder.

* * *

When I came to, Michael was leaning over me. In my dazed state, I just wanted to kiss him, and was reaching for him when I realized we were still near the stock pens. "How long have I been out?"

"Long enough," Michael said. "Charlie has gone to get help to get Larry out of the pig pen."

* * *

I've had a shower. I'm sitting in the chow hall. It's like an all-night restaurant. People are everywhere. Recruits, staff, Josh, the preacher from the church in Carlsbad, church members, reporters, the police. None of the so-called "residents" of the ranch are allowed to leave. That's me and Brian, and Donald, and Jerry, and the other recruits who came in on the same bus I did exactly forty-six days ago. Michael and Charlie have gone back to Carlsbad. In the morning, Michael will tell the people at the furniture factory that he is needed out here to give his statements to the police. They have set up temporary headquarters in the activities building. I guess until they gather what passes as evidence for them, they prefer to be here. That's all right.

Paul and his five soldiers are in jail, tonight, in Carlsbad, for suspicion of murder.

K. O'K.

XV

Barbed Wire for a Crown

Lion's Mouth Christian Ranch
Thursday, July 23

The Chow hall, around midnight
Charlie and I rode out to the miner's shack, again, earlier this time, then beyond, still looking for evidence of what happened to Larry. We came back empty-handed, again. I began to think that Paul (if he did take Larry from the tent in the dead of night) had another hiding place where he kept Larry, while the search for him was going on.

How did Larry die? When did he die, and who killed him? These questions frustrated the police and were on all of our minds. These same questions were asked of Paul and the others. The little Nazis have kept their traps shut, even though, at this writing, the police have a lot more information than they did have. I'll explain later in this entry, but I want to get the day's events down in order.

Michael was here earlier in the day, but as soon as he had another session with Rafferty and retold that blind man what he'd already told him, Michael talked to the police. He told Charlie and me that the police are trying to get Donald and Brian to press charges of rape against Paul and the others. If we can't get Paul on murder, yet, we can at least put him away for rape. I hope. When it comes to homosexual rape in a small town like Carlsbad, New Mexico, I doubt whether there's much that will be done to the rapists.

Yes, Paul, I have a basic anger problem.

Of Larry's death, they've been able to determine the cause, even though there was so little of his body left. They say he bled to death. How do they know that? Well, part of it has to do with what Charlie and I found earlier today. I'll get to that. But the forensic specialists have also verified that he bled to death. They have established that Larry's body must've been dumped in the pig pen some time on the 20th, probably before dawn. I wondered how, in our search, we could have missed finding him at the stock pens, but it's like many things that are lost. One doesn't think of looking close by. In Larry's case, we all assumed he was trying to get away from the ranch, so we tried to find his trail away from the valley.

Part of their reasoning in placing the time of Larry's death on the 20th, they say, is because by the time we found his body on the 22nd, late in the afternoon, there just wasn't that much left. The hogs had had plenty of time to make a meal of him.

My theory is that Paul did abduct Larry the evening of the 19th. That night is when Larry met his death, too. Then, when Paul was through with him, he dumped the body into the pig pen. The next morning, he only pretended to be surprised that Larry was not in his cot. All our searching, therefore, was in vain, and Paul allowed it as a smoke screen—even in volunteering his group to conduct a search. They must've taken that opportunity to dispose of Larry's clothes, burn his shoes, and cover up the crime scene, to ensure against future discovery.

* * *

Rafferty stays away from the hustle and bustle of the chow hall, where everyone congregates. He has meetings off and on with the staff and with the church members, I suspect, to feel them out about continuing the ministry once the investigation about Larry is over. I don't believe I've ever seen a more stubborn individual at hanging on to a dead, lifeless, utterly lost cause.

From what Charlie and I have learned, the church in Carlsbad is very reluctant to have the program continue here—especially since this incident.

Charlie had said that some people in the church were trying to find a way to continue the program, since Rafferty did contribute a lot of money and paid for so much repair and construction at the ranch, which the church owns. But he also said that people like Les Hunter and Sharp Jones are calling Rafferty's money, "blood money."

Charlie and I met about this just after lunch, on our way to the stock pens. We had decided to take a hand with the livestock, since no one else seemed concerned about them.

It was hot out there. And creepy. There were flies everywhere; and the stench of manure, pig shit, and muck still made me want to puke, as I remembered seeing Larry's body buried in it. I got a very unpleasant feeling, climbing into the pen with the pigs to dump the filthy water from their water trough. Their grunts and their beady eyes watching me seemed like a threat. I tried to tell myself that they are carnivores, just like I am, that they do not have a conscience, or need one. A meal to them is still a meal, but it gave me the willies, anyway.

Charlie watched me while he ran the hose over the fence and began filling the water trough. He was grinning. "You're as white as a sheet," he said.

"I can't stop thinking about what these hogs did to Larry."

"Well, you better, because they can smell your fear."

He laughed loudly as I fairly leaped out of the pen. Then he put his arm around my shoulders as we made our way to the cows.

"Charlie? What are you going to do if the program ends?"

He squeezed my shoulders then dropped his hands. How can I describe how it felt to witness the blossoming of a gay identity in that man, or how charged his touch was? I let the moment pass, rather than exploring it, and I don't know what Charlie was feeling, either. But he separated himself a little from me.

"I've thought about that, Kelly," he said, picking up my question. "I have you to thank for getting me to take a look at things. My life. I can't believe I've lived so long and don't know the love of another human being. Guess I'll take a vacation from the farm. My brother can run things for awhile."

"You mean you're going to look for romance?" I teased.

He took me seriously. "Maybe. Probably. Only, I don't know where to look."

"Will it be with another man, or do you think it's a sin?"

Charlie chuckled, but there was an undertone of bitterness in it. "I think it's a sin to have wasted that part of my life. Of course it will be with a man."

"But how do you know you're homosexual?"

He looked at me as if I'd said something in Chinese. "That's a dumb question, Kelly. Because I know. I've always known. And because of that one night you gave me—that was the capper. If I had any doubts about it, I couldn't after that."

I felt embarrassed about that one night, when I'd had sex with him—not that I didn't enjoy it. I didn't want him to think it meant more for me than it did, and I was about to try putting my feelings into words when he slugged my arm.

"Besides…" he said, grinning. "How did you know before you had your first sexual experience? Did you have sex with a man, and then think you were gay, because you liked it?"

"You got me there," I said. "You're right. My own feelings for other guys came long before I lost my virginity. By the time I had the sex, I already knew I was gay."

"Exactly," Charlie said.

We fed the cows, then tried to do a little work on the cow shed. The runoff from the rain had made it collapse when it washed out the ground around one of the corner poles. It was dug into the ground only about two feet. The ground was sandy and had washed away like sugar melting in water. The other three poles had been weakened in the ground, but did not give way when the corner pole fell. The structure sagged to one side, causing the corner pole that washed out to snap in two.

"Think I'll run up to the building site and grab a couple of two-by-fours," Charlie said, when we saw we couldn't make any repairs with the material at hand. Then he left me.

I walked around the area. The cow shed is south of the pig pens. All the stock pens are lined up north to south. Between them and the cliffs is a narrow alley about six feet wide. Because of the way the cow shed collapsed to one side, the area between the pens and the cliffs was temporarily widened. The way the pole fell against one of the fence poles, kept it from falling all the way to the ground. Part of that pole fell crossways on the fence pole and, as I looked at it, I was reminded of a Christian cross.

I took a closer look at the cross, trying to figure out a way for us to push the shed upward with the least amount of effort. To do so, I had to step amid the manure and piles of hay that had blown into the area. That's when I saw what had to be blood, soaked into the manure. With the toe of my shoe, I dug a little deeper, and saw that a lot of blood had soaked into the manure. Then I took a closer look at the pole, lying crossways on the fence post. Baling wire had been wrapped around the left- and right-hand ends.

What clicked in my mind at that instant was not only the source of Larry's death, but the sick mind that dreamed it up. Larry had been crucified, right here, and somewhere on his body—probably the carotid artery—he had been stabbed. That explained how the blood got on his

T-shirt. Cutting the carotid artery would account for the massive amount of blood that ran down the T-shirt and soaked his Levi's.

By the time Charlie got back, I was sure I had the crime figured out. Paul must have taken Larry from the tents when he stepped outside to do his nightly walk. I could imagine him coming up to Larry, at first startling him, then soothing him. "I've noticed you're terribly unhappy, here, Brother Larry," I could imagine Paul saying, and Larry crying in return, "I don't belong here! I want to leave! My parents sent me, but I don't belong!" And so the conversation might have gone. Then Paul devising a plan, inviting Larry to go into hiding. "Just for tonight," he might have said. "We'll keep you at the stock pens, okay?"

Paul must have told the others in his cadre that they were due a reward, or some hellish thing, for their loyalty. Or maybe all of them were feeling long overdue for some of their torture play. Who knows what their motives were?

I tried out my theories on Charlie, and he kept nodding as I talked. "That all sounds reasonable," he said.

* * *

The police accompanied Charlie and me out to the stock pens. They did their thing with evidence bags, taking samples of the blood-soaked manure. One of them said, "This could also be calf's blood. Wasn't one of them killed when the shed collapsed?"

While that was true, Charlie pointed out that the calf was found farther below the shed, not in the corner of it. The police did find more blood in the area where the calf was found dead. They said they would do a comparison.

I guess the whole thing is now in the hands of the police. There can be no relief or satisfaction in knowing Larry died a horrible death, but it's better than not knowing.

The thing that frightens me, or repulses me, is the devious way Paul carried out his plan. He almost got away with it. If he hadn't stripped Larry's body before dumping it in the pig pens, the clothing would have turned up. Maybe the bones would have too, but by getting rid of the clothing, he did ensure that the body would be fairly eaten, and the hogs' rooting would have buried the bones.

* * *

July 23

Larry's parents arrived at the ranch today. Such ordinary people, with that same look as William's parents, the one time I ever met them. How can I describe that "look" of the Texas or Oklahoma religious fundamentalist? A couple out of the 1950s, when everything was in black and white, and the wives were housewives and the husbands were the head of the household. Except Larry's mother and father looked stricken and ashamed, whether it was for sending their child to this place where he was killed, or for having to be here at all; shamed by the fact that everyone here knew that their son was one of the damned. I hated them and their tormented looks of grief and shame all commingled, judging everything they saw, no doubt as I was judging them for being parents like William's. What would *they* tell their fellow church members back home? How much of a scandal did it arouse there in Ft. Worth, Texas? They were appalled at the living conditions, but I wonder if they had the conscience to be appalled at themselves. They were herded here and there, and left about a half-hour after arriving. Rafferty tried to talk with them, but they waved him away.

From Les Hunter, I learned that the parents plan to sue the ministry. While I feel sorry for Larry's parents in losing their son, I do not share in the sympathy heaped on them by the church people.

Larry must have begged not to be sent here! How cruel, then, that he suffered so much humiliation; then was murdered in so foul a way—crucified (if that's how he was killed). Charlie had said my earlier theories about Larry's abduction didn't make sense. Again, neither does this, nor Paul's motives for doing it.

Around noon, today, the rest of my speculation was finally brought to an end. We were all assembled in the chapel. The recruits were asked to sit near the front; then behind us, the staff of the ranch, then the church people from Carlsbad. At the podium was Rafferty and the preacher from the Assembly of God Almighty Church. The preacher spoke first.

"Today ends what we started a little over a year ago, when the Rev. Rafferty came to us, by our request, to tell us more of his ministry. We had read of his plans to establish a retreat for homosexual men who desired to be delivered from their sin. We had this plot of land in these mountains and offered to lease it to the ministry. In addition, the Rev. Rafferty offered to pay so many staff to help with the operations—such as farming, caring for livestock, and such.

"There was much to pray about, much work to do before the first of you young men could come. We were buoyed by the thought that we could perform an outreach to you, by helping to establish this retreat. Our role, once the program was underway, would be minimal, as we did not consider ourselves expert in this field of ministry. We would make our congregation open to you throughout the program, and in the end our reward would be knowing your feet had been set upon the path to salvation. That's all we wanted for you.

"Unfortunately, we did not examine the program in enough detail to realize that certain aspects were cruel."

When the preacher said this, Rafferty twisted uneasily in his chair. I looked from him to Brian and Donald, who were sitting side-by-side. Brian bowed his head, no doubt thinking of the cruelty he'd been subjected to.

"We did not realize," the preacher continued, "that you would be subjected to unthinkable tortures, hard, uncompromising labor, without adequate rest..." He paused and slipped a page from a sheaf of papers on the podium in front of him. He held the page out to us in a self-conscious gesture, looking at it himself, as if it had just been handed to him.

"I have a whole list of the things we think were either bad judgment on the part of the planners and participants in this ministry, or despicable acts of inhumanity. But why enumerate them to you, who have suffered them? You poor children of God.

"I am here, today, not only to extend to you our heartfelt apologies for those aspects of the ministry that no doubt did you harm, but to tell you that the two young men who were entombed together in the coffin were housed by one of us for a week or more, before we sent them back where they came from. It did take time for them to recover from the ordeal of their entombment; it was an act so heinous as to outrage even the most enthusiastic supporters of this ministry in our congregation.

"Many of us still think the basic concept of this ministry is sound. Some of our number would like to continue the program; others object. After weighing the options, we have decided that we are withdrawing our support. Reaching this decision has been extremely difficult. There was much praying and soul searching.

"We realize that some of you will want to continue trying to overcome your sin. That is why we are allowing the Rev. Rafferty to speak to you. We thank you."

When Rafferty rose to speak, I studied the movements of the recruits. Some of them fidgeted, some cried, others held their heads high as they listened. Others bowed their heads.

Rafferty spewed the same junk he'd been spewing, asking us to weigh the value of a Christian-centered life over a life spent on the edge of the abyss.

"In conclusion," he said, "our ministry will continue, if God so wills it. For now, we will return the program to Albuquerque, where it began. Perhaps we tried to expand too soon, too fast, and the Lord was not ready for us to do so in this most difficult of ministries. Thank you."

* * *

That's the way things stack up as of this writing. The ministry at Lion's Mouth Christian Ranch is finished. But the ministry to "cure" homosexuals is not. I wonder if Rafferty, himself, has had his fill of this dead valley in the middle of nothingness. Perhaps Rafferty would have stayed on if the church in Carlsbad hadn't withdrawn its support. Maybe, if I can write up a good enough report about what went on here, other churches will decline Rafferty's offer when it comes. Who knows?

We'll be packing up and leaving tomorrow. I'll be riding to Carlsbad with Charlie, although I would also like to make my exit the same way I came—on the bus with the rest of the guys. That way, I could get some sense of how they feel as they leave this hell behind.

Maybe later, I'll gain enough perspective about my experiences, here, to know exactly what it was that happened to me and to the rest of us. I think I finally know what happened to William. It seems like a lifetime ago that he committed suicide. Over what?

It may be I cannot put into words how places like this generate such psychological force over a person. I know my own thoughts have been limited to this small valley for several weeks. I have not wondered about people elsewhere, except in cursory moments, because of the intensity of my attention on this place.

Who was the villain here? Was it Paul, a homosexual who hated himself and, by extension, who wanted to punish others because of that self-loathing? Was it Rafferty and all programs like this, or just this one? Is it the fundamentalist Christian impulse, itself, to want to stop homosexual behavior?

Or is it our own weakness as human beings that is the true villain, here? Have we been successfully cowed so that we hate ourselves? Do we gay people live lives on the edge of society because we have been banished there—or do we ultimately banish ourselves because we don't feel that we belong in ordinary society?

Does Rafferty's eighteen-steps really add up to a cure for homosexuality? Or, is the program just successful in producing unbearable guilt in those like my William? Had he chosen to live, would William have ever been free of the guilt enough to enjoy the basic pleasures of a life that included sex—with men or women? Who knows what damage was done to each of us because of this experience? What strengths of character were debilitated or destroyed?

For Larry, this program, this place meant death. I cannot imagine his fear at the last moment of his life when Paul and his goons strapped him to that cross, running baling wire around his wrists. I cannot imagine how he felt as he lost all hope in those last few moments. For Paul Romaine, I hope there is the God of the Bible and that the fundamentalists are correct in their interpretation of that God as being angry and spiteful, and that Paul will spend eternity in hell, where there is literally fire and brimstone and Satan, who takes delight in the suffering of the lost souls such as Paul.

There has been no tidy end, as in those hour-long cop shows, where the killer is caught and brought to justice in the last ten minutes of the program. Instead, the end is getting messier by the day. Thank goodness the people who have been doing the cooking continue to do so. They've thrown the budget out the window, since there are so many people at the ranch, including us, the staff, the police, and various church members, who are coming to show concern. It's ten miles to the nearest farm, another thirty miles to Carlsbad, and so the people eat here. Some have brought sleeping bags and have turned the activity center into a hotel.

The recruits are directionless. With the program suspended and people more or less not paying attention to them, they go about their own activities. Brian and Donald made no pretense or excuses today among the recruits that they're falling in love. It bothers some (those who will probably stay with the program if it gets back on track). With Paul and his five goons gone from the ranch, there are only nine old recruits in the other tent. With Leo, Sidney, Michael, and Larry gone, there are only seven recruits in ours.

Of the old recruits, those I used to call the S&Ms, I only have a passing acquaintance with Jerry and a guy named Alex, with whom Michael was occasionally paired. I see the other guys, know their names, but I haven't taken time to start conversations with them.

I just go about my own business, here, which is to listen in on as many conversations as I can among the church people, Rafferty's staff, and the police.

I'll write more once I get off the ranch. But for tonight, I think I'll go back to the tent, lay back, and close my eyes and listen to the whispers among the others.

Except this:

Donald and Brian left this afternoon. Charlie gave them a ride after our last meeting in the chapel. I'm sure Charlie told them about himself on the way to Carlsbad. This afternoon when I saw him off, he said, "I'm going to tell my brother who I am, Kelly. I can't live the rest of my life in a lie, especially to him." I guess once he tells the people who matter to him that he is gay, it will be easier to tell others. Anyway, Charlie seemed delighted to have such young and beautiful charges in tow this afternoon. He was kind of like a father-figure to them, as he loaded their baggage in the Jeep. He was beaming as he waved good-bye to me.

K. O'K.

XVI

Look Who's Laughing Now

The Hays Farm Friday, July 24, 1998
Carlsbad, New Mexico

July 23/24

After I'd finished writing last night and sometime after I'd fallen asleep on my cot for the last night at LMCR, yet again, someone woke me up—this time by shaking my shoulder, not sucking my dick.

With Paul Romaine gone, I didn't care if the rest of the tent woke up, so I sat up and said in a normal voice, "Who is it?"

"Uh—Alex."

Aside from knowing who Alex was as one of those recruits I called S&Ms, one of the people whom Michael was paired with occasionally, I couldn't for the life of me figure out why he would have to talk with me so urgently as to wake me up in the middle of the night.

"Well, Uh—Alex, what do you want?"

"I—uh—have to talk to you."

"Can't it wait until morning?"

There was no answer. Then I heard sniffling, so I assumed the guy was crying.

I'm a sucker for men who cry, so I got up, slipped into my sneakers, and accompanied Alex outside. He was fully dressed. I was wearing my briefs. We could see each other plainly under the moon that had risen sometime after midnight. Sure enough, his face, lit by the moonlight, was streaked with tears.

"What is it, Alex?"

Alex wiped the tears from his face with the heel of his hand. "Some of the guys are saying you can be trusted. Can you? They say you never were here for the program. Is that true?"

"Yes…and yes."

"They say you're the one who found Larry's body."

"I did, but it was dumb unluck."

"And they say that, from the start, you hated Paul."

"Well, not right from the start, but that's essentially correct. I didn't like the way he looked, talked, or acted."

"And it's not true about Michael, is it? He didn't try to—ah—accost Paul that day, did he?"

"No, Alex, it isn't. He didn't. I never told anyone, but I saw the whole thing. Paul, Eugene Baker, Alton Drigger, and some of their close buddies abducted Michael and took him behind the stock pens among the cliffs. I followed them along the ridges and could see the whole thing. They stripped Michael down, and *Paul* tried to rape *him*. He was the ring leader, incidentally, and not the victim he made himself out to be that night I was in the hot seat, remember?"

Alex nodded.

"Anyway, Charlie Hays caught Paul and the others before they could do anything to Michael. And that's the truth. That's how it happened. Now, why are you asking me all these questions?"

"Sorry," Alex said, "I just wanted to be sure about a few things before I told you. Remember the day Larry turned up missing?"

"Yeah."

"Well, the night before, Paul was outside when Larry was. We knew Paul liked to stay outside the tents a lot. He used to say it was instructive. He said that those who have something to hide can't sleep. He stood guard, more or less, most nights. I never saw anybody who could stay awake as much as he could."

"But you digress," I said. "So…Paul was outside that night, and…?"

"I heard him and Larry talking."

"Could you make out what they were saying?"

Alex nodded. "You could hear Paul's whispers clear across the tent, if he wanted you to. It used to give me the creeps. Anyway, he tells Larry he'll help him get off the ranch, but for now to go down by the stock pens and wait. Then after about thirty minutes—don't ask me what Paul was doing after Larry left—he comes into the tent and taps on the cots of several guys. I saw them get up one by one and leave the tent. They stayed out until it was time to wake everybody up. And what got me?" Alex said, his voice ending in a question, choked off by a sob.

"What, Alex?"

"When we were waking you guys up, Paul acted surprised that Larry was gone."

"Anything else?"

Alex sucked in a ragged breath. "I should've told somebody how funny that looked to me, Paul pretending he didn't know where Larry was."

"But this is hindsight, Alex. You couldn't have known anything bad was going to happen to Larry. Is that what's got you upset?"

He nodded so slightly, I wasn't sure he'd done it. "It doesn't matter, anymore. But I had to tell someone what I heard. I should've done it sooner."

The moon was bright in the clear sky above the valley, as it had been the night Larry met his death. Alex' face shone in its light, and I could make out striking details—the way his eyes were focused on me, the sheen of his neck, the contours under his jaw, his throat—

I shuddered, imagining how Larry's face, contorted with fear, would have been rendered in such light—how the blood would have glistened, its color, black.

Again, I was repulsed to know part of Larry's fate, but relieved to know it. Although it didn't indicate that Paul had killed Larry any more than all the other circumstances we'd put together—like finding Paul's name tag near the place where we found Larry's bloody clothing—it was another piece of the puzzle put together.

I thanked Alex. I wanted to ask him what he'd be doing with his life, now that the program at LMCR was over, but I didn't. I had been too personally involved with too many of these guys already and knew I wouldn't be seeing most of them again.

I was reminded, yet again, of boot camp. We went through hell together, it seemed, during those few weeks. We made what felt like close friendships; then, when it was over, we talked eagerly of staying in touch, with promises like "You better believe it, man. I'll write." "Damn straight, dude, we'll cross paths somewhere down the line." All that kind of close-buddy crap never amounted to anything. I didn't want to raise my expectations about Michael, much less this guy, Alex. This place was finished. It was time to say good-bye.

* * *

There was one more breakfast in the chow hall. This time, there was no prayer, no one to guide us in our thoughts for the day. Rafferty stayed away. In fact, he might have already left the ranch.

The chow hall seemed empty with all the church people, police, and Rafferty's staff gone. Someone had cooked the breakfast. There were piles of pancakes, solidifying lumps of scrambled eggs, gnarled strips of bacon, biscuits, pitchers of syrup, milk, and orange juice—all laid out along the serving counter.

The recruits were helping themselves to the food, completely disorganized and random. The regimentation of lines, the orchestrated breakfast events, like prayer, little speeches, work roster changes—all were gone, as if a storm, the breath of an angry god, had blown all our leaders away, leaving us alone in this valley. In the emptiness, you could hear the recruits all over the chow hall. Some were chatting as if they'd just gone through a wonderful experience in this ministry at LMCR. They were misty-eyed, I guess, realizing it was over. They made the usual promises we'd made in boot camp, to stay in touch. Some said, "See you in Albuquerque." These recruits intended to follow Rafferty down the path he had prepared for them. Others looked as if they'd just gotten out of prison on parole. They cried. As I looked around the room, I wondered which of the guys were on the real "path to salvation"—those who would continue to trust the ministry of Josh Rafferty, or those who would shake off the dust of this place and never look back, their damnation be damned.

I wondered about Jerry. I couldn't resist asking him. He was sitting alone at a table as I wandered over. He smiled nicely when I sat down. We talked for a little while about nothing. Then I popped the big question.

"So, Jerry, will you go on with the program, or have you discovered you can't change what you are?"

He looked at me with such a confused face, I didn't know what to make of it.

"Why are you asking me that?"

"It's not obvious whether or not you are."

"I don't know," he said, after a silence. "You?"

"Isn't it obvious I'm not?"

"Nothing is obvious to me, Kelly."

"What d'you mean?"

Jerry just shook his head. "A few days ago, if you'd asked me that, I would've said I was staying in the program. But with everything that's happened, I don't trust Josh any more."

I was surprised by Jerry's comment, and a little thrill coursed through me at the thought that he, of all the people I'd met here, just might be coming to his senses. Still, I was doubtful I'd heard rightly. "But you're not supposed to put your trust in people, Jerry," I said, then shut up, realizing I was falling back into my teasing routine with him, messing with his head. It seemed mean, now.

"But if you can't trust people, who can you trust?"

"I just try to trust in myself."

Jerry began to cry—not loudly or full of sobbing, nothing like that, just tears that welled up on his lower lashes. "How could he let Larry die?" he said, after swallowing a few times and wiping his eyes. "If we were doing what was best out here, shouldn't we have all been safe? Shouldn't this have felt more like a religious experience, where everybody is good to each other?"

"That's what I would've thought, Jerry." As I said this, I remembered the outrageous lies I'd told him about how I came to realize I was gay. I'd also never told him about William. "But after my lover of five years committed suicide..." I began.

Jerry looked surprised. "You never told me about that!"

"I know, Jerry. I didn't tell you the truth about anything. I was never abused by any uncles. I didn't hang around toilets at the university."

"But why didn't you tell me the truth?"

I sighed to myself. This was going to take awhile. I got myself another cup of coffee, and brought Jerry back one as well. I began with William's suicide after he'd gone through Rafferty's program in Albuquerque. "So..." I said, after five minutes of nonstop talking, "I went into Rafferty's program to see what had happened to William. I wanted to know how he could be made to believe he'd become heterosexual and what drove him to carry on for those few months afterwards as if he had."

"Well, Kelly, maybe he was cured for a little while. Wasn't it what he wanted?"

"Oh, no doubt that's what he wanted, Jerry. But I don't believe for a minute he'd suddenly become attracted to women. I think he was afraid *not* to believe he'd become cured. When he took his life, I think he realized he hadn't been cured and was engulfed in such horrible guilt he couldn't pray himself out of it. If that makes any sense."

Jerry was silent, sipping thoughtfully on his coffee. Then he smiled wistfully. "It makes more sense to me now, Kelly."

"What does?"

"Why you were so angry. I wanted you to like me, you know. But you handed me that line of bull the first morning we talked."

"You were so damned sincere, Jerry, about your questioning. I wasn't about to let you get close to me."

"I know that, even if you did snow me about your uncles. I knew you were angry and you were pushing me away."

I liked Jerry, at that moment, and I felt sad we would probably never see each other again. I would certainly never take the time to look him up. I was afraid he wouldn't overcome his guilt or the brainwashing he'd gone through, either. I was afraid that if I ever saw him again, he would still be looking for a way to escape what he was and would be more messed up than ever. So I came full circle to my original question.

"You think it's a sin, don't you?"

"What?" he asked. "Being homosexual? Don't you?"

"It's not a sin to be born, Jerry, unless you buy into Original Sin, which I don't."

"But what does that have to do with being homosexual?"

"I believe I was born gay, Jerry. I've never doubted for a moment that my attraction to men was innate. Do you think it's something you chose? Did you get up one morning and say to your yourself, 'Hmmm. I think I'll be a queer. I'll get crushes on men and turn my back on my upbringing.'"

Jerry laughed, but his eyes didn't reflect the laughter in his voice.

I pushed. "Can you honestly tell me, Jerry, that in your past, you didn't already know you were gay, whether you wanted to be or not?"

Jerry looked pensive. He was staring blankly at his coffee cup. His hands wrapped themselves around it. Then he looked up at me. "I knew something was wrong with me, all right, when all the other guys were dating girls. But I didn't think I was homosexual."

"Did you ever think maybe nothing was wrong with you?"

He shook his head. "No. I knew it was wrong. When I finally realized I wasn't interested in girls like the other guys…" He trailed off, his beautiful eyes moistening again. "I realized I was probably homosexual. And then I met Rick…this guy in Oklahoma City."

It was Jerry's turn to talk for awhile.

Jerry talked of his doubts, his guilt, his being in love with this man, Rick, and fighting his love for him at every moment. It brought tears to my eyes listening to his tale, because it reminded me so much of William.

"Then I came home one day," Jerry said, sighing, his voice dropping so low I had to lean forward to hear him.

"What happened, Jerry?"

Jerry's fist hit the table. "Oh, God!" he said softly, tears running into the corners of his mouth. "I'd been out that day, picking out a present for him. It was his birthday. He'd stayed home from work. So I pretended I went off to work, as usual, but instead, I'd gone shopping. I'd found the perfect shirt to set off his green eyes. Silk. And I came home around lunch, thinking I'd surprise him. But when I came in through the back door, I could hear voices, as if the house was full of people."

"Was it?"

He waved my question away, his eyes lowered, not looking at me. "So I went into the living room from the kitchen, angry that he'd have a party when I was at work—or when he thought I wouldn't be coming home—and could do what he did without getting caught." He looked at me then, his eyes narrowing, as if he were accusing me of something.

"He was throwing a party, all right, Kelly. An orgy. There must've been a dozen guys on the floor, all of them naked, writhing like a nest of snakes, tangled up with one another. And then I saw Rick fellating one guy, while another one was humping him from behind and another one was fellating Rick. And it smelled like a locker room.

"I didn't say a thing. I just backed out of the room. And Rick never knew I'd been there."

"So you left him?"

"Yes, I left him! What would be the point of staying? I didn't even bother to come back to the apartment for my clothes, or anything else. It was all dirty. So filthy. So evil."

"So after that, you joined the program?"

He nodded. "I wanted to cleanse myself. I wanted to rip out my eyes for having seen. I wanted to scrub my mouth for ever having kissed him."

There wasn't anything else to be said, after that. I hated to leave him, then. But I got up from the table and offered him my hand, and we shook.

"I'm sorry," I said, feebly, and felt like a fake, like those offering condolences at a funeral.

"I'm not," he said. "At least I've been able to get over any feelings I ever had for him. I've been able to see a way out for myself."

I sat down again, flabbergasted. "You mean trying to cure yourself? Jerry, it wasn't your fault. Why are you punishing yourself?"

"I'm not punishing myself. I'm trying to save my soul."

"From what?"

"From turning out like him. I can't live that kind of life."

"But you don't have to!" I wanted to shake him. "Do you think you have to participate in orgies, just because you're gay?"

"Is there really any hope of a real life, one that God would approve of?"

"I think there is, Jerry. I'm sorry, but if there is a judgment day, and if I meet God, I'll have to argue with Him about it. That's all I know. I intend to meet another man and show him all the love I can."

Jerry smiled sadly. "I wouldn't expect any less of you, Kelly. I hope you're not disappointed, though. Take care."

* * *

Charlie took me through Lion's Mouth Canyon in his pickup about mid-morning. Already, it was hot as we entered the canyon and began our climb out of the valley. I turned around in the seat and looked out the window at LMCR. For almost two months, I had lived in that valley. As we climbed I could see the entire ranch laid out, from the tents on the north side, to the hill on the east end of the valley beyond which lay the stock pens. They were empty, now, some of the farmers in the Church in Carlsbad having taken the beasts for their own. As the canyon swallowed us, I almost missed seeing the chow hall, activities center, and chapel on the south side of the valley.

How forlorn they already looked, since all of the recruits were gone as well. The barracks we had worked on would likely never be finished, unless the church could find a use for the property. As a church camp for young people, it was too harsh of an environment; it would never make a vacation spot, either, because it would repel those who wanted a lovely place to relax. Yet, I felt sad leaving—whether it was because of what had gone on there, or because Larry had died and it seemed he was being left, alone, on the ranch he'd died trying to leave, or because in some way, I wanted to see Jerry and Donald and Brian and the others again and my leaving meant I would not—I don't know. But I swallowed back a lump in my throat as we rounded a curve to the south and the valley was swallowed up by the terrain.

"Something troubling you, Kelly?" Charlie asked. He tapped my knee a couple of times, letting his hand linger over my thigh as if he wanted to leave it there.

Our eyes met briefly before he had to look back to the road in front of us. "I was just wondering what would happen to everybody," I said, then straightened in the seat.

The Guadalupe mountains all around us shimmered in the heat. Cliffs of skyscraper proportions cast shadows on the worn down hills over which they hovered. The sky above us was almost white in the heat. A few clouds drifted overhead, casting other shadows on the land. As we curved steadily south then east, we climbed over rises and fell into valleys, sometimes passing through scraggly pine growths, sometimes hugging the sides of mountains where, on one side the mountains rose above us, and on the other, dropped away.

But as we traveled, growing closer to Carlsbad, the terrain became rolling hills, then stretches of plain. As we came out on the east side of the Guadalupes, I suddenly felt all the pent up sadness escape as I scanned the horizon in front of us, which stretched on into Texas and became the great plains.

Charlie and I had spoken little, except for an occasional comment about Michael. During one stretch of the journey, Charlie had talked about Brian and Donald. "Can't tell you how nice it was, Kelly, to have those two boys share a bed in my house," he said, then laughed. "Made me feel real proud to have them. A little horny, too…"

I wanted to laugh, but I reigned in my grin, realizing it would embarrass him.

"I even slept in their bed without changing the sheets, the night they left," he said. "Those boys'd made it smell so sweet, I knew they'd made love in it."

"I know what you mean, Charlie," I said, thinking of how William's smell had lingered on his pillow in my apartment for a few days after he'd left, how the aroma of his cologne remained in the closet where he'd forgotten a couple of shirts he'd worn.

Then the town of Carlsbad came into view, glass reflecting sunlight, trees sweetening the air in its neighborhoods, and the highway widening and smoothing out as we entered the outskirts. That's when I was suddenly struck with an idea.

I sat up in the seat, leaning forward. "Charlie? You don't suppose Paul Romaine and the others are still in jail, here, do you?"

Charlie nodded. "I know for a fact they are, because it's in the papers about the murder. They're being held until the investigation is complete. Why?"

"Because I have a little unfinished business with that bastard."

* * *

The police station was off the main drag, but still impressive compared to the low-slung buildings around it. The people in the county probably paid high taxes to keep their peace keepers happy. When we walked into the station, it was as if we'd entered a hospital. At first, there was little sign of activity. If I had been in a hurry to report a robbery, I would have had to scream bloody murder. Then I caught sight of a spiffily-clad cop, so young looking, I figured him for a rookie, cocked back in a rickety swivel chair in his cage, next to a bank of telephones and CBs; he was reading a magazine and scratching his shoulder.

"Uh—officer?" I said to the plexiglass shield between him and me. When I got no response, I knocked on the window.

He looked up, coming out of a daze, then slowly came to his feet, and sauntered over to the counter. "Yeah?"

"You got someone I wanna see."

Without speaking, he pointed to a printed sign above my head. Visitor's hours weren't for another two hours.

"I'm leaving town in a few minutes," I lied. "Wouldn't it be all right to have just a few words?"

He looked at his watch, then at Charlie, who was standing behind me. "Hey, Uncle Charlie!" he said. "This guy with you?"

Charlie squeezed my shoulder and pushed me gently out of the way, speaking lowly to me: "My brother's youngest son." Then he smiled at his nephew. "How 'bout letting him have a few words with the murderer you got in there."

"Romaine fella?"

"You got any more?"

Charlie's nephew grinned, his smooth face looking attractive for the first time. "Be all right, I reckon, Uncle Charlie. But you stay here with me, case Tubbs comes back from Denny's. Fart'd stick me in with the prisoners if he thought I'd made an independent decision." He turned to me. "Go stand in front of the metal door down the hall. When it clicks, push it open. When you're ready to come out, ring the bell."

I did as he said, wondering how friendly Charlie's nephew would be if his father ever told him about Charlie. I wandered down a twenty-foot hallway, flooded with florescent lights, then stood before the door at the end. There was a tiny window with criss-crossed wire reinforcement in the door just barely low enough for me to peek into. I could make out the iron-gray walls and the rows of cells on the other side; I was thinking how much it looked like a dog pound when a scraping-metal click sounded—a dead-bolt being pulled back electronically.

I pushed open the door and walked into the jail area. The hallway narrowed to about six-feet wide, with cells on both sides of me. It gave me the creeps to walk down the gauntlet; it would have been worse had prisoners lined both sides. I would have had to walk a narrow path down the middle to avoid being touched, or grabbed.

Paul Romaine was in the third cell on my left. His goons were in cells farther down. When I walked up to his cell, he stared at me from his cot. "Brother, Kelly O'Kelley," he deadpanned. "What a fucking surprise."

Gone from his face was any glimmer of what he'd tried to pass off as Christian demeanor. Now his beady eyes penetrated the gray gloom and locked on mine. He hadn't shaven in several days and his little chipmunk face looked even more ludicrous with the growth of gray whiskers.

"What have you gotten yourself into?" I said, smiling. "Everybody thinks you're guilty of murder, you know."

"Yeah, well," Paul said, getting up from his cot and walking over. He was wearing orange pajamas, like his goons in the next few cells. "We were just in the wrong place at the wrong time. People could accuse you of the same thing, with all the evidence they haven't got."

"That's not what I hear, Paul. In fact, Alex…you remember Alex? He said you were the last person he knew of who saw Larry the night before. Said he heard you tell him to meet you down by the stock pens. Said you'd help him get off the ranch."

Paul stuck his hands into the pajama pants and scratched his crotch. "Hearsay. What do you want? You finally want to tell me why you were at the ranch? I never figured you were like the rest of those lambs. You're what…close to forty years old? Maybe you're a chicken queen."

"I wasn't the one plucking the chickens, Paul. I regretted never being able to tell you that I saw you take Michael off behind the stock pens. Did you know that? I saw Drigger and Baker strip him, and I saw you squeeze your little pecker into a cock ring."

"So? Big deal. What does that prove?"

"Proves you're a liar and a pervert, Paul."

Paul turned away and looked over his shoulder. "Fuck yourself, Brother Kelly. You tire me out."

"I'm going," I said, grasping the bars of his cell and pushing my face between them. "But I didn't come here just to tell you I saw what you did to Michael. I came to send you greetings from a couple of old enemies of yours. Do you by any chance remember Tom Allen and Joel Reece from Common, New Mex—"

Paul lunged at me. I jumped back in surprise, then took hold of the bars again.

"Those two!" Paul said, his snotty face twisting into utter hatred. "How I would've loved to get my hands on them."

He said this quietly, after his initial outburst, and I felt like laughing, realizing I had touched a very sore spot.

"Joel would've ripped your pecker off, Paul, regardless of how many goons you surrounded yourself with."

He took hold of the bars and snarled at me. "Yeah, well I could've handled Tom. That one needs to have a baseball bat shoved up his ass."

I did laugh, then. "I take it you haven't seen him in some time. But you sure are fixated on him, aren't you?"

"I hate him!" Paul shouted.

"Yeah, I know, Paul. You see...I did come to the ranch to do a little work. I stayed with Tom and Joel about a week, long before I joined this program. Tom had plenty to say about you, too. Did you know that? So when I got here, I figured out you were the same guy Tom had talked about."

"He remembered me?"

"You could say that, Paul. But only how foul you are."

He slumped to the floor, whining suddenly, rocking to and fro. I watched him for a moment, about to turn around and walk out without another word. Then he stopped rocking, raising his face to meet my eyes. His irises were like two black beads surrounded by the whites of his eyes. In the gloomy gray of the jail, I shivered and couldn't look away.

"You think you've won, don't you?" Paul said, his voice a low rasp.

"Not until you fry," I said, breaking eye contact.

Then he smiled. It was an insane smile. "What happened at the ranch is just the tip of the old iceberg, you know. There's more where I came from—a lot more—and we've got plans."

"Yeah? Well, we'll meet you head on," I said, turning away.

"We're training our people well, Kelly!"

I didn't look at him. "You hear that, guys?" I said, calling over my shoulder, as I began walking out of the jail, meaning my words for Paul's cadre. "I'm not in jail, and you wouldn't be, either, if you'd testify against this little chipmunk. Look where he's led you." I didn't wait to hear what they said, if they said anything at all. I had been able to get back at Paul Romaine by mentioning Tom and Joel; and it had seemed to crush his ego—for awhile. But his insane words still rung in my ears, and I left feeling depressed. No doubt there were others out there, like

Paul Romaine and Josh Rafferty, and the founders of other such ministries. But worse, there were other Williams, and Jerrys, and Donalds, and Brians, and even those like Michael.

* * *

July 25

It's now Saturday, and I am at Charlie's house on the Hays farm. Although theirs is not nearly as big as the farms Tom and Joel Allen-Reece run, the Hays brothers seem to make a good living. I suppose they worry over financing every year, over rising costs, but both houses are comfortable, if not extravagant. I think Charlie's is the older house. The roof is pitched more steeply than modern houses. And if the furniture isn't genuine antique, it's genuine old. The only things that look new are the appliances in the kitchen.

This isn't a travelogue, but I've re-entered the world with new eyes. I want to drink in every detail. Ah, the smell of freedom. I was at the LMCR only seven weeks, but it truly does seem to have been a lifetime. I cannot imagine what it would have been like to stay there another eleven weeks! I didn't even make it through half the program; yet my sweet dead William lived through all eighteen weeks. No wonder he was unable to shake the guilt, or to admit (maybe) that it had all been such a waste of time. I think now of Jerry, and the horror he was running away from that brought him here.

I suppose I will never know what happens to him, or to any of the other guys. But I think I'll check those ex-gay sites on the world wide web, and perhaps even those ex-ex-gay sites to see if anyone I know pops up on any of them.

Here's to life!

Michael, Charlie, and I took in the night life of Carlsbad last night. But compared to the ranch, it could've been some large city. The teenagers were out dragging the town's major through streets, typical of teens everywhere, I suppose, in small towns. Charlie took Michael and me out for steaks. Then we went to a bar and all three of us got a little drunk.

Michael is still working on his butch image. He still maintains that, if nothing else, the ranch helped him with that. Charlie is so regular looking, I'm not sure where you'd put him on a butch-fem scale. His drag (if you can call it that) is of the southwestern farmer and nothing else. What you see is what you get, as they say.

We've made plans to travel together. I'm going to try to get my job back at the garage where I was working before I went to LMCR. I guess Michael, Charlie, and I will be friends. Who knows, now, what the future holds? We're planning a trip out to see Tom and Joel—hopefully before the snow flies. And if Tom and Joel come see us, maybe by then, we'll have the courage to take them to the ranch and show them where one can begin a descent into Hell.

For now, I think I'll let Charlie hold onto my journal for me. One day I might have the stomach to tell this story.

Kelly O'Kelley

Afterword

The Salvation Mongers 2000—The Real Thing

I do not know of any physical violence that has occurred within the ministries of the ex-gay movement—either past or present. Yet, during the same time that such ministries have been operating, there has been increasing violence against gays, lesbians, and transgendered individuals by hate groups and hate-filled people. A step-father kills his gay step-son, just because he doesn't like his step-son's homosexuality; a gay college student is robbed, pistol-whipped, and tied to a fence post to die, because one of the attackers was allegedly propositioned by him and suffered "gay panic"; a gay soldier is bludgeoned to death in his sleep with a baseball bat, because his attacker is embarrassed to have lost a fair fight to a gay man and doesn't think gay people should be allowed to serve in the United States military. Such hate crimes are increasing, yet across the country, legislators refuse to pass hate-crimes legislation because they don't think homosexuals deserve "special rights." Moreover, religious organizations are in the forefront of the move to prevent such legislation, at the same time adding to the hate-rhetoric by claiming that it's the homosexuals in the country who have a frightening and dangerous "gay agenda."

But they go even further, because they have an agenda of their own—nothing less than the extermination of homosexuals, themselves.

Is that too blunt? Too disturbing to consider? Too reminiscent of the "Jewish Solution" in Nazi Germany of the 1930s and 40s? Perhaps it is too far-reaching to make such a claim; certainly no right-wing religious organization with a real voice in this country would admit to such an outrageous program of extermination. No, these organizations simply want to deny housing, jobs, protection of civil liberties, and marriage to homosexuals. And during the AIDS epidemic, when gay men were dying by the thousands of this affliction, it wasn't beneath Pat Robertson and others to declare that it was God's fitting punishment.

Further, the right-wing Christian organizations eschew any responsibility whatsoever for causing the increase in gay bashing. Yet they are silent when vicious murders actually occur, claiming instead that they *love* homosexuals and only want to *save* them. Again, I do not say that ex-gay ministries are responsible for the rise in violence against homosexuals. But I believe that whatever spawns the ex-gay ministries also spawns the hate groups; and I believe that "whatever is behind it" is the view held by the religious right that homosexuality is always a sin, is "unnatural," and that it ought to be a crime to "practice" homosexuality.

Also, ex-gay ministries are often sponsored by the very same right-wing religious organizations that hold this negative view of homosexuality. It is, indeed, from the pulpits and pamphlets of the most right-wing churches that comes hateful rhetoric and spiteful agendas against the homosexual and their sympathizers. Again, I believe that hate groups take their inspiration from such religious organizations.

The Salvation Mongers

To illustrate my point, I wrote *The Salvation Mongers* to represent the physical violence done to homosexuals in the name of Christianity, or in response to the hateful rhetoric of the religious right. I based the incidents of violence in my novel on actual events that have taken place within the last thirty years in the United States and elsewhere, incidents I read about or witnessed in the real world. For example, the "death of the spirit" demonstration in my novel was inspired by the real-world religious leader, Jim Jones. He sentenced two men to a "spiritual death" when they were caught having sex in his late 1970s cult; they were locked together inside a coffin for 24 hours, which was on display in the compound for all to see. Another example of a real-world incident in my novel came from Anita Bryant's "Save Our Children Campaign" (SOC), which took place in 1977 in Dade County, Florida. The genesis of the Bryant anti-homosexual campaign was an attempt to overturn gay-positive measures that had been adopted in Dade County. Threats of violence were made against homosexuals during the same time that the SOC campaign was active. Bumper stickers on cars in that area advocated "Death to Homosexuals!" and urged: "Kill a Queer for Christ!" In the novel, these slogans are written in pig's blood on the inside walls of the tent where the ex-gay recruits sleep and spend several hours each night before lights out reading their bibles or praying.

The rhetoric of Bryant's plea to "save our children" was quite shrill, characterizing homosexual men and women as child molesters. Since homosexuals cannot have children, the argument went, they have to recruit other people's children into the homosexual lifestyle. In all fairness to the SOC campaign, I feel certain that individuals from the lunatic fringe displayed such bumper stickers and were *probably* not condoned by SOC. But today, religious leaders have gone much farther than the SOC campaign. Although none publicly call for the *death* of homosexuals, they've dropped the distinction between loving the sinner and hating the sin.

One example is a Baptist minister, Fred Phelps, out of Kansas, who makes it his business to appear at the funerals of AIDS victims and at gay churches with signs that read: "God hates Fags!" In the most well-publicized activity of this minister, of course, was his unseemly and hateful appearance at the funeral of the Wyoming college student Matthew Shepard, who was robbed, beaten, and crucified by two young men who had lured him out of a bar, themselves claiming to be gay. Then there are the more accepted lunatics like Pat Robertson, founder of the Christian Broadcasting Network. Smiling into the camera with the happy face of repression, Robertson blithely announces that natural disasters, such as earthquakes and hurricanes, are sent by God to punish homosexuals and the communities that protect the rights of its gay citizens. Yet, not a word was whispered about God's wrath on that bastion of fundamentalist Christianity, South Carolina, when it was battered by hurricanes and flooding in 1999. If nothing else it shows that God is wildly democratic in His targets. If San Francisco goes under because it harbors homosexuals, South Carolina goes under because it harbors religious fanatics—and many of the religious-right organizations.

Today, in fact, the religious right blames the gay-rights movement for the breakdown of civilization, itself. How such a movement actually destroys society is not made clear.

Another theme in *The Salvation Mongers* is the way in which the characters deal with the question of whether or not homosexuals can become heterosexuals. The ex-gay ministry I created is only a mirror held up to actual ex-gay ministries that have arisen and have operated within the United States since Anita Bryant's 1970s crusade.

Treatment Options and Attitudes Toward Homosexuality

To understand why ex-gay ministries fail to convert their recruits, it is a good idea to understand the narrow range of dynamic options (treatment methods) available and core concepts held by the ex-gay ministries when attempting to bring about change within the homosexual. Treatment options are based on "reparative therapy" from the field of psychology, or some form of multiple-step program, based loosely on the 12-step Alcoholics Anonymous program. The steps are tailored to fit the core concepts of the ministry. One core concept most ex-gay ministries have in common is the idea that they "love the sinner, but hate the sin." I assert that the very human leaders within the ex-gay ministries cannot draw such precise lines between hate and love and that they sometimes hate the sinner as much as the sin. Another core concept shared by most ex-gay ministries is the necessity of embracing the Christian concept of Jesus as Savior, and expecting God through Jesus to cure homosexuality. One of the other mainstays of the ex-gay ministries is that homosexuality is always a sin, without exception, based on the literal and "inerrant" Holy Bible—more clearly a sin, without exception, in *The Good News* version, however, than other versions, where the word "homosexual" is inserted into biblical text. Curious since "homosexual" is a nineteenth-century construct. For example, the word "effeminate" becomes "homosexual" in the *Good News Bible*, yet it has also been interpreted to mean one who is an out-of-control womanizer.

Perhaps the most dangerous (and cult-like) core concept many ex-gay ministries share with their religious-right sponsors is that Jesus, the Christ, often speaks with them—albeit two thousand years after his death and from "off-world," as it were. It is also curious but telling that the words from Jesus and God spoken to these modern-day religious leaders sound suspiciously like their own hate-filled rhetoric. Their view of scripture is narrow and therefore incomplete because they discount how other religious organizations (middle-ground to liberal) have come to grips with the issue of homosexuality, supposedly using the same scriptural referents as do those on the right. One does not have to speak with Jesus through some divine internet to know that the Jesus of the Bible might not *want* to cure or kill homosexual persons, although given the time in which Jesus the man lived, he just might have considered it a sin (as a waste of seed, perhaps) and told them to go and sin no more. But we have no way of really knowing what Jesus might have done, since he never addresses the issue. This lack of "policy" by Jesus, therefore, makes it necessary for us to either believe that modern-day ministers of the religious right have a direct line of communication to Jesus (which I assert is highly doubtful) or that we are thus left to make sense of the issues ourselves.

The Dark Side of the Ex-Gay Ministries

Beneath the seemingly benign core concepts of most ex-gay ministries, there is a dark side that is common (if not universal) among the ministries. It is an unacknowledged, toxic by-product, which poisons the psyche of homosexual men and women when they seek a "cure" of their homosexuality. In many cases, these individuals are worse off after going through the ex-gay programs than before (one disillusioned ex-gay reportedly emasculated himself after failing to overcome his homosexual nature by pouring acid on his genitalia). When the ex-gay recruit fails to rid himself or herself of homosexual desire, there is an increase in self-loathing and a greater feeling of isolation. To minimize both the self-loathing and the sense of isolation, most ex-gay ministries encourage praying partners and regular attendance at ministry sessions with other ex-gays. The ex-gay's social world eventually narrows to a few single-thought companions. They commit themselves to a daily regime of denial of their homosexual feelings and seek to sustain their religious conversion. Or they wrestle honestly with these feelings (believing that homosexuality is a sin) and accept celibacy as their only alternative to being cured. But celibacy is a cheap solution for the so-called ex-gay. In no way does it mean that the homosexual individual has been fundamentally changed—only that his or her behavior is restricted, even if the urges are still present. It is disingenuous and cruel for those in the ex-gay ministries to sell this as a real cure for homosexuality.

In my estimation, what really happens to homosexual individuals seeking a cure is that they suppress many natural impulses. But if they give in (on occasion) to these same feelings, they will likely blame their behavior on demonic influences. This suppression can cause true psychic disconnection from one's inner self. Individuals thereby give up free will when engaging in homosexual acts, and blame it on Satan or some other influence beyond their power to control. Without accepting true responsibility for their own actions, these individuals might continue to "engage in homosexual acts," yet (with a straight face) claim to be *ex*-gay.

But most striking about the ex-gay movement and something I sought to illustrate in *The Salvation Mongers* is what self-loathing homosexuals do to themselves—and to others as their surrogate selves. Self-loathing homosexuals organized many of the ex-gay ministries and recruited other self-loathing gay men and women. For an ex-gay ministry to wield influence over its members, the members must be willing to embrace any program, any doctrine—using almost any method—if it promises to "cure" them.

Prior to the ex-gay ministries, psychiatrists and doctors on the fringes of the medical profession held out the same cruel hope of a "cure" to which self-loathing homosexuals went for help. Some homosexuals willingly subjected themselves to barbaric medical treatments; among these is lobotomy (a long metal object much like an ice pick is inserted into the eye socket and rammed into the frontal lobe of the brain, where it supposedly scrambles the homosexual sex drive); some were even castrated. Like celibacy, the cures of the psychiatric and pseudo-medical professions were fake but much more violent. Lobotomy and castration killed the person's ability to *feel*—period.

While there are dozens of ex-gay programs active at any given time within the United States, a few examples of some of the more widely known ministries will serve to characterize the methods and activities of their less well-known counterparts.

Exodus (later called Exodus International) was founded in 1976 by two homosexual men, Michael Bussee and Gary Cooper. Their ministry used the psychologically-founded method known as reparative therapy. And even though this ministry still exists (in fact has well over a hundred sub-ministries under it in the United States, alone, it should be known that the founders, themselves, failed in their attempts to become ex-gays and, after three years in the ministry, dropped out and became lovers. They claimed that rather than curing the homosexual individual, Exodus only succeeded in exacerbating members' feelings of guilt and personal failure. And even though the psychiatric community has eschewed the use of reparative therapy to cure homosexuality, Exodus International continues to use it and extol its efficacy.

A man by the name of Guy Charles, who founded "Liberation in Jesus Christ," has become a former ex-gay, as has Roger Grindstaff of "Disciples Only." Grindstaff was also a consultant to "Teen Challenge." If his methods failed to cure him, one can only grieve that the teenagers who sought his help were likewise disillusioned and wasted their formative years fighting, rather than learning to understand and celebrate their true nature. John Evans of "Love in Action" and Jim Kasper of "EXIT" are also former ex-gays. The point is that, as of today, in 2000, many hundreds of members and many leaders within the ex-gay ministries have become disillusioned with the ex-gay movement.

Even current leaders sometimes worry aloud about the ineffectiveness of their ministries. Yet leaders within the ex-gay movement continue to grasp tightly the idea that a change in *behavior* makes one ex-gay which, itself, is based on the erroneous premise that affectional and sexual attraction is a choice. Even if they know they are not *really* offering *hetero*sexuality, their followers are often deluded into accepting celibacy as a "cure." The leaders then report that their members are ex-gays, and convince them that, "by committing themselves to Jesus," as one ex-gay leader put it, "the converts take on the heterosexuality of Jesus as their own"—even while admitting that their converts really have few heterosexual responses or feelings.

It is therefore not surprising to me that while my work, *The Salvation Mongers*, is fictitious, the experiences of the ex-gays in real ministries do not differ much from those in my fictional account.

In summary, self-loathing homosexuals still subject themselves to years of self-torture and heartache; some commit suicide; others choose self-mutilation; but most self-loathing homosexuals just fail to actually convert from homosexual to heterosexual and continue to live tortured private lives. These are the ones for whom *The Salvation Mongers* was written.

About the Author

Ronald L. Donaghe lives in a 93-year-old adobe house in a historic district of Las Cruces, New Mexico, with his mate. When he is not working at his day job as a technical writer, or pursuing his career as a novelist, he enjoys working in the yard, taking day trips with his mate and friends, and reading.

LaVergne, TN USA
17 December 2009
167362LV00001B/96/A